SOULED

Diana Murdock

Souled is a work of fiction. The events and characters described herein are imaginary and are not intended to refer to specific living persons or experiences. The businesses, however, are or have been a part of Sandpoint, Idaho, and are only included in this novel as locales and have not endorsed the opinions/imagination of the author.

The opinions expressed in this fictional piece are solely the opinion of the author. The author has represented and warranted full ownership and/or legal right to publish all materials in this book.

PROLOGUE

450 A.D.

Fingertips of fire seared his flesh as Silura trailed her hand along the length of his heavily-corded arm.

"In exchange for your body and soul, I offer you the world and all that it holds. You will know immense power and you shall want for nothing." The violet of her eyes glowed under his gaze. "What say you?"

He flexed his muscle instinctively, recognizing the power in her touch. "You wish that I forsake all others and become your consort?"

Her fingers curled slightly, her nails pressing lightly onto his bronzed skin. "You find that distasteful?"

The corners of his lips raised in amusement. "Quite the contrary. I find it to be... most interesting." He raised his hand to stroke the line of her jaw and followed it back to the nape of her neck. Leaning toward her, he drew her face close to his, holding himself a breath away.

When he spoke again his voice was honey-sweet, sending a shiver up her spine. "So, my body and soul. That is the only price?"

Her brow rose in a graceful arc.

Laughter rumbled deep in his chest. "There is always a price for everything, is there not?"

Yes. There was always a price, she thought. She would do anything for him. She wanted his heart to be hers, and would gladly give him her own. She knew she could not compel his loyalty, for only true love could command that. But, she vowed, she would give him reasons enough to remain at her side. She felt a pull of possessiveness she had never before known.

She winced at her weakness. A powerful sorceress, reduced to a love-sick fool! But to have his body and soul was well worth the title of Fool.

"The price is mine to bear," she whispered. She dared not ask for his love, for if he refused, it would shatter her. But surely love would come with time.

It must...

SETH

"I Will Not Bow"

Now the dark begins to rise
Save your breath, it's far from over
Leave the lost and dead behind
Now's your chance to run for cover
I don't wanna change the world
I just wanna leave it colder
Light the fuse and burn it up
Take the path that leads to nowhere
All is lost again
But I'm not giving in

I will not bow
I will not break
I will shut the world away
I will not fall
I will not fade
I will take your breath away

Watch the end through dying eyes
Now the dark is taking over
Show me where forever dies
Take the fall and run to Heaven
All is lost again
But I'm not giving in

I will not bow
I will not break
I will shut the world away
I will not fall
I will not fade
I will take your breath away

And I'll survive, paranoid
I have lost the will to change
And I'm not proud, cold-blooded fate
I will shut the world away

Chapter 1

*The desires of the boy are many. In him, I see the
chance to regain my strength. I must convince him of
my power. Total control of his mind must be mine.
That is the only way that I can be released.*
~ Maksim

My girlfriend, Dani, stood very still with her
elbows pressed against her sides, apparently oblivious
to everything going on around her. The bowling alley
was always packed, always loud on Friday nights. In
our little Idaho town of only 6,000 people, about the
only place to go on the weekends during the winter
and spring months was the bowling alley. Despite the
other bowlers' laughing and shouting and the noises
coming from the arcade, Dani's focus was on the
solitary pin staring her down from the far end of the
lane.

"She's good." The voice slithered over me—a
voice I'd know anywhere.

The muscles in my back cinched up and my
shoulders squared off when I heard Dirk's voice, but
my eyes never left Dani.

Beside me, Justin, my best friend, glanced over
his shoulder at Dirk and lifted his chin a fraction
before turning away.

"Yes! Beat *that*, Seth!" Dani turned and sauntered
towards me, smiling at her pin takedown, but the
corners of her mouth dropped when she saw Dirk.

He was one of the best wrestlers at Sandpoint
High School, by far the cockiest, and, hands down,
the biggest jerk. Inexplicably, a lot of the girls at the

high school saw him as some kind of god or something.

Fortunately, Dani wasn't one of them.

"Nice one, Dani," said Dirk.

He was so full of shit. The only time he gave out compliments was when he wanted something. In this case, it was Dani.

Her eyes narrowed. "That's *Danika* to you." The words smacked the air like a rubber band.

One of the many things I loved about her: she could handle herself.

"Okay, *Danika*," Dirk grinned. "I'll take you up on your offer to beat that."

"I wasn't talking to you," she said, flipping her long brown hair over her shoulder and turning her back to him.

But *I* couldn't keep my back to him. I didn't trust him. He played dirty both on and off the wrestling mat, getting serious pleasure in whatever pain he could inflict. There was no question which side of the line of good and bad he walked. Dirk had probably carved up dead cats when he was a kid. No, I had no doubt he'd stab me in the back, given the chance. Hell, he'd stab me in the chest.

And he'd probably get away with it. His parents owned one of the biggest houses on Ponder Point, right on Lake Pend Oreille, and they knew all the important people in Sandpoint, including the police chief.

I'd been to Dirk's house once when his family had a housewarming party a few years ago. They'd just moved here and he'd invited everyone in his classes. We'd been in algebra together during our freshman year.

That was before we had gotten to know each other. Before we realized we hated each other.

I stood and faced him. Both of us were about the same build—big, around six feet tall, with wide shoulders—but his muscles were a little thicker, a lot like his head. His dark, short-cropped hair made him look like he'd come straight off an army recruiting brochure.

"I don't remember inviting you," I said.

Dirk very deliberately sized me up and smirked. As if that would intimidate me.

"Go back to your own lane," I said quietly, tipping my chin in that direction. My hands ached from fisting up. I wanted so badly to knock that smirk off his face.

Dirk looked past my shoulder. "Maybe some other time then, huh, *Danika?*" He laughed and turned around.

It killed me to let him walk away. But I had to. I refused to let him provoke me.

"Hey." Justin stepped in front of me and punched my shoulder.

Justin may be shorter than I am, but he packed just as much muscle on his body.

"Forget about him, man. He's just being a dick, as usual," he said. "Let's finish the game." He turned and headed toward the carousel. "Besides, we can't let a *girl* win, can we?"

Dani reached up to hit him upside the head as he walked by, but Justin ducked right before she could make contact.

"You might as well give it up, boys," Dani proclaimed. "This *girl* has this game in the bag." Then she tugged on my arm and pulled me into a hug. "Let it go, babe," she whispered.

I took a deep breath and the tension in my back eased up a little. She was everything in my life, and I was pretty sure she felt the same way I did. Why,

9

then, couldn't I shake the feeling that she'd find someone better, someone who could give her more?

"I hate the way Dirk looks at you," I said, wrapping my arms around her and pulling her close.

"Hey, he's not worth the energy," Dani shrugged.

Okay. I'd drop it for now, but I would never let it go.

I looked over Dani's head at the scoreboard. "Looks like I have some catching up to do." I turned Dani around just in time to watch Justin's ball knock down all ten pins.

~ ~ ~

After school that Monday, I pulled my truck into my driveway. Man, I was still wound up about Dirk. He had enough girls to choose from. Why did he have to go after *mine*? *Let it go, let it go,* I thought. Right now I had more important things to think about. Like finding a birthday present for Dani.

I pushed open the front door of the house and stepped into the small hallway leading to the living room, walking past the family photos that hung on the wall, past the photos of Mom.

I really missed her; some days more than others. I missed the way the three of us hung out together every Friday night—our family movie night. That was our routine. After a week at work and school, we'd pop in a movie and have popcorn and ice cream—vanilla ice cream with hot fudge and heaps of whipped cream. That was the one night Mom would let me eat as much ice cream as I wanted.

But life was different now. School, homework, and wrestling practice all week hadn't changed, but coming home every day to an empty house was now part of my life. It took getting used to at first, but now the silence wasn't so loud.

A lot of kids at my school have it far worse than I do, but then again some have it better. Since Mom died, Dad has tried to make ends meet the best he could. He drove a semi, logging enough miles so we could live comfortably. I told him I'd get a job to help out, but he insisted I focus on school and wrestling so I'd have a better chance at getting a scholarship for college.

After turning the heater on just enough to break the chill in the air, I headed to my room to finish what I'd been doing for the last couple of weeks: obsessing over finding the right birthday present for Dani. I had done the same thing the last two years for her birthday, and both years I'd made myself crazy trying to find her the *perfect* gift. I never had much cash to work with, so I always needed to make every penny count. I'd lost track of how many hours I'd spent on my computer surfing through page after page of ads and sites. I'd seen just about everything a girl Dani's age could possibly be interested in—and a whole lot she wouldn't.

Pulling the chair back, I sat down, turned on my computer, and started my nightly routine. My email inbox displayed the usual stuff. There was a message from my dad, notifications from the social media site and eSouled. I always opened my dad's email first, just to make sure everything was okay.

A sidebar ad next to the email caught my eye. *Power and Control.* I'd seen that one before. In fact, it'd been there every day for the past week. Had to be some woo-woo thing, some New Age self-help crap. I ignored it.

The last email was from eSouled, with their latest on-line auction recommendations. Usually those had nothing to do with what I wanted, but I opened the email anyway.

Draw others to you. Same address as the "Power and Control" ad in my sidebar. There was probably a warehouse full of the books or DVDs, or whatever the ad was selling.

I deleted the next two emails without even opening them. I opened the last one, a notification that Justin had posted some pictures from his family's Hawaiian vacation this past summer. I had to check those out. He and his family always took some amazing side trips wherever they took a vacation.

Power and Control. It popped up in my social site sidebar now. They were pushing that ad heavily, weren't they? Who would be stupid enough to fall for it? I could use both power and control, but this had "quick buck" written all over it. There was no way you could sell, or buy, control or power.

Another click and I was on eSouled's home page. What I *really* wanted to get Dani was jewelry. She never wore much, except for the necklace I gave her last year, and I wanted her to have more. Something really nice.

An hour later, though, I still hadn't found anything. *Damn!* This definitely wasn't easy.

An email came in from Dad, letting me know his next route.

"Have. A. Safe. Trip. Dad," I said out loud as I typed the words. "Send." I pressed enter. Hunger gnawed at my stomach, but I decided to take one more look before I made dinner. Going back to eSouled, I typed in "earrings." At the top, that same stupid ad was featured. The words *Power and Control* pulsed yellow, almost like a heartbeat. My fingertips instinctively touched the pulse in my neck. Like *my* heartbeat. Wow! That was pretty cool. How did they do that?

"I might have to check it out," I said. What price would someone put on something like control? Huh. Apparently not much, because the bidding started at one dollar. Big time scam. But still… To have *some* power, *some* control over things in my life... How great would that be? Laughing at myself, I put it on the Watch List. Watching it didn't mean I was buying into the idea. I was just curious.

A shiver worked its way up my spine even though the house had warmed up. I shrugged it off and reached for my backpack. Right now, all I had control over was getting some food into my stomach and getting my homework done.

Chapter 2

Love. Desire. Power. A potent mixture. A formula that inspires mortals to perform deeds of greatness... or deeds of destruction. It leaves a trail with a scent so compelling, it calls to the primitive core of Man, cutting through him with the ease of a freshly-honed sword. His desire for these things called me to him. This boy's desires will be his undoing.
I know.
Because they were mine.
~Maksim

"Dude, come on! Spot me."

Justin shifted his body on the duct-tape-patched weight bench that sat in a corner of my room, gripping and re-gripping the bar, waiting to finish our workout.

"Yeah, okay." I said, running my palm across my chest, trying to ease the tightness that was building in my muscles. I'd been looking at the *Power and Control* auction from my Watch List. I still wasn't sure exactly what the deal was, but it'd definitely gotten my attention. I mean, the page had totally sucked me in. Maybe it was the colors. Maybe it was the description. Just the title alone had me thinking.

Power and Control.

"You can look for Dani's present later. I've gotta get going," Justin said.

He was usually quiet, watching everything around him in that way he does, his arms crossed in front of him, keeping his mind and opinions to himself. Justin and I grew up next door to each other, totally inseparable since age five. We were so close, people thought we were brothers. We even looked like we were from the same family. I was taller by a few inches, but we both had brown eyes and sandy blond hair that we preferred to keep as long as the wrestling regulations would allow. We were easy-going for the most part, but Justin was harder to read, even for me, who knew him better than anyone. Right now, though, I knew he was running out of patience.

Justin was right about the auction not going anywhere right now, so I dragged my heels off the edge of the desk, snagging a picture frame with them. I lunged, but wasn't quick enough to catch it before it crashed onto the hardwood floor.

"Crap," I said, picking up the frame.

"Isn't that seven years of bad luck?" Justin joked.

"That's for a broken mirror," I said. I flipped the framed picture over and ran my fingers over Dani's image. She was the best-looking girl at Sandpoint High and, being a runner, she was in incredible shape. Thin, in a healthy-thin way. The sharp angles of her jaw made her look determined, but when she smiled, those angles always softened. Her eyes, an amazing shade of jade-green, looked out at me from behind the broken glass. I remembered she'd been laughing at something I'd said when I took this picture last summer. Yeah, she was something special.

I set the frame on the desk along with the other stuff that had fallen. Scooping a stray sock from the floor, I threw it towards the corner of the room, just missing the laundry basket, before rounding the bed to the weight set.

"You good?" Justin asked.

I widened my stance and held my hands directly under the bar, in case Justin needed help. "Yeah, I'm good."

16

Justin pushed the bar up and off the brackets and eased it down to his chest to begin the last set.

I forced myself to focus on him. I had to, because one slip...

Power.

Something pushed at my brain, almost like a whisper that brushed under my skull. And it came from...

The sudden weight of the bar across my palms snapped my focus back to Justin. His arms were starting to wobble with fatigue under the weight of the bar.

"Come on, you wimp." I grinned, now completely focused on him. "It's not that heavy. I didn't even put the extra plates on yet."

That hit a nerve. Justin could never resist a challenge. His eyes locked with mine and with a yell, he shoved the bar away from his chest, locked it out, and dropped it onto the brackets. Man, he was quick—that was his strength on the wrestling mat. He caught me totally off guard when he whipped himself off the bench and ducked under the weight bar.

He had his hands locked behind my knees before I knew it. My feet lost contact with the floor a second before my back hit, his shoulder pressing hard against my chest.

"Okay, okay!" I grunted. If he hadn't knocked some of the wind out of me, I would have laughed. "I'm tapping out!" was all I managed to say.

Out of the corner of my eye, I saw a spark of black flash on the computer screen, but when I snapped my head around to look, the screen was just as I had left it.

I know black can't flash, but I would've sworn it had just done that. It was as if a black hole sucked in a bunch of color and spewed it out, like the taste of the colors was too disgusting for it to ingest. Maybe Justin hit me so hard, I was seeing stars. Maybe, but I was pretty certain that wasn't it, because being knocked flat didn't usually result in me hearing voices, and I *did* hear a voice. Distant, but clear.

You need me.

I shoved Justin off and scrambled over to my desk. I switched from screen to screen, looking for... I don't know *what* for. I pulled up my auction watch list and checked the time remaining in the auction. Fifteen minutes left. What the hell? I thought there was more time. Hadn't it just said there were two hours left?

"What's that?" Justin looked over my shoulder.

"I don't know. I've been watching something. It says 'Soul for Sale.' Crazy, huh?"

"Yeah, well," Justin answered, "you definitely need soul. Have you ever watched yourself dance?"

I could see Justin's reflection in the window as he danced, looking like a malfunctioning robot, his arms flailing and head twitching in every direction.

It looked like he was enjoying himself too much at my expense, so I reached around and punched him hard on the shoulder.

"There's not even one bid on it," I said, turning back to the computer. I nodded towards the screen and crossed my arms over my chest. "Only one dollar. It's probably a scam. Still..." I leaned closer to the screen. "Listen to this: 'Power. Seduction. Control.' Wouldn't *that* be sweet?" I leaned back into the chair and started imagining what I'd do with all of that. "I could get Dad off the road, get Dani something cool for her birthday, and have her wrapped around my finger..."

"Instead of the other way around?"

That earned Justin another punch.

Justin leaned in to get a closer look, rubbing his shoulder. "*Power Over Your Enemy*," he read aloud.

I grinned. "I might need some help with my dance moves, but *you* could use help with your enemies on the mat. Maybe *you* should buy this, whatever it is."

This time I had the element of surprise. Standing up and spinning around to face him, I stepped forward and snatched Justin's ankle, lifting his foot high. I tripped him backwards until he landed with a thud on the floor.

"Dude, not cool!" he said, laughing.

We grasped each other's forearms as I pulled him up.

"You're lucky I have to go home and finish my English paper. Otherwise, I'd stay here to kick your ass," Justin said, shoving me back. He grabbed his jacket and put it on. "Did you finish your paper yet?"

"Yeah, this morning." I crammed my hands into my pockets. "Dani's coming over. Movie night."

Zipping his jacket, Justin nodded. "Cool." He turned to the door. "See ya," he said over his shoulder. His footsteps faded down the hall and within a few seconds the front door closed.

I looked at the clock. Not much time before Dani would be here.

I sat down at the desk and put my hand over the mouse. The item seemed to be glaring at me, as if I had some nerve to keep it waiting. Great, now it had a personality.

Ten minutes remained in the auction. The picture on the screen wasn't very clear, but if I squinted really hard, I could almost make out an image flickering in the photo box. Not quite enough, though. It was more like I could *feel* it, rather than *see* it, but that made absolutely no sense. I rubbed the frown between my brows. Why did I even care about this? I scanned the description again. *Soul for Sale. Power. Seduction. Control. Nothing will be beyond your reach.*

That's why I cared. There was everything I needed to make me happy.

Down at the bottom of the screen, I read the shipping details. *No shipping fee. Immediate delivery upon completion of transaction.*

Leaning back in my chair, I propped my foot up on the desk, narrowly missing Dani's picture again. "It *would* be nice to have a little edge once in a while," I said to her photo.

It wasn't that my life was so bad. My room, like the rest of the house, like the neighborhood—hell, like Sandpoint—wasn't very exciting. But it was a solid world, and it was mine.

But then again, to have control! I could *really* take care of Dani. I could give her anything she needed. If I had control over everything I wanted, I'd get a scholarship and have enough money to keep Dad from driving all over the country. We could live in a newer house, my old truck would be history…

All of that for only one dollar.

Oh, what the hell. Why not? Even as I clicked on "Bid Now" and even after I entered my debit card number, *knowing* this was bogus, I couldn't stop hoping that my bid would win. Hey, a little desire never hurt anyone.

Time started taking bites out of the five minutes left, and still no one else had placed a bid. Probably for a good reason, I thought, shaking my head, suddenly losing the excitement that I'd had. More than likely, a month from now I'd get some stupid token made in China or a cheap booklet with philosophical crap on the meaning of life or the power of the mind. Maybe a hokey statue made in an obscure Third-World country.

Even so, I couldn't help but imagine the things I could do with this… soul… or whatever it was. I leaned back in my chair and waited the longest five minutes of my life. Dragging my hand over my face, I let out a sigh. I couldn't believe I was taking this so seriously. How much of an idiot was I?

The screen glared at me again. Five seconds, four, three, two, one, zero.

Congratulations! You've won!

Waves of heat poured through my body and my skin crawled with sharp pinpricks that made the hair on my arms stand up. I wanted to rub the goose bumps off, but my muscles clenched up and I couldn't move my arms. My breathing sped up and my eyelids felt like lead. I let them close, focusing instead on trying to make the pain in the pit of my stomach go away. I was seriously close to puking.

Crap! This was not the time to be coming down with the flu. Not that any time was good for that, but especially now. With the state wrestling championships coming up, getting sick was not an option.

The second my chin hit my chest, my eyes snapped open. I couldn't get air into my lungs fast enough as I fought a feeling of panic that pressed against my ribs. I held the air in, taking back control. The tingling stopped, my skin cooled off slowly, and the waves of nausea finally eased up. Relief washed over me, but was it because the waiting was over or because I'd won the bid? I dragged my fingers through my hair again. Maybe a shower would help. I stood and leaned against the desk before moving, feeling suddenly worn-out. Whatever "power" I had just bought had better get me through the next month.

~ ~ ~

"Seth?"

The front door slammed shut.

"In the kitchen!" I called to Dani. I shook the skillet around to mix the rice with the sauce. I liked to cook, especially in the winter. Mostly comfort food. Since it took a lot of food to fill me up, I figured I should learn to cook something more than spaghetti and frozen pizzas.

Dani came through the living room and poked her head around the corner. "Mmm! Smells great! Whatcha got cooking there, babe?" She tossed her keys on the counter and stood behind me, wrapping her arms around my waist.

"It's nothing special," I said. "Just chicken, rice, and veggies. Oh, and corn muffins."

She kissed my shoulder. "What you cook is always special, Seth. Don't sell yourself short." Her arms tightened for a second and then she stepped around me to lean up against the counter. "You spoil me, ya know?"

I gave her a half-grin and shrugged. "Can't help myself. You deserve to be spoiled."

I turned down the temperature on the stove and opened the oven door. "Hand me that, would you?" I asked, pointing to the oven mitt behind her.

Dani grabbed it and tossed it my way. A perfect pitch, but it slid off my hand just as I grabbed the hot baking tin. Yanking my hand back, I waited for the pain. Small, shiny lines ran across the tips of my fingers and thumb, but quickly faded, as if they'd never been there.

"Oh, my God! Are you okay?" Dani pushed herself off the counter and stood close. She grabbed my hand. "Did you get burned?"

We both took a closer look. Nothing.

"Huh," I said. "Must not have touched it as long as I thought I did."

"You're supposed to put your hand *in* the oven mitt, Seth," she teased. She took my hand and pressed her lips to my fingers. Then, picking up the mitt from where it had fallen, she slid her hand inside it and took the muffins out of the oven.

I looked at my hand again. There should have been at least some pain. I'd felt the heat coming off the tin when I grabbed it. I stretched my hand and angled it toward the light. I *know* my skin got burned. I *saw* the marks. Maybe it wasn't as bad as I had thought.

I took two plates from the cupboard and handed them to Dani so she could set the table while I started on the salad.

Opening the refrigerator, I poked around. "Lettuce, tomatoes, avocados, and..." I raised my voice so Dani could hear me, "this week, Madame, you have a choice of ranch dressing or blue cheese." My hip bumped the fridge door shut as I turned to face the only counter space in the small kitchen. There was one problem with the way I cooked—I always managed to use every utensil, seasoning, pot and pan we have, and leave them on the counter, giving me hardly any counter space to work.

I elbowed dirty pans to one side and everything else to the other to make room. Dani's keys were pushed to the edge of the counter, and teetered for a second before slipping over the edge. Dropping the head of lettuce on to the counter, I reached to catch them. Just as my palm was right over the keys, a single thread of heat shot from my shoulder to my fingertips, just like a pinched nerve, numbing my entire arm.

The keys hovered for a fraction of a second before my fingers wrapped around them.

Yeah. Hovered.

Which was exactly what my heart felt like it was doing.

"Nice catch!" Dani appeared behind me. "You've got great reflexes."

"Yeah," I said, staring at the keys in my hand. "I guess I do."

Dani scooped the keys out of my hand and tossed them back on the counter, leaving me to stare at my empty palm.

"Here," Dani said, getting two knives out of the drawer in front of us and handing one to me. "I'll help you."

We made the salad in silence, which was okay, because my mind was spinning with thoughts I couldn't ignore. My reflexes weren't that fast, and the keys would have dropped had they not… maybe it was my imagination.

Maybe not.

"What?" I looked at Dani. "What'd you say?"

"I didn't say anything." She smiled up at me, then went back to chopping the tomatoes.

That was weird. I could have sworn I'd heard a voice. Again.

With the salad finished, Dani carried the salad bowl to the table. I hung back, though, staring hard at the keys. They sat where Dani had tossed them, nothing out of the ordinary.

But something wasn't right. Flexing my hand and straightening my fingers, I passed my hand over the top of the keys. Nothing happened. I lowered my hand until it was almost touching the metal.

Still nothing. I'm not exactly sure what I was waiting for. This was nuts. Dani was right. I just had great reflexes.

Chapter 3

*Compelling this boy has not been easy. Fear
follows closely on the heels of his curiosity. I indulge
him by letting him perform simple tricks. Soon he will
believe. He will see the usefulness of my power. For
now, I merely shadow him. Soon I will be his equal.
Then I will be his master.
And finally...
~Maksim*

"Come on, come on," I twisted the key harder in
the ignition, as if that would force the engine to turn
over.

My truck didn't usually have trouble starting
when the temperatures dropped down into the 20s like
they did last night, but this morning the battery had
only enough juice in it to sputter before dying.

"Damn!" I slammed my palm onto the dashboard.
I didn't have time for this. Dani was waiting for me to
take her to the animal shelter where we volunteered
Saturday mornings, something she had recently talked
me into helping her with.

I pressed my forehead against the cold plastic of
the steering wheel. God, I was tired. Just how long
does it take for three cups of coffee to kick in? I'd
never had nightmares before, but last night I'd had a
long string of them. Not the zombie or disaster-type
nightmare, just the really disturbing, confusing-type. I
didn't remember much more than screams and
maniacal laughing and… shadows, I thought they
were, moving in darkness.

Looking up and rubbing my forehead, I stared through the windshield at the quiet street ahead of me. Sandpoint was slow to wake up on winter weekends. On Sundays the town pretty much shut down and Saturdays weren't much more alive than that. There were hardly any tourists in town now, especially since the ski mountain wasn't getting a lot of snow this season. Boring. Nothing ever happened here. I couldn't wait to graduate and go to college, to go somewhere a little more exciting.

I blew out deep breaths and stared as the moisture stuck to the windshield, the edges spreading until I couldn't see the street in front of my car anymore. What was I doing? I *had* to get over to Dani's house.

Reaching down, I pulled on the hood release and then shoved the door open with my shoulder, carefully stepping over the thin ice on the street. I unhooked the latch and the hood opened with a quiet groan, reminding me once more how old my truck was. I knew my way around the wires and belts on this engine better than I wanted to, but I was glad that it was the battery giving me trouble and nothing more than that.

A flash of red from the corner of my eye caught my attention as a brand new, cherry-red truck drove past my driveway. A totally sweet ride. I didn't stop staring at it until it turned the next corner and drove out of sight.

Depressing. My truck was nothing compared to that—not even in the same league. *Crap!* I needed to get a new battery, and soon. How much would it be? Seventy-five bucks? I didn't have that kind of cash and I couldn't ask my dad for any more money.

There is no need.

"Huh?" I looked over my shoulder, expecting to see my neighbor, but there was no one there. Whatever.

I glared back at the battery. "Stupid thing," I mumbled. As I jiggled the connectors and checked the bolts to make sure they were tight, pinpricks stabbed at my palm. I tried pulling back, but my hand froze over the battery. Stabbing shots of energy broke against my skin and oozed heat that spread across my entire palm. Blue light arced across the battery and clung to the cables. It was damn near impossible to flex my fingers, but I finally pulled my hand away, and when I closed it into a fist, the heat broke somewhat, but not completely. Gulping down the thudding of my heart and rubbing my hand against my pant leg, I took a couple of slow steps backward to distance myself from the truck. I'd always been under the impression that unless I'm touching metal to exposed terminals on the battery, the chance of getting shocked was fairly small, but okay, next time I'll use gloves.

Well done.

What? This time I spun around quicker, but I was still alone.

"I'm losing it because I'm tired. That's all. I'm just tired." I couldn't get the hood shut fast enough. That was just too weird. Yanking the truck door open, I slid behind the wheel. Dragging in a deep breath of the cool air, I wiped my sleeve across my forehead. This was going to be okay. If I couldn't get the truck to start, I'd just have to get my neighbor to help me with jumper cables. Not a big deal.

Turn the key.

Okay, I *definitely* heard a voice that time, but it was just my own voice *inside* my head... wasn't it?

"Come on, man," I muttered. "Get a grip." I turned the key, and the engine rolled over without a hitch, the battery sounding fully charged. Huh. The connectors must have been...

A satisfied smile lifted the corners of my lips. But the smile felt... wrong... like it wasn't mine. Like strings attached to my mouth had pulled my lips up, forcing the reaction.

I shook my head hard, then scrubbed my mouth to rid myself of whatever the hell *that* was all about, and shoved my truck into gear.

~ ~ ~

Dani and I stepped into the lobby of the animal shelter and headed to the reception desk.

"Hey, Gracie! Taking good care of my babies?" Dani asked the receptionist.

Gracie, years of experience sunken into the lines of her face and in her gray-streaked hair, looked up from her computer screen and smiled.

"Hey, kids!" She took her glasses off. "Good news! Sasha was adopted Wednesday."

"Really? Oh, Gracie, that's great!" Dani squeezed my hand tight and gave me a huge smile. "Isn't that great, Seth?"

That, I thought, was what I lived for—her smile, her happiness. These dogs meant a lot to her. It never seemed to occur to Dani to be anything *but* happy, and I'd do anything to keep her that way.

Anything? What would you do?

I was beginning to annoy myself. This brain chatter had to stop. It wouldn't do me any good to keep questioning myself.

"Why don't you two head on back?" Gracie nodded in the direction of the doorway behind the front counter. We could hear the barking and whining of the homeless dogs from the back. "I'm sure the dogs can't wait to see you."

"Come on, babe," Dani said, tugging on my arm. "It sounds like they know we're here." She dragged me along behind her.

Gracie called, "Oh, and there's a new one that came in last night. Real friendly. Last suite on the left."

We made our way back to the cages, aware of being the focus of each and every one of the dogs.

"Hey, you guys." Dani walked ahead of me, dragging her fingers along the wire cages, letting the dogs catch her scent. "Are you all ready for a walk?"

The barking bounced off the walls, ricocheting in every direction, drowning out Dani's voice.

To me, it seemed louder today and was of a different pitch, like the dogs were afraid. But that didn't make any sense. Why would they be afraid?

I walked over to the cage of my favorite dog, a chocolate Labrador. Max was brought in about the same time I started volunteering here. We hit it off the first time we met, but then again, Labs love anyone who will show them attention. I squatted down and poked my fingers through the wire. "Hey, Max."

The dog wagged both ends of his body at the same time, his tongue trying to reach my face through the wire.

"You're always glad to see me, aren't you, buddy?" I stretched my fingers to reach his ear. "You're too good to be in here." I leaned closer to the cage. "I'll walk you first, okay?"

"Hey! I heard that," Dani teased. "No playing favorites." She stood close behind me and eyed Max. "Unless, of course, that favorite is me. You understand, Max, don't you?" She reached down and squeezed my shoulder. "Come on, Seth. Let's check out the new kid in the neighborhood."

Two cages down, a Schnauzer wiggled his bobbed tail excitedly. His eyes were pinned on Dani, his nose frantically sniffing her fingers as she squatted and brought her face down to his level. As soon as he caught a whiff of my scent, though, his nostrils flared and his excitement died completely. The dog went perfectly still except for a ridge of hair on his back that slowly rose, along with a low, deep growl that vibrated in his throat.

"Whoa." Dani looked up at me, her eyes wide. "Gracie said he was friendly."

I squatted beside her and placed my palms against the wire. "It's okay, buddy."

The dog stood still, his body tense. The edges of his nose flared again as if my presence offended him. With his ears flattened against his head and his eyes fixed on my face, it didn't look like he trusted me at all. Taking two steps backwards, he sat on his haunches and whined.

"Losing your touch, Seth?" Gracie said as she walked toward us. "I've never seen a dog that didn't like you."

I stood up and turned to face her. "Yeah, well, I just haven't turned on the charm yet."

"What's up with this dog, Gracie?" Dani asked as she moved next to me, linking her arm through mine. "Is he usually like that?"

Gracie looked past me at the dog and frowned. "Hasn't been until now."

Dani bit her lip, staring first at the Schnauzer and then at me. "Okay, I have an idea," she said. "Why don't you walk… what's his name, Gracie?"

"Blaze," Gracie said.

"Seth, you walk Blaze and I'll walk Dakota and Lady."

"But I promised Max," I protested. Besides, I wasn't sure it was such a good idea to get too close to Blaze.

Dani laughed. "I'm sure Max will understand. Come on, Seth. It's bonding time." She turned to the Schnauzer, who had backed himself into the corner. "Don't worry, Blaze. Seth won't bite."

"Nah," I said, smiling at the dog. "We're going to get along just fine."

~ ~ ~

My truck rolled to a stop alongside the curb outside Dani's house. She hadn't said much on the way back from the shelter. She seemed to be bothered about how the morning with the dogs went down, because she'd gotten quiet right after we'd taken them for their walk.

As for me and Blaze, I wouldn't say that the bonding session had been a complete success. In fact, it was a total failure. After having to practically drag Blaze outside, he'd distanced himself from me as far as the leash would allow the entire time we walked. Dani had gotten so discouraged watching the two of us interact, she finally traded dogs with me. The difference in his behavior after that was like night and day. Even though it *looked* like he'd forgotten about me, he'd glance back and step up his pace if I was too close to him. I didn't understand it, but I knew it wasn't a good thing.

Anything you desire can be yours, the voice in my mind whispered.

Yeah, right, I thought. I was starting to sound like the one-dollar promise I'd been stupid enough to buy.

I still couldn't believe I'd fallen for it. As if anything I bought online could possibly change things.

The voice barely had time to fade before electric shocks pooled in the tips of my fingers, like needles pelting against my skin. I squeezed the steering wheel, trying to get rid of the tingling, but that just made it worse. The muscles in my hands and forearms tensed up, shooting threads of pain to both sides of my neck. My shoulders automatically shot up. Shit, that hurt.

"You okay?"

Letting go of the steering wheel, I flipped my hands back and forth, looking at them. What the hell? It took me a few seconds to focus and realize Dani was talking to me.

"Seth, are you okay?" she asked again.

"Huh?" I turned to her and forced a smile. "Yeah, sure, sure. Just a cramp or something." I clapped my hands once and rubbed them together, trying to stop the tingling and heat. "Ready?" Without waiting for an answer, I shouldered my door open and jogged around the front of the car, stretching to open Dani's door.

"Thanks." Dani's voice came out in one white puff and disappeared into the cold air. "Hey, I'm thinking about getting my mom a new camera. The one she has takes the worst pictures, but she refuses to get a new one. Will you help me look for one online?"

"Sure," I said, sliding my arms around her waist and pulling her against my chest. "But there's a price."

She laughed, playfully slapping my shoulder. "There's always a price, isn't there?"

"Well, we could start with a down payment," I said, leaning in to kiss her ear.

Take her, my mind whispered.

There was no question about it. I definitely wanted to, and had for a long time. But she had it in her head to wait until marriage. We'd messed around a lot, but she had definite boundaries. I didn't necessarily like those boundaries, but I respected them.

My hands cupped her face and I ran my lips against her cheek until I found her mouth. Her lips moved against mine, slowly at first, then her arms wrapped behind my neck, pulling me closer. A lot closer, like she couldn't get close enough. Not holding back wasn't like her, especially out in front of her house in broad daylight, but I wasn't about to turn her down.

Seduce her...

I didn't need to tell myself that. Hell, she was doing fine on her own. Her fingers were all of sudden at the zipper of my jacket, yanking it down and reaching for the buttons of my shirt

My fingers slid down her throat, over her pulse. It was racing as fast as mine was. If we kept this up, I was going to have to go for a run or something later. But for better or worse, I didn't know which, she stopped and pulled back, her chest rising and falling with her breath.

I looked down at the undone buttons of my shirt. "You know, I really don't mind what you're doing, but I'm thinking we should go somewhere else..."

"Oh, God, I'm sorry." Her hand covered her mouth. "I didn't mean to give you the wrong idea." She ducked her head and her hair hid her face so I could hardly hear her. "I really haven't changed my mind... I mean, I still want to wait until... I'm sorry. I don't know what got into me." She pulled the edges of my jacket together and backed up. "I'd better get going."

"What's wrong, Dani?" I reached for her hands and leveled my face with hers.

"There's nothing wrong. That was just ..." She blinked a few times. "Wow, I need to go inside. I've got to finish some homework."

"Hey." I held her hands tighter as she turned away. "I love you, Dani. I really do."

She squeezed my hands and a faint smile pulled at her lips. "I know you do. I love you, too."

As I watched the front door close behind her, I stood for another minute. What the hell was that all about?

~ ~ ~

"Another simple trick," Silura said, taking his hand and turning it upward.

"Trick?" His brows raised. "Simple, perhaps, but certainly not a trick."

The sorcery she taught Maksim had opened a portal to a new world for him. What he discovered fed his imagination, and he feasted on it by day and dreamt of it through the night.

A smile played along her lips as she placed her other palm a slight distance above his.

Unseen pressure upon his skin startled him and he tried to pull away.

Her grip tightened on his hand. "Be still," she whispered. "Do not be hasty in your perception of what you feel."

The pressure rolled within itself, forming a transparent ball of heat. Mimicking her movement, he curled his fingers around the energy that pulsed between their hands. Palpable, yet intangible. Heavy, yet weightless.

"How can this be? What is this?" he whispered, awed.

Her smile widened, but she said nothing. With outstretched fingers, she pressed down on the now pulsing heat, until the space was no longer there.

Again, he tried to pull back as the energy flowed up his arm, caressing like a lover's touch, over his shoulder, up the sinuous muscles of his neck, across the high bones of his cheek, and resting over his lips.

Silura had not moved, yet he felt her touch; a seductive, slow touch that left him weak and vulnerable. Such an unfamiliar feeling, one he did not wish to feel again.

"What is this?" he asked again.

Releasing his hand, she shrugged. "Transfer of energy. From me," she touched her fingers to her lips before placing them on his, "to you."

His eyes lost their focus and drifted into a calculating haze. He had proven to be an eager student and was determined to quickly learn the ways of sorcery. One day, she thought, he would be the one to command such power—and many would come to fear him.

Her smile dimmed. "I will continue to teach you what I know, but you must remember two things."

The focus returned to his eyes as he gently lifted her hand and brushed his lips across her fingers.

"What might they be?"

She flushed, then squared her shoulders, once again regaining her resolve.

"First, this knowledge I bestow upon you is powerful. You must be extremely careful when using it. It is not the way of our kind to abuse sorcerer magick. And, second," she said, pulling away her hand and reaching to touch his cheek, "you must remain committed to me only."

He dipped his head in acknowledgement. "As you wish," he said lightly.

But they both knew his lie for what it was, for a man such as he could never abide by such constraints.

~ ~ ~

Chapter 4

I grow impatient, for he resists. His mind has not yet accepted me. None of their puny minds really ever do. The unknown and untried frighten them. They ignore the obvious, and look for an explanation that suits them. But in the end, there will be no explaining me away.

~Maksim

"…Five…six…seven…" The bar settled back onto the brackets before I stood up. What the hell? I wasn't even straining and these were the same plates I'd put on only three days ago. They were almost too heavy then, but now they were too easy. How could I have gotten so much stronger in only three days?

I grabbed a couple more plates and slid them onto each end of the bar. Then I threw on two more ten-pound plates before lying down on the bench. Wrapping my hands around the bar, I tested my grip and took a few seconds to psych myself up. With my wrists rigid and shoulders tensed, I pushed up on the bar and lifted it up and over the brackets. I hardly felt the added weight. How could that be, though? I guess it was possible I hadn't been keeping track of how much weight I'd been putting on the bar. I pumped out the rest of the set, dropped the bar back on the brackets, then sat up.

Across the room, the mirror reflected a body that I was not used to seeing. There was no way that could be me. Getting closer to my reflection, I took a hard look at myself from head to toe. I hadn't noticed before that the sleeves of my shirt were pulled too tight against my arms. I pushed a sleeve up over my shoulder and flexed my biceps.

No way.

I yanked off my shirt.

No *way*!

I straightened up, pushing my shoulders back, and *stared*. I'd never had that much width before. Cut muscles, but not *this*. I'd definitely gained some mass. Not weight, I thought, hitting my fist against my stomach. Just bulk. Major muscles.

Whatever program I was doing, I'd better stick with it. This was cool, in a disconcerting way. Kind of like a Spiderman transformation. Just to be sure, I flipped my hands over and checked my wrists. Okay, I was good. No webs shooting out. Shoving my hands through my hair a few times, I checked the clock on my dresser.

Running late. Always running late. Time moved too fast. With one last look at my reflection, I grabbed my shirt and headed out of the room.

~ ~ ~

Dani's voice was a welcome interruption to vacuuming because the drone from the motor was starting to give me a headache.

She said something again before I had a chance to turn off the vacuum.

"What?" I asked.

Dani slung her backpack onto the couch and unzipped it. "We're only studying, remember? You don't have to clean up for me."

"I know. That's not the reason I'm doing it." I grabbed the cord and yanked the plug out of the wall.

"Dad is coming home tonight. He switched routes so he could be home for a couple days."

I swiped at the beads of sweat on my forehead with the back of my hand, and rolled my shoulders to loosen the tension in my back. This living room wasn't that big and I hadn't been moving the few pieces of furniture we had, so I doubted my sweating was from the vacuuming. Since this morning I'd been feeling hotter than usual and my skin felt tight, almost like my insides were trying to bust out.

"You okay?" Dani stared at me, concern in her eyes.

"Yeah, I'm okay. I must be coming down with something." I smiled, hoping to mask how crappy I felt. "You sure you want to hang out with me?"

"Are you kidding? Of course I'm sure." Her books hit the coffee table with a thud. She rounded the table and stood toe-to-toe with me. "I'm not afraid of any big bad germ you've got going on inside," she said, poking at my chest. "Oh!" Her brows raised. "Wow, Seth, working out has been paying off." She smiled and reached under my shirt. "I like that."

I would've kissed her if my stomach hadn't lurched. I held back a groan, but I guess my misery showed on my face.

"Seth?" Her brows pulled together.

I managed a smile. "I'm glad you're not afraid of me."

The front door opened, then slammed shut.

"Hello?"

"We're in here, Dad!" I called. Normally I would be rushing to greet him, but not this time. I felt like I was going to pass out.

"You should tell your dad you're sick," Dani said.

"No," I said quickly. "I don't want to worry him. He has enough to think about." I reached down and started to coil up the vacuum cord. The throbbing in my head was getting worse. "He's only here for a couple of days."

"I don't know, Seth." Dani didn't look convinced.

I lowered my voice. "I'm fine. Really. Please don't say anything to him."

"All right." Dani said, raking me with narrowed eyes. She turned toward the hallway. "Hey, Mr. Thompson!"

"Hey, Dani!" Dad grinned at her, but his smile grew even wider when he spotted me. "Seth!"

With each forward step he took, his arms spread out wider, ready to pull me into a hug.

It hadn't been long ago that my dad, Martin, Marty to his friends, had towered over me, but now I towered over him. He looked the part of a trucker: worn jeans, nylon jacket over what looked like a new t-shirt, and a baseball cap that hid his graying brown hair. His skin clung a little tighter to his cheeks, but below his eyes, it hung looser than the last time I'd seen him. He looked tired tonight and I felt the usual stab of guilt. I took a step towards him and braced myself for one of his bear hugs.

"It's good to see you, buddy!" he said, slapping my back.

"It's good to see you, too, Dad." I pulled back and stared down at his shirt, lifting the edges of his jacket to get a better look at the words. *My wrestling champ can pin your honor student in 3.14 seconds.*

Dad grinned, obviously thinking that was the greatest line ever. "Get it?" he laughed. "3.14 seconds. Pi? Math? Wrestling?"

I rolled my eyes and groaned. "Geeze, Dad. I hope nobody saw you wearing that."

"What's wrong with it?" He turned to Dani. "Do *you* see something wrong with it?"

42

She giggled. "It's adorable. Really."

I glared at her. "Don't encourage him, Dani."

"I want everyone to know what a great kid you are!" He pulled me into another hug and laughed.

I could do no wrong, as far as Dad was concerned. It was sometimes hard to live up to. I looked over his shoulder at Dani, who seemed to be getting a kick out of the whole thing. Even though I was a little embarrassed, I wouldn't have this moment any other way. Who could complain that his father cared too much?

"Okay, Dad," I laughed. "You win."

"Hey, listen," he said, holding me at arms' length. "I grabbed a pizza for tonight. It's still out in the truck. I'll get it—oh! I almost forgot! Dani, your birthday is coming up, right?"

"Uh-huh," she nodded.

"I thought so. I have something for you," he said, patting his pockets. "I thought I'd be a bit early, but… Where is it? Oh, here." He reached into the inside pocket of his jacket and pulled out a small plastic gift card. "I don't know what teenage girls want these days…"

"Tell me about it," I mumbled.

"So I got you this." Dad handed the card to Dani and shrugged. "Sorry it's not wrapped or anything. I've never been good with that kind of stuff."

"Oh, don't worry about it!" Dani said, taking the card from him. "Thanks, Mr. Thompson!" She stood on her tip-toes and gave him a hug. "That's so cool!"

"You're welcome." He laughed, obviously relieved. "Okay." He clapped his hands together. "So, let me go get the pizza. Be right back, kids."

I shoved my hands into my pockets. "Looks like he beat me to it," I muttered. "I wanted to be the first to give you a gift."

"Hey, it's not a big deal." Dani said, moving close. "Besides, I've told you not to worry about it. But," she said, wrapping her arms around my waist and giving me a lazy smile, "if you insist, you still have until next week."

"I know." A strand of hair clung to her mouth, and I pulled it away, smoothing it back where it belonged. "I'm looking for the perfect present."

Dani tilted her chin up to look at me. "It doesn't make sense to get something perfect for someone who isn't."

"I think you are." I leaned over and kissed her, hooking my fingers through her belt loops, drawing her closer. This was where I wanted to be, close to Dani—all the time, my body against her...

...in her, around her.

A burning heat trickled out through my fingers and warmed her skin where I touched her waist.

She leaned into me, sliding her arms around my neck. "Seth." My name was a whispered breath against my mouth.

I tugged her closer, having to practically holding her up.

"Eh-hem..." Dad cleared his throat. "Who's hungry?"

Whoa! That was intense. Even when she pulled away and buried her face into my chest, the connection between us was still smoking hot. I stooped to look into Dani's face. She looked a little dazed, a little confused, but she... glowed. And *I'd* made her feel that way. Not Dirk, not anyone else. Whatever had been going on between us in the last couple of days was really heating up and it was definitely helping me feel more secure with her. Looking over the top of her head, I couldn't help smiling.

"Sorry, Dad. I was going to grab some plates but Dani stopped me."

"Hey!" She snapped out of her daze.

I laughed, dodging Dani's reach as I headed to the kitchen. "So, Dad," I called over my shoulder. "How's the studying going?"

I was really proud of him. Dad never had the chance to finish high school because his dad, my grandpa, in one of his drunken stupors, had kicked Dad out of the house after beating the crap out of him. Dad could have gone back home when Grandpa had sobered up, but he just kept walking, never looked back. He did okay for himself over the years. He met Mom and had a pretty good life after that. But now he'd decided to get his high school diploma.

"Great!" my dad said loud enough for me to hear. "I'm getting close. And after I have my G.E.D., I'm going to sign up for some online college courses. By the way," he added, "I have some questions on my math assignment. Can you help me later?"

I walked out of the kitchen carrying forks, napkins, plates, and leftover salad in my hands and cans of soda tucked under one arm. "Yeah, sure."

"Here, Seth, let me help you." Dani grabbed the cans and handed one of them to my dad.

Putting everything else down on the table, I pushed the plates in their direction so they could help themselves to the pizza and salad. Just as my hand got closer to the forks, electric shocks spidered out across my palm and splintered up my arm, tightening my fingers until they locked up like a claw. Flexing my fingers only intensified the tingling in my hand. I closed my eyes and took a deep breath, held it for a second, and tried to relax my arm, but couldn't. Straightening my arm made a little bit of a difference, but not much. Less than an inch away from my fingers, a fork spasmed off the table and shot into my hand, and my fingers reflexively wrapped around the cool metal.

"Holy *shit*!" I looked from the fork to Dani and then quickly to Dad, whose jaw hung open just a little bit, but I think it was because he'd never heard me say something like that, not at what just happened with the fork. At least I'd hoped so. I handed the fork to him and got another one for Dani.

A trail of sweat inched down my back. Man, it was suddenly *way* too hot in the house. "Dig in. It's getting cold," I said, gesturing at the pizza and salad. "Oh, I forgot the dressing, didn't I?"

"I'll get it," Dani offered.

"No, no," I said. I needed to get up and move around. Actually, I wanted out of that room. "You eat." I leaned over and kissed her cheek.

Dani stared at me a second longer before turning back to Dad. "So, what classes are you thinking of taking?"

I hurried to the kitchen. I was wound up—like one of those toy cars that you spin the wheels back further and further until they wouldn't move anymore; and then you let the car go, letting it fly. I felt sort of like that—my heart sped up and my muscles tightened, as if ready to explode out the starting gate. I steadied myself against the counter. I'd swear my heart had found its way up to my throat and was trying to jump out of my mouth. And the way my hands shook? I was lucky I didn't drop the dressing when I finally took it out from the fridge. Maybe eating something would help.

"... hopefully that will land us both at the same college, or at least in the same state," Dani was explaining to my dad when I got back to the dining room.

When she reached across the table and squeezed my hand, my insides settled down almost as quickly as they had gotten fired up.

She looked at me, her eyebrows slightly raised. She mouthed, "You okay?"

I nodded and pulled a slice of pizza from the box before sitting down. Using my plate instead of my hand, I pushed my fork away from me, then pushed it farther away. I waved off the bowl of salad my dad held out to me. No forks. I wasn't about to risk that one again. The fork, just like Dani's keys, had looked innocent enough while it lay on the table, but I wasn't going to let my guard down, at least not until I figured out what the hell was going on.

I let my dad do all the talking through dinner. Fortunately, he was never at a loss for stories. I just nodded and smiled, all the while keeping an eye on the fork, half expecting it to lift itself up and stab me in the heart. What had I done to all of a sudden become a metal magnet?

~ ~ ~

I leaned back in my chair, my feet propped on the edge of my desk, my computer screen switched into screen-saver mode. Dani had gone home about an hour before. She'd studied while I sat across the couch from her and analyzed how crappy I felt. I couldn't believe this. I never got sick. Maybe a cold, but even then I never felt like a furnace about to explode. It seemed that I had all the symptoms of the crud—stomach pain, headache, squeezing in my chest, tingling in my hands. I supposed it was possible I had a cold or the flu. The flu would have been a great explanation, except for the fact that I wasn't coughing or sneezing, didn't have a runny nose, sore throat, or trouble breathing. There was no explanation for the sudden strength and size I had. No way I should've been able to pull the keys and fork into my hand. And then my truck; it had been running fine—better than ever—since the day the battery almost gave out.

There will be no explaining me away.

I jumped at the sudden intensity of the pinprick sensation on my arms and scalp.

Congratulations! You've won! Faint laughing tickled the back of my mind.

No! I moved my head back and forth in denial. My thoughts raced to the place I'd been avoiding for the last few days, and this time I couldn't stop them.

There's no way. It's not possible to buy a soul, online or anywhere else. A soul isn't a tangible thing. I wiggled the mouse to wake up the screen, and glared at the eSouled page. What exactly had I bought and when was it going to be delivered?

Then I shook my head. What was I thinking? This was nuts. The sale was bogus. What exactly would buying a soul *mean*? Nothing. I *was* getting the flu. At this time of year, there was a lot of crud going around.

Pulling my feet off the desk, I closed down the auction page and grabbed my math book. I needed to do something normal, and studying was the most normal thing I could think of, but when I saw the words and numbers on the pages, they didn't register. Resting my head in my hands helped steady the throbbing in my forehead, but not the speed of my heart pounding against my chest. I took a few quick breaths. *Get. A. Grip. Thompson.* I bit down hard. *Control. Control.* I cleared my mind, keeping it as blank as I could. Nothing in, nothing out. A little trick I used in wrestling to block out any insecurities or distractions. Okay. No voices, no doubts. Just white noise.

"Hey, Seth?"

I was really glad when my dad knocked on my door. I wasn't sure how long I could hold my mind blank against the million thoughts pushing to get in.

"Come on in, Dad!"

He opened the door and stuck his head inside the room. "Is now a good time to go over my homework?"

"Sure." I put down my own book and pulled up a chair for him. "Let me see what you've got."

Dad flipped open to a page and put his book on my lap.

"Now, what I don't get," Dad said, pointing, "is how to get from this part of the problem to here."

Stretching behind a stack of books piled on my desk, I said, "I know there's a pencil back here." My fingertips brushed the side of the pencil and it rolled away. Stretching just a little more, I almost had it. The closer my hand got, though, another round of tingling fired up the tips of my fingers. The front legs of my chair came off the floor as I leaned back quickly and grabbed the pencil.

I will not be ignored.

The chair legs landed back on the floor with a thud. "Did you say something?" I looked at my dad.

He put on his reading glasses. "Yeah. How do I get from here—"

"No," I interrupted. "I mean, did you say something *after* that?"

He glanced at me and shook his head.

I straightened and stared down at the problem again. Freakin' A. I *did* hear something. I knew it. I wasn't crazy. Or, maybe I was. The pencil cracked under my grip.

"Okay," I said. "You start by…" I managed to get through the explanation between wiping away the sweat on my forehead and rubbing my eyes. I hoped Dad understood what I said, because I didn't have a clue whether it had made any sense. Words came out of my mouth, but I'd been more focused on listening for more whispers—inside my head or out.

"Okay, I get it," Dad said. "That's simple. Now, how about… Seth, are you okay?" He leaned closer, trying to get a good look at my face.

"Yeah," I nodded, looking up at him. "No." I shook my head. "I mean…" Shadows crossed my eyes, dimming the light, like something had passed across the sun.

"Let me feel your forehead." The coolness of his hand and the concern behind his gesture made me feel less alone.

"You're a little warm, Seth." He dropped his hand to his lap. "Wow. I can't remember the last time you were sick." He grabbed my chin and turned my face towards him. "Your eyes are a little glazed over." He straightened up and sat with his hands on his knees, studying me. "I'll tell you what. I'll work on this stuff on my own for now. We can try it again tomorrow, okay? You'd better get some rest."

Rest. Yeah. That's what I needed. I wanted to go to bed and close my eyes and have this all go away.

"I'm sorry, Dad."

"No, it's okay. We'll see how you feel tomorrow." He leaned over and ruffled my hair. "Can I get you some Tylenol?"

"No, thanks." I gestured to my desk. "I have some in my desk." The queasiness twisted my stomach in a knot before climbing up my throat. I forced myself to look at my dad and smile. I didn't want him to know how I really felt.

"Okay. Let me know if you need anything." He picked up his book and closed the door behind him.

I wiped my face with my hand again. I was feeling worse every minute. My chest and stomach were too tense, and taking a deep breath was like pressing my ribs against a brick wall. It felt like there was no space in my lungs for air.

A hot, prickly sensation scratched at the back of my scalp. *Oh, God!* Not again. I sucked in a breath and shook my head back and forth, trying desperately to stop the feeling. I stood and paced the room, trying to walk it off, but it wouldn't go away.

You can do it again.

I stopped pacing and held very, very still. What. The. *Hell?* This time, it was very distinct, very much a *voice.* Outside on the street, I could see how I could have been mistaken. But here, inside my room, in total silence, there was no doubt. I scanned the room.

"What… can I do again?" I said out loud. Then I held my breath, waiting for an answer I hoped wouldn't come.

Get your keys.

The breath I had been holding shot out of my lungs. I scrambled to my chair and sat, facing my computer again. Hitting the mouse, I brought the screen to life and restored the eSouled page. Okay, the night I thought I burned myself when I grabbed Dani's keys, the night I started feeling sick. That was the same night I made the bid for the soul. But there was no way that could be real, I reminded myself. Besides, souls are just dead people. And dead people can't talk.

"Let's see exactly what I bought," I whispered, as I searched my account page.

Control. That's what I remembered the description had said. Control I had - over my body and my workouts. Being stronger on the mat would mean control over my opponents. Bottom line – scholarship.

Power. The keys. The forks. I made those things come to me. Wasn't that like telekinesis or something? Definitely power.

Seduction. Dani. The way she melted when I touched her. Yeah, we were definitely getting hot!

I dragged my hand down my face, taking the dampness away. I needed to talk to the seller, like now. I scrolled through my past purchases, but I couldn't find anything that mentioned *"Soul for Sale."* Damn! Maybe the seller had another soul for sale, or other strange stuff, and I could track him that way. After a few minutes of clicking around, though, I realized there wasn't going to be anything on the seller *or* the sale.

My keys. They sat on my desk just like Dani's keys had lay on the kitchen counter. They had hovered. I *knew* they had hovered. It wasn't my quick reflexes, it was like something *had helped me* grab them. I pushed my chair back and stepped away from the desk and the keys, until I felt my bed against the back of my knees.

Did I *really* buy power? Was this an Aladdin's lamp kind of thing? I spun around. "Who are you? *Where* are you?"

Silence radiated from the walls and wrapped around me like a blanket. My gaze slid around the room and stopped at my desk. Could I *really* do it again? The muscles in my jaw tightened. Out of anticipation? Out of fear? Maybe a little of both, but, as much as I hated to admit it, I really wanted to find out if I could.

As if holding a catcher's mitt, I lifted my arm with my palm flattened to give the keys a perfect target. Man, if I could do this....

"Come to me," I ordered.

The keys didn't move.

"Now. I command you. Come."

Still nothing. I felt so stupid.

My arm landed hard against my body. What was I doing wrong? In the kitchen I didn't have to say or do anything.

Try again.

I stood straighter and listened. "Who the hell *are* you?" My eyes narrowed, as if that could that would give me special vision. "Are you some kind of ghost or... an... angel?" Oh, my God. I couldn't believe I'd asked that.

But it laughed like there was some secret joke. *An angel. Yes. Of sorts.*

"But... why? Why me? Why now?"

Try again. The voice insisted. *Focus.*

Then the possibility hit me. "Wait a minute! Am I in trouble or something? Angels don't just pop into someone's life unless they're going to save them from something, right?"

There was no answer for a few heartbeats, then it spoke again, very patiently, like a father to a child. *The keys.*

The keys. Why was it so insistent about the freakin' keys? I might get hit by lightning or something, and all it can think about are the keys?

"Okay." I whipped around, looking in every corner of my room. "If I play along with this, then will you tell me what's going on?"

The keys. Focus.

"I need to know."

The room turned quiet again. I wasn't sure how to take that. Was I going to get an answer or not? After another slow turn, with no more hints invading my mind, I decided I wasn't going to have anything to lose, so I locked my door and went back to where I'd been standing.

So I'd try again, but this was nuts. Really nuts.

Just like I did before a wrestling match, I filled my lungs with as much air as they could hold, then let it seep out through my clenched teeth. This time, though, a kind of heavy fog swirled through my body, pressing down on my shoulders and weighing me down. My eyes narrowed until everything disappeared from my line of vision except the keys. I held up my hand again, ready to catch them.

The keys didn't move.

Focus on the stream of energy between you and the keys.

My concentration broke and my hand dropped to my side. "I can't." I shook my head. What was wrong with me? "You're not even real," I said out loud.

Try. Again. The voice sliced the air with obvious impatience.

I spun around again. "What is going *on*? Who *are* you?"

An angel. Your angel. It said too quickly. *Come. Try again. I will help you this time.*

"*Why* are you helping me?"

You asked me to.

"I did not!"

Again, quiet laughter rippled around me. *You most certainly did. I heard your desire. I answered. Try again,* it said, a little more insistent this time, but the edge was gone.

My breath came out with a small quiver. "Okay." My stomach got tangled up in my nerves and tripped,

54

landing with a thud. But I was willing to try again. I flattened my palm toward the keys one more time. "Like this?" I whispered.

All things are energy. All energy is connected. Imagine the connection.

The muscles in my arm, from my shoulder to my wrist, pulled in tight and a small tremor intensified as I pictured a silver thread stretching between my hand and the keys. In the center of my palm, a very small part tingled before a sensation of warmth melted the tingling away. A ball of heat, about the size of a BB, then growing to the size of a ping-pong ball, filled my palm. The invisible thread widened and stretched, reaching a few inches beyond my palm. My whole body tensed. Every cell in my body convulsed until the tension clawed at me, screaming to get out.

Yessssss.

I could see, I could feel, but for a few seconds it didn't feel like my body was mine anymore. I felt furious and impatient, and at the same time, scared and excited.

The keys quivered where they sat, the metal tapping against the surface of the desk before they rocketed off, bee-lined across the room, and slammed into my palm. My breath caught as the metal tore at my skin before dropping in a heap on the floor.

The heat cooled, the tingling slowed to almost nothing, and my lungs found a shallow, steady pace until I was breathing normally again.

The stillness of the air was eerie. There was no movement at all, anywhere, until I let my hand down once again.

Oh. Wow. That was crazy. Heh. Harry Potter lands in Idaho.

Well done.

My body jerked at the voice as if I had been shocked. Like an echo, the sound bounced its way around my mind, making the hair on the back of my neck stand up. My first impulse was to run—far away. But away from *what* and to *where*? I hardly thought I could hide, let alone outrun it.

My palm began throbbing—not like thorns or needle pricks—more like claws had sunken in and raked down the skin. But my palm was the least of my worries. Because, though I didn't want to believe it, I felt it. Something was inside me. Something… other. Very other.

A second pulse inside me beat steady, strong, and disturbingly close to mine.

And then the truth hit me. Hard. I knew.

The soul *had* been delivered.

Chapter 5

*I allowed the boy to rest this past night to give
him time to adjust to what he already knows. I settled
around him, weaving in and out of his consciousness,
blending our souls and reinforcing the ties that bind
us. I have chosen him as my eyes, my ears, and my
touch. He will be the one to fulfill my destiny.*
~ Maksim

The sky was just beginning to lighten when the
alarm went off. I must have slept hard because I
didn't have any dreams, good or bad. None that I
remembered, anyway. I sat up and ran my fingers
through my hair, trying to identify what it was that
felt different this morning.

Different, but in a good way. I rolled my
shoulders and turned my head from side to side. I
guessed I'd managed to shake off whatever made me
so sick last night.

Last night. Man, I hadn't felt good at all. How
much of that really happened? I couldn't help
questioning myself. I *felt* something then. I *know* I
did. But now… nothing. Could I have imagined all of
it?

The rattle of my cell phone on my desk made me
jump. Throwing back the covers, I jetted across the
room, half expecting the phone to levitate or the
tingling in my fingers to start again. Flipping my
hands back and forth, I checked for anything unusual,
but my hands and fingers looked normal and felt fine
when I flexed them. But just to be sure, I wiped my

hand against my leg, and before anything had a chance to change, I snatched up the phone.

Dani had sent a text: *Have 2 go in early. Meet u in 1st. XXOO*

I hadn't realized I was holding my breath until my chest ached from the pressure of caging it in. Nothing happened. Nothing was *going* to happen. I'd imagined the fork and the keys taking flight... *and* the voice.

And I wasn't bummed out all. Well, not really.

I texted Dani an answer and tossed the phone on my bed, grabbed a t-shirt off the floor and yanked it over my head.

The smell of bacon and eggs slipped through the crack under the door. I hadn't realized how hungry I was. No wonder. I don't think I even finished my pizza last night. I couldn't get my door open fast enough.

Dad hummed to himself as he stood in front of the stove pushing bacon around in a pan. He looked totally content to be home. I wished I could do something to make that permanent.

"Hey, buddy! How are you feeling this morning?" he asked, giving me a once-over.

"I'm feeling pretty good, actually," I said, peeking over his shoulder at the strips of bacon that curled and spit in the grease.

"Great!" Dad grinned. "You had me worried. I didn't want to hit the road again if you were sick." He turned down the stove and reached for the oven mitt. "I have a plate of eggs in the oven."

"Here, Dad, let me do that for you." I reached for the mitt.

He held the edges open and I pushed my hand in. "You do that and I'll make the juice." He took a can of frozen juice from the freezer and started opening

58

the cabinets, looking for something to put it in. "Ah, here we go," he murmured, taking out a pitcher.

I opened the oven door and visually traced the red-hot curved rods that snaked below the rack. It was like a miniature hell that sent its heat up to wash over my face.

Dad rambled on, his voice a background buzz. "I know what you're thinking about the bacon, it not being good for you and all, but I figured once in awhile it'd be okay."

I stared at the rack, thinking about how only a few days ago it had burned me—or so I'd thought. I slid the mitt off my hand and touched my fingers to the plate. There was no squeezing of my brain or chest. No voices in my head. Heh. I guess I *did* want it to have been real. It might have been nice to have an angel looking over my shoulder.

"Are you still there?" I whispered, hoping that the voice would answer.

I've never left.

I flushed hot, then cooled just as fast. My brain had registered panic before the relief hit. The angel was still here. I looked out of the corner of my eyes to both sides of me, thinking maybe I'd see him. Of course, I didn't. How do you see a voice? I knew nothing about angels, but I was pretty sure they didn't just materialize. But maybe I could make him show himself.

Touching the plate with one finger at a time, I tested the heat until I had a firm grip on the plate, letting the burn seep into the layers of my skin. Fighting the rational urge to pull away, I did the irrational and tightened my grip. *Let's put this to the test*. I waited, expecting my skin to burn and my arm to shake from the pain. Okay, any time now my angel should be saving me.

Behind me, Dad stood at the sink filling the container with water. "I wanted to go all out and get you fresh-squeezed juice, but I couldn't find any decent oranges at the store last night. Wrong time of year, I guess."

I pulled the plate out of the oven and set it on the counter just as Dad walked over and placed the pitcher on the countertop.

"I should have gotten a bag at the produce stand the other day, but I thought for sure I could get some in town. I hope this is okay for you." He looked around the kitchen. "All righty, now," he said. "I think that's it. Let's get you fed so you won't be late for school." He pushed the plate of eggs over. "Ow!" He sucked in a quick breath and looked at his hand. "That plate is hot!"

I gestured to the mitt and smiled. "You should use the mitt next time, huh?"

"I'll say." Dad nodded and smiled back. Grabbing a spoon from the drawer, he piled the eggs and bacon onto two plates, gestured for me to bring the juice and a couple glasses, and headed to the dining room.

I hung back, studying my hand.

No burn mark. No pain. Just like before.

Who are you really? What is your name? I asked in my head.

I am a friend, came the answer. *Long ago, they called me Maksim.*

~ ~ ~

The school parking lot hadn't filled up yet so I easily found Dani's car and a space close to it. Grabbing my backpack, I slammed the truck door behind me.

"Seth! Wait up!" Justin skirted around a few parked cars before catching me. "Hey, man. How's it going?"

I nodded. "Good. My dad is in town. Came in last night."

"Really? How's he doing?"

"Awesome." I grinned and patted my stomach. "He made me breakfast." I looked at my hand again, opening and closing it. "Hey, when you buy something on eSouled, isn't the seller's info right there?"

"Yeah. Why?"

I shrugged. "I must have just missed it." That's what I thought, but didn't bother going into any more detail. No one knew I had made the purchase and I saw no reason for that to change. This issue was mine, and mine alone. Besides, I didn't want Justin to think I was crazy, talking about buying angels online.

Once inside the building we slowed our pace to match everyone else shuffling down the halls. We pushed around those who'd decided to stop and talk by their locker.

"So, is the big search for Dani's gift finally over?" Justin asked. "What'd you get her?"

Fortunately, I didn't have to answer because Justin got ambushed.

"Hey, Justin." Shorter than Justin by at least six inches, a blonde girl with big blue eyes cut him off by stepping in front of him. I'd seen her around before but couldn't remember her name. She stood there, holding her notebook against her chest, looking up at him.

"Hi, Seth." Her eyes darted to me for a second— and then another—before moving back to Justin.

"Hey, how's it going?" Justin tipped his chin in her direction as he moved past her.

"Good!" Her face lit up. She spun around and called to him. "I'll see you in class, okay?"

I moved around her and kept pace with Justin. "When are you going to ask her out?"

"I doubt I ever will." He shrugged. "See you at lunch."

Inside the classroom, Dani sat in one of our usual chairs, going over her notes. I stood inside the door for a moment, enjoying the sight of her. I loved the way she pressed her lips together when she was thinking about something, and the way she absentmindedly hooked her hair behind her ear. Hell, I loved everything about Dani.

"You're blocking the doorway, Mr. Thompson," said the teacher from behind me.

"Sorry," I mumbled. I moved over to let her pass before making my way to Dani.

"Oh, hey!" She looked up. "How are you feeling?"

I bent down and gave her a quick kiss. "A lot better."

"Good," she said, patting my hand. "I was worried. Wasn't sure if you'd make it to school today."

I leaned into her touch when she placed the back of her fingers against my forehead.

"All right, people. How 'bout we get started?" The teacher adjusted her glasses and began her lecture.

~ ~ ~

We didn't feel like going off campus for lunch, so Dani, Justin, and I walked into the Commons, the lunchroom next to the gym, and headed to a table in the far corner. Against two walls were trophy cases, displaying the athletic trophies won throughout the history of Sandpoint High. Behind us, the line to the student store was growing. This room was where a lot of events happened: meetings, banquets, dances, and, everyone's favorite, lunchtime.

I pulled a sandwich out of my backpack and Justin dropped a small bag of chips in front of himself before sitting down. Dani sat between us, watching as members of the student council put up signs about the upcoming dance.

As usual, the muscles in my neck tightened up at the sight of Dirk, who walked through the doors and headed toward us. I bit into my sandwich and watched him, relieved when he stopped at the next table. I really wasn't in the mood for his crap right now. I shook my head when Justin offered us chips.

"Want to go skiing Saturday?" he asked.

"Nope. No cash." I forced myself to drag my eyes away from Dirk.

"What about you?" Justin turned to Dani.

"I can't. I'm helping my mom this weekend."

"Hey, Dirk!"

The three of us looked up at the loud, sing-song call from across the Commons room. Jessica, a freshman, swung her legs from under the table, stood up, and swayed her hips in Dirk's direction.

She moved in close to him, snaking her arm around Dirk's waist and pulling his arm over her shoulder, because apparently he wasn't going to do it himself. She looked at me to see if I was watching, but instead caught Dani staring at her. Jessica's smile slid off her face before she turned away.

Then it was Dirk's turn. He glanced over Jessica's head at Dani, shooting her a pointed sneer. Then he puckered up and kissed the air, sending it directly to Dani.

"Eww." Dani grimaced, pretending to shove her finger down her throat as if to puke.

I glared at Dirk, who threw his head back and laughed before pulling Jessica closer and walking away.

He believes you are weak.

Pfff. I'm not weak, I thought.

But it is what he believes.

My chest tightened up, making my breath come out fast and shallow. It felt like snakes were pressing against the inside of my ribs, looking for an opening, trying to get past my skin. Damn, the guy really got to me.

Dani reached over and squeezed my hand. "Hey." She shook my arm a little to get my attention. "Don't worry about it. He's just being a jerk." She grabbed a chip out of Justin's bag. "Here, have a chip."

"Yeah, come on." Justin reached around Dani and shoved my shoulder. "Let it go."

The pressure in my chest eased up some as I watched Dirk disappear around the corner. My smoldering hot anger dissipated and my breathing slowed down. I had to blink a couple of times before I could focus on the chip Dani held in front of my face. I couldn't believe Dirk pushed my buttons so easily.

"Yeah, I know," I said. "He *is* a dick." I opened my mouth and took the chip from Dani's hand.

Chapter 6

The boy named Dirk... he causes the boy to feel
anger. Anger is good, for it weakens the boy's
defenses, allowing me to grow stronger. It is through
this crack in his armor that I am able to feed from
Dirk, the dark one. I can use this energy to hasten the
task that I have been condemned to complete.
~ Maksim

"Okay, gentlemen. I want doubles to high legs for
five minutes. Then rotate to your next opponent."

Upstairs in the wrestling area above the basketball
court, the coach waited for everyone to pair up.
"Technique, gentleman. Remember your technique!"
He checked the clock on the wall. "All right...
Begin!"

Justin and I faced each other, shaking loose our
legs and arms, and crouched down into a stance. We
shook hands, signaling we were ready. I took a
penetration step and snaked my arms around his
calves. Then I drove forward off my front leg, pulling
his legs from under him.

Justin twisted and landed on his stomach. I went
right into the high leg, grabbing his wrist and pulling
it under him, then hooked his leg and stretched his
arm across his back.

Justin grunted.

"You good?" I asked.

"Yeah."

I pushed myself off and we went through it again,
switching off.

The third time, I went for the pin.

I stretched his arm across his back and kept pushing until he rolled over, then hooked his head and used my weight to pin his shoulder. I nailed it. Too easy.

After helping Justin up, I rested my hands on my hips, catching my breath. Against the wall, off the mat, a dozen or so people stood. Some parents watched, some students talked in the corner, but one person in particular had her eyes on Justin. I tipped my chin up, showing Justin the girl in the corner.

He looked over his shoulder just long enough for the blonde girl to wave to him. He rolled his eyes at me and shook his head.

"I'll let you pin me next time," I teased. "It'll make you look good."

Justin leaned in to push me, but I stepped out of his range and shoved him away.

"Next guy! Let's go!" The coach's voice filled the practice area.

I already knew who my next round was with, and I couldn't stop the tension from dripping down my spine.

Right on cue, Dirk gave me his usual cocky grin.

"Oh, good, it's you. I needed a rest," he said, shaking out his arms.

I crouched low and planted my back foot, keeping my mouth shut. He wasn't worth running laps for.

"Bet you $50 bucks I can get Dani to go to the dance with me," Dirk sneered.

He wants what is yours.

"What?" I started to straighten, but sunk back down when I realized who—or what—it was. It was unnerving to have that voice come out of nowhere. Sometimes I couldn't tell if I was talking to myself or if Maksim was saying something. Either way, it was annoying when what the voice said was pointing out something obvious. Like now. I knew Dirk wanted Dani. I'd known that for a long time. Just because he had money, Dirk thought could have anything he wanted. But not this time; Dani was mine. I took a quick glance at the coach, who was busy working with a freshman on the other side.

"Hey, but that's not very fair of me, is it?" Dirk taunted. "You won't have $50 to pay me when you lose, will you?"

Show him how powerful you are.

I never felt it coming. My muscles coiled a split second before I lunged, ducking low, wrapping my arms around his legs. I had dumped him on his back before either of us realized what was happening.

Dirk let out a harsh *humph* as he hit the floor.

"I don't remember giving the signal, Mr. Thompson." The coach's voice blasted across the practice mat.

Dirk smirked, throwing his hands back in surrender.

I knew what was coming next, but I didn't care. It felt good to knock Dirk on his ass.

"That will be ten laps after practice, Mr. Thompson." The coach glanced at the others. "Okay. Begin."

I went through the motions of the high leg, getting myself face down on the mat, with Dirk sprawled on my back.

His breath was hot and stale against the side of my face. "Give it up, Thompson," he murmured. "You don't have what it takes. It'll just be a matter of time before Dani sees it, too."

My peripheral vision clouded and darkened, like a fast moving storm, and my focus fixated until all I could see were pinpoint red spots on the mat. But even from that narrowed vision, images exploded in front of me of Dani and Dirk, wrapped around each other, hands everywhere, Dirk with his freakin' smirk, and Dani loving every minute of it. My lids snapped shut.

Use me. I am here for you.

Beginning in the pit of my stomach, shooting to my hands and feet, a tremor flashed under my skin and fire shot through my veins. If I could give it a color, it would be black, an inky jet of bad vibes, and they were strong. And fast. Too fast for me to stop them from erupting. I arched my back and swung my feet over Dirk, wrapped my arm around his waist, and leaned in hard, pinning his shoulders against the mat.

"Finally, you're getting some balls." Dirk grunted.

"Say anything else about asking Dani out and next time I won't hold back," I hissed. I let him up and we stood toe-to-toe for a few seconds before he shrugged and walked away.

He didn't look back. No smart-ass remark this time. Huh. I was beginning to really like this angel of mine.

~ ~ ~

As soon as practice was over, I booked it over to my truck. I slouched a little bit in the driver's seat, hoping no one would see me. I couldn't talk to anyone. I was still too fired up—even after pinning five more guys to the mat, even after the ten laps. I needed to go home and work out again. Maybe that would help me settle down. I grabbed my cell phone from my pocket and called Dani's phone.

"Come on, come on. Answer." My fingers drummed against the steering wheel.

"Hi, Seth!"

I let out a breath of relief.

"Hello? Are you there, Seth?"

"Yeah, sorry." I rubbed my hand over my face. "How's it going, Dani?"

"Good," she said. "How was practice?"

"The usual. Hey, will you go to the dance with me?"

There was silence on the other end. My hand tightened over the phone. Had Dirk already asked her? Why was she hesitating?

"Um… Yeah." She sounded confused. "Of course I will. You didn't have to ask."

"I know," I said, breathing easier, "but I just wanted to make sure."

I could hear the smile in her voice. "I love you, Seth. Forever."

"Me, too. I'll see you tomorrow, okay?"

"Okay. Goodnight, babe."

~ ~ ~

I pulled into my driveway and turned off the engine.

Okay, I felt a little stupid for asking her to the dance, but I had to make sure she'd go with me.

I got out of my truck and stood beside it. I *was* good enough for Dani. And this neighborhood wasn't a bad area; not like Dirk's side of the tracks, but still pretty nice. It was older, tucked in a corner of town, right down the street from the hospital. And we had good neighbors. There was nothing wrong with it at all.

I grabbed the mail before going inside. *Crap!* Who was I kidding? We didn't have much money and the neighborhood wasn't that great. I hated feeling so damn insecure.

Dad was setting up a stool under the light in the kitchen when I walked in. "Hey, Seth! How did school go today?"

"Good," I said, leaning against the counter. "Dani said she'd go to the dance with me."

Dad grabbed a light bulb off the counter and stepped onto the stool. "Yeah? You didn't think she would?"

I shrugged.

Dad looked over his shoulder at me. He didn't say anything, though I could tell he wanted to. After a moment, he turned towards the ceiling and twisted in the bulb. "You had practice today?"

"Yeah." My forehead compressed into a frown. I pushed off the counter and swung the refrigerator door wide open, staring into its depths.

"Hey, hey, hey," Dad chided. "No snacking. I have dinner in the oven." As he pointed towards the oven, his heel slid off the edge of the stool.

I spun around just as he lost his balance. I knew I wasn't close enough to catch him, but my hands came up instinctively anyway. The air around me crackled like fireworks for a few seconds before going completely still, as if someone flipped a switch to silence it. The kitchen felt weighed down with a thickness that pressed against my ears and squeezed my body; yet, I moved easily, as if there were no gravity, nothing holding me back. I was behind Dad in an instant, holding him up; breaking all the rules I'd ever learned in physics. He was no longer falling… and the image of the hovering keys flashed across my mind.

Then everything stopped, including my breathing. My gaze dragged across the kitchen and I did a quick check of the appliances. The refrigerator motor had cut out and the second hand of the clock was suspended at a little past the four. I supposed it'd be no big deal if it ran on electricity, but it was battery operated and I'd just replaced the batteries last month.

Something like panic squeezed my throat.

Something like satisfaction forced the corners of my mouth up.

Time had stopped.

Only trying to help.

Before the sound of the voice faded, my dad's back pressed against my palms and the clock above the sink ticked away the seconds again.

"Whew! Thanks, Seth," Dad said, stepping carefully off the stool and slapping my shoulder. "For a second there, I thought I was going to fall."

I could only stare at him. *Holy shit!* He had no clue what had just happened.

But then again, neither did I.

~ ~ ~

"Here," Silura invited, patting the stone bench on which she was seated. "Sit with me."

His steps were swift.

She welcomed his excitement and brought his energy close, melding it with hers. She would gladly share her secrets with this man if it brought him happiness, for what he had done for her, to her body and soul, was beyond ecstasy.

"Today we begin with the elements. Fire, air, water, and earth," she said. "It is all energy, all matter that can be manipulated. Each element intertwines with the others and we with them. Everything is connected."

Her slender hands cupped the air before her and she shifted her gaze to her palm, encouraging him to look as well.

His gaze flitted across the space above her hands, as if looking for something he had missed.

Seconds passed. Then the air above her hands visibly shifted and swirled, slowly at first, then twisted like small ghostly serpents, the air sliding silently against itself, rolling around until the joining was complete. The center mass radiated its brilliant light outward into spiked tendrils, until the tips faded into the evening air.

His eyes widened, reflecting back the now white glow of the orb she'd placed in his hand. She had never seen him quite so filled with awe. It was wonderful to share her world with him! Having lived the life of a sorceress since learning to speak her first words, she had forgotten how much wonder and beauty there was in magick.

"See? It is really quite simple," she murmured, watching him closely.

"But where did it come from?" He held the orb as if it would shatter.

"It is all around us." A graceful arc of her arm brought his attention to the grass and trees that were bathed in dusky reds and yellow from the setting sun. A gentle breeze startled the blades of grass beneath their feet and shifted strands of glossy black hair across his face.

"We need only to turn our focus inward before turning it outward, allowing us to harness the energy that is ever-present." She closed her eyes briefly before reopening them and focusing again on the orb. With one pass of her hand, the light burst into flame.

"Ahh!" Quickly dropping it, he looked at her in disbelief.

She laughed, taking his hands in hers. She blew upon the seared skin of his palms, and the flesh healed instantly. "Very simple."

He looked upon the flawless skin of his hands. Slowly, he smiled and snaked his arms around her waist. Leaning close, his whispered. "It appears, Mistress Silura, that I have much to learn."

~ ~ ~

Chapter 7

*I breathe easier knowing the boy's acceptance
has taken root. I am firmly anchored, though I am
still a mere shadow behind his will. But a shadow is a
beginning. A shadow can obscure and cloud. It can
kill the brightest of lights. There will be no denying
me now.*
~ Maksim

"What's the matter, buddy? Come here, boy." I
pulled my hand back when Max shied away. I patted
my thigh, inviting him to come to me.

Each paw stretched behind him until his body
pressed against the wall of the kennel, a whimper
quivering in his throat. He crouched low, and the hair
on the ridge of his back began to rise.

"Aww, Max, come here." Dani stood next to me
and reached her hand out. "What's the matter, boy?"

He skirted a wide perimeter around me, edging
around to the other side of Dani, then sat next to her,
still eyeing me.

I'd been dissed by a dog. Ouch.

Dani looked first at me, then at Max. She leaned
over and cupped his ears in her hands, giving him a
good scratch. "Hey, Gracie?" Dani called over her
shoulder. "Is Max not feeling well?"

Gracie looked around the corner, a phone cradled
against her ear, and mouthed, "Hang on."

Dani nodded and turned back to Max, giving him
a reassuring pat on his back. "It's okay," she
murmured.

Max was fine around Dani. It was me he was reacting to; that much was obvious.

Max looked scared and, at the same time, ready to rip my face off. Like Blaze, he wasn't about to let his guard down.

"You know," Dani said, still soothing the dog, "animals can sense things about people, like their emotions." She turned towards me. "Are you okay with coming here, Seth? I mean, you do like it, don't you?"

I forgot the dog for a minute because Dani was staring at my hands. I hadn't noticed but they'd clenched themselves into fists. I slowly uncurled my fingers, releasing the tension that had built up. The uncertainty in Dani's eyes pulled me back to the moment.

"He sure is keeping his distance, isn't he?" Gracie walked up behind us, reached down, and gave Max's fur a jostle. "He's fine. Maybe he just doesn't recognize you today, Seth?"

I stood and faced her.

She squinted, scrutinizing my face. "Did you change something about yourself? Your hair? You look a little pale. You feel okay?"

My jaw clenched, I sucked in a deep breath, then pushed it from my lungs. "I'm just getting over the flu." I crouched down beside Dani and turned her face towards me and waited until her eyes finally looked into mine. "I'm totally good with being here, Dani, really."

I could see by the way she searched my eyes that she wanted to believe me.

Then I reached across the front of her and held my hand out to Max. "Friends?"

Max growled low in his throat.

"Maybe you should get completely well before coming back," Dani said, gripping my arm and pulling it back. "I don't like the dogs—especially Max—acting this way towards you." She shook her head. "It's just so weird. I don't understand it."

I'd never given her reason to doubt me. I'd never lied to her.

But when she looked at me with just a little bit of doubt, I felt what would be the first crack in our relationship. I couldn't do anything to stop it. All I could do was try to keep it from getting bigger.

~ ~ ~

It was quiet that night. No calls or texts from Dani. Maybe she was a little upset about what happened at the shelter today. Justin had called after I'd gotten home, but it wasn't enough of a distraction, so after we talked, I pressed the weights to the point of exhaustion, trying to wear myself out, trying to work out the tension that had returned. So far it hadn't helped

My cell phone rang. It wasn't Dani.

"Hey, Dad."

"Hey, Seth. How are you feeling?"

I flopped back on the bed and stared at the ceiling. "I'm good."

I lied. I wasn't. I was beginning to feel a dull ache inside my stomach. I couldn't quite put my finger on it, but it was like there was just too much inside of me for my skin to contain it all.

Sometimes it hurt, like tips of knives stabbing everywhere all at once. I felt as though my bones and muscles were being crushed and kneaded, then molded into something they weren't meant to be.

Other times I felt… good. Like a new life was growing inside me.

Dad's voice filtered through my thoughts. "Glad to hear that. You're a strong boy. Ever since you were little, you've always been able to fight off sickness like it was nothing."

I rested my arm over my eyes. Not this, whatever it was, I thought. I can't fight this off. I wondered if angels healed this kind of sickness.

"So," Dad went on, "what did you end up getting Dani for her birthday?"

I sighed. "Nothing yet."

"I've been thinking about this. I know she means a lot to you. Go ahead and get her something special and I'll cover it for you. Okay?"

Guilt slapped me hard across the face. Dad was always making sacrifices for me, and he never complained. He was right, though. This *was* important.

"Thanks, Dad. I appreciate it. I'll pay you back, I promise."

"Don't worry about that right now. Well, I'd better get some sleep before I hit the road again. I'll call you tomorrow, okay?"

I looked at the clock. It was late. "Okay, Dad. I love you."

"I love you, too. Good night, Seth."

I hung up.

What the hell *was* happening to me? I shook my head and raised my hands above my head, stretching out the tightness that cramped my body.

I'm here to help you, whispered the voice in my head.

Bolting upright, my hands came down instantly, and I wrapped my arms around my chest, as if I could protect myself from something I couldn't see.

"I still don't get it," I said. "Why me?"

We've discussed this already. You asked for me.

"I don't remember asking for any angel."

I am watching over you. Maksim said. *I am helping you.*

"Helping me with what?" I slammed my fist into the bed. Damn! None of this was making any sense.

There was no way I could ask my dad about what was happening. I couldn't possibly tell him I'm not as together as he thought; he'd be way too freaked out.

I reached for the only thing I was sure of—the picture of Dani that I kept on my nightstand. I stared back at those eyes that always kept me grounded. Maybe I was going crazy, but there was one thing I was sure of, the only thing I knew was real—I loved her and she loved me.

Unless, of course, I did something to screw us up.

Chapter 8

*His trust is imperative to our relationship... and
to my ultimate goal. But he does not trust me. I
cannot imagine why.*
~Maksim

Overcast skies allowed only a little sunlight to
break through and splash across the top of the table.
Dani, Justin, and I sat at our usual spot near the back
door of Dub's, a favorite fast-food hangout of
Sandpoint teenagers. During the summer, the burger
place was usually packed with tourists, but during the
winter and spring it was mostly locals who came in.

The snow was melting fast, in a hurry to
evaporate into the already too-wet air or disappear
into the saturated ground. This winter had been like
one continuous wet spring.

Dani sat with the window on one side of her and
me on the other. We sat in silence while Justin and I
powered down burgers and fries. Dani drank coffee,
reading the *Sandpoint Newsline*.

I stopped mid-chew and pushed the basket of fries
in front of her.

"Here." I said. "Eat."

She stopped reading for a second to look at the
fries, then smiled and shook her head.

"You sure?"

"Yeah, I'm sure. Thanks," she said.

Cold air filtered in as the back door pushed
opened and three girls stumbled in. Their laughter
turned into smothered giggles as soon as they saw me,
and, as if on cue, they stopped in a huddle next to our

table. I recognized only one of them. As for the others, well, sometimes you can go through an entire year and run into students you've never seen before.

"Hi, you guys," the redhead said to me, a little too breathlessly.

And with that breathlessness came an unexpected wave of energy soaked with lust. It rolled up and over my shoulder, snaked around my back, across my chest, and tightened itself like a noose around my neck. There was no mistaking what the redhead wanted, and my body burned with her thoughts.

Before I could begin to wrap my mind around what was happening, I was struck by a frigid energy that clashed against the redhead's heat. I snapped my head around to look at Dani, half expecting to see her fingernails turning into claws. Dani was smiling, her expression bland, but she was shooting off a mix of anger and possessiveness.

She is jealous.

Jealous? Why?

Dani nudged me with her foot. "She asked you a question, Seth. Why don't you answer her?" Her voice dripped sugar.

I turned to the redhead.

"Your next match, Seth. Where is it?" She flipped her hair over her shoulder and smiled.

She wasn't interested in the wrestling match. She wanted *me*. I swallowed hard. How could I tell what she was feeling? How was it that I knew what all of them were feeling?

Maksim? What's going on?

If he answered I didn't hear it through the rush of warped white noise that poured into my ears. The vibes of the redhead and Dani collided and crushed me. My head swiveled from one girl to the other.

Then I felt another emotion... and it came from Justin.

Your woman. He wants her.

My jaw went slack. *Really? No! He wouldn't...*

"Justin? Post Falls, right?" I managed to say. "On Thursday?"

"Yeah. I think so." Justin's gaze broke away from Dani and landed on the redhead. "Last match of the season."

"Hey, Justin." This girl was the one I recognized, the blonde from practice. Her lust—not quite as strong as the redhead's—slid behind my neck, circling my shoulder before it anchored onto Justin.

"How's it going?" Justin looked down at his plate, but not before sneaking a look at Dani.

The redhead tapped her painted fingernails on the table. "Maybe we'll show up. You know, it being the last match and all," she said. "See you around, Seth."

They left, taking their emotions with them, leaving me sitting next to the full force of Arctic cold from Dani. I felt my cheek to make sure that side of my face hadn't turned to ice. Wow. So she *was* jealous! I'd never given her a reason to be. But then, I'd never had girls hitting on me this way before. Everyone knew I was with Dani. So why all of a sudden was it happening now?

The frigid energy cut back, thawed out by a small, but palpable pulse of heat coming from the space between Justin and Dani.

You feel it, don't you?

"Yeah, I feel it," I muttered.

"What?" Justin said, looking at me, the muscles in his shoulders suddenly tense.

I shook my head. "Nothing." I reached my arm around Dani's shoulders and pulled her close to me. It had never really bothered me that Justin didn't have a steady girlfriend... until now. "So who are you taking to the dance?" I asked him.

Justin stabbed a fry into the ketchup that had pooled next to his burger. "Haven't decided yet."

Dani looked over his shoulder at the girls, then smiled at Justin. "Are you going to ask the blonde?"

"Probably not."

"Why?" Dani asked. "She was practically begging you to ask her out!"

"Yeah, she was," I agreed.

Dani placed her elbows on the table and leaned toward Justin. "Couldn't you tell? Didn't you see the way her body was angled towards you, her smile..." Dani took a sip of her coffee, peering at Justin over the top of her cup. "You've got a lot to learn about a girl's body language, Justin."

Ha! I wanted to point out to her that body language didn't always reflect what someone was thinking. I wanted to tell her that *her* body language was hiding the jealousy I hadn't known she felt.

"He has plenty of girls to choose from, don't you, Justin?" I said.

"Yeah, right," he said, pushing away his plate. "So, who's up for lit class?"

Dani laughed. "Changing the subject?"

"Yes, I'm changing the subject," he said. "Come on."

~ ~ ~

Stepping out of my truck into the school parking lot was like stepping out of a cigarette smoke-filled room, then walking through the Grand Canyon. The air smelled cleaner, felt cleaner, and whatever toxic emotional fumes that had been clinging to my clothes disappeared into the space around me. I filled my lungs with the purity of it. I wasn't sure I liked being poked and prodded by everyone's emotions. I really could have gone through the day without knowing what that redhead was thinking about me. Now, whenever I saw her, I'd know.

Once inside the building, though, the clarity disappeared. Without warning, I was pelted by a jumble of thoughts and emotions that pressed all around me. It was like some floodgate had opened up and I happened to be downstream when the water was let loose.

I feel her.

Pressing against my eyes didn't stop the feelings. I felt it all. Katie was mad at Mark. Shane was afraid he'd failed his test. Ms. Anderson had just had a fight with her husband.

"Are you okay?" Dani tugged on my sleeve.

Keep searching. Do not stop.

Like I had a choice! A wave that felt like a two-by-four across the back of my head stopped me in my tracks and I spun around in its direction.

Yes.

The girl could have been mistaken for a shadow, the way she pressed herself flat against the wall. If it weren't for the pulsing darts of energy shooting off her, I probably wouldn't have noticed—her irises were like tropical pools contained only by the thin line of black encircling her eyes. Her black lipstick and nail polish were like extensions of her intensity. She didn't even blink when I nailed her with my own piercing stare.

That is her. That one… she is a problem.

"Who's that?" I whispered to Dani, pulling her closer.

Dani followed my stare. "That's Alyx, from my math class."

"She's staring at me."

"Yeah, like all the other girls in the school," Dani said under her breath.

I peered down at her and then back at the girl. "Jealous?"

"No, I'm used to it. Besides, you're too smart to let me go." She took hold of my hand and pulled me down the hall.

I didn't look back. Whatever was up with that girl, I didn't want any part of it.

~ ~ ~

After my last class I walked the halls, still unable to turn off the battering assault of energy from everyone around me, especially the girls. The air around me felt slightly musky and just this side of raw. Girls had never looked at me that way. Some were daring; others sneaked glances out of the corner of their eyes, but the vibes were definitely there, strong and almost overwhelming. And Maksim was being too quiet. I needed his help and I needed it now. I didn't understand any of this. The closeness of the people in the hallway and the overpowering emotions and sensations were suffocating. It was like listening to everyone's problems day in and day out, and there were more depressing thoughts than happy ones. If only I could just tell everyone to stop thinking until I could get out of the building!

Today Dani had a meeting after school, which, for the first and only time I could remember, was okay with me. I wasn't feeling so good again. The headache that had started out as a small pulse in my temple was gaining strength and was now a throbbing band around my head.

I went down Senior Hall to the drinking fountain and gripped its cool porcelain edges. "I can do this," I muttered.

Of course you can. I will teach you how to control it.

Teach me. Yeah. That would be nice. Why don't you just take it away? I thought back to him.

"Hey, you okay?" Justin appeared beside me with his books tucked under his arm.

I sucked in one more breath to steady myself and straightened up to face him.

"Yeah. Why?"

Justin shrugged. "It just looked like something was wrong."

"Headache," I said.

"Oh, that sucks. Are you going to make it to practice?"

I dug a Tylenol out of my backpack, swallowed it down with a gulp of water, and nodded. "Let's go."

~ ~ ~

That night I headed down one of the main aisles of the big box store, between the women's clothes and the kitchen appliances, feeling the stares of the female shoppers. My skin flashed hot and tingled all over as I soaked up their energy. I couldn't help it. I drank it in.

I stopped in the electronics section. "Okay, teach me to control this," I whispered, cringing at the constant pressure in my head.

A couple of guys stared at me, looked at each other and laughed, then walked away.

Do not resist. Be ready.

I relaxed my mind as much as I could. That was the easy part. The hard part was not falling over when

I did relax my mind. If I thought it was bad before, this new onslaught of everyone's energy was a punch to the stomach—it stole my air, and I had to force myself from buckling. The emotions surrounding me were jumbled up in one big murky fog. It was impossible to tell where one began and the other ended. Kind of like what my watercolor tray used to look like when I was a kid. I rubbed my throbbing forehead.

Focus.

Focus? Focus on what? It would be easier to focus on a single raindrop falling out of the sky!

Find your center, the core of you! Feel me. Use me!

Okay, okay. You don't need to get so uptight. I closed my eyes and pressed my hands against my ears. My core. Where do I find my core? What exactly *was* my core?

Silence yourself. Feel, rather than think. Focus on one strong emotion.

I tried for a couple minutes. I really did. In fact, my focus was so intense that I felt like I developed a permanent crease between my brows. The battering kept up, pelting me with shots of emotion. But finally, walls began building up around my mind, blocking out one emotion after another, until there was only one feeling left: elation. I dropped my hands to my sides and my eyes slowly opened, waiting. Then my gaze tore through the crowd like a predator sensing its prey. The source was close. Very close.

Ah, there it was, behind me. At a cash register stood a boy, twelve years old maybe, his face dominated by a toothy smile. On the other side of the counter, a clerk slapped a receipt onto a brand new Xbox.

The boy's scrawny arms wrapped around the box and pulled it off the counter. He sprinted, the box crowding his arms, and headed straight towards me, his mother trailing behind. I ignored the woman and instead focused on the boy.

My energy tapped into his and sucked it in like a vacuum. To me it felt wondrous, exciting; he didn't feel the same way. He looked as though he'd smacked into a wall. He froze, his eyes latched onto mine, his mouth dropped open, and in a moment his head cocked to one side as if he were looking at something he didn't quite understand.

I smiled.

He forced his eyes shut, for a minute covering them with his arm as if the darkness wasn't enough. Then, grabbing his mother's sleeve, still struggling with the box, he ran in the opposite direction.

Ha! That was freakin' awesome

~ ~ ~

The onslaught of thoughts and emotions from the people in the marketplace pressed hard across his back. It radiated down his legs and caused his knees to buckle beneath him. Like fire, the energy spread to envelop his shoulders and chest before creeping up his neck and face.

Emotions from every direction throbbed in his temples. He raised his arms to encircle his head, trying to create a barrier between the emotions and his mind. But it was a futile gesture. Once his mind had been opened, the rush of energy prevented him from closing the door again.

"Focus, Maksim. Focus."

Silura placed a gentle hand on his shoulder and squeezed the muscles that had coiled with tension.

"Pick a feeling," she encouraged, "and follow its trail."

Maksim's face contorted with discomfort. An easier task to say than to do, he thought. But he was determined to succeed.

Tight with tension, his neck muscles protested as he lowered his arms and raised his chin, exposing his face to the pelting energy around him.

He flinched as if struck. There were so many emotions! How could he possibly choose one?

Wait—there it was, the one with the strongest pull. It tugged against his mind and he latched on, focusing solely on strengthening the bond.

Anger. Yes. Such a strong emotion.

"Trust your instincts only and do not believe all that you see," Silura murmured.

Maksim's eyes opened to narrowed slits, and tracked the source of the venom that was now swirling through his own veins. It became him, empowered him, and heightened his senses.

The man was leaning against a tree, partially hidden in the shade provided by the leaves and branches. A husband, no doubt, of one of the village women Maksim had bedded. The man's face was a mask of serenity, his fingers pulling gently on his beard, as if lost in thought. But there was no doubt that the anger came from him. Maksim frowned. The man's face held no animosity, yet his feelings shouted otherwise. In confusion, Maksim looked to Silura.

"Yes," Silura said, looking pleased. "You have discovered him. Well done."

Maksim followed her gaze back to the man. Maksim gave a slight nod, then Maksim dismissed the man from his mind.

~ ~ ~

Chapter 9

*He toys with the possibility of power and so my
presence within him expands. He does not yet realize
what is really happening. Or perhaps he does not
care*
~ Maksim

"Eight ball. Corner pocket."

The Dive wasn't much of a hangout, but with two
pool tables, a dozen or so video games, and a
mechanical bull, we were able to kill time between
now and the time we graduated from high school.
Justin, Dani, and I came here when we needed a
change up from the food at Dub's.

This was about as exciting as Sandpoint got.
Pathetic, but it was a tourist town, with visitors
coming from all over for skiing in the winter and
playing in the lake during the summer. Sandpoint
wasn't geared for high-paced action. It was a place
where people escaped the cities to live the simple life
alongside moose, elk and other wildlife.

I leaned over the pool table with the pool stick
threaded through my fingers splayed over the felt.
With four striped balls scattered across the table and
the eight ball tucked snugly in the corner, it was a
sure thing. This was the best game I had ever played.
The pool stick felt solid in my hand and one by one
the balls had dropped into the pockets. There was no
way I could miss this shot.

"Yeah, we'll see," said Justin.

Heat flooded my arms and hands as I pulled the
stick back.

Shall I assist you once again?

Sure, I answered. *Why not?* I could always use a little help.

I drew the stick back in perfect alignment with my shot—the eight ball practically begging to be put away—but the stick was pushed from behind and it hit the cue ball at an awkward angle, sending the ball careening against the wrong side of the table.

"Oops! Looks like your pool game is as bad as your bowling."

I straightened and slowly turned.

Dirk slapped me on the shoulder before walking to the mechanical bull, Jessica hanging on his arm. "Better watch your back next time, hot shot."

You allow him to behave that way?

I don't allow him to do anything, I answered. *What am I supposed to do? Start a fight?*

Get his attention. Focus. Just as I taught you with the keys.

And if I don't want to? I argued.

Trust me. Let me show you.

Okay, I figured it couldn't hurt to play along. So I focused, just like I did the other night with the keys, imaging a silver thread beginning in my chest, slowly stretching the distance between us like a ghostly finger.

But somewhere along the way, I lost control and the thread took on a life of its own. It tugged hard somewhere behind my ribs, hooking my breath as it pulled. The closer the thread got to Dirk, the faster it went. In the span of about a second the thread bore into Dirk's back like taser lines from a stun-gun. At the point of connection, the silver turned murky dark and reversed direction, heading back to me at lightning speed—too fast for me to do anything but brace myself. But when it hit me, all it did was melt, or rather evaporate, into the lining of my jacket.

Stopping in mid-step, Dirk wavered, a little unsteady on his feet, before slowly turning and looking directly at me, his eyes blinking, as if he was trying to clear his vision.

The corners of my mouth curved upwards into a smile that didn't feel like my own, followed by a grunt as the energy stream that tied the two of us together tugged at my ribs again.

Confusion, and a shred of fear, flashed in Dirk's eyes as he took a step forward. Then he stopped and took a few steps back. He pulled Jessica closer to his body, turned, and walked away.

Well done, Maksim laughed.

"What was that all about?" Justin asked over my shoulder.

I had forgotten he was there. Squeezing my eyes shut, I took a deep breath, and shook off whatever it was that lingered between me and the one guy in the entire world I hated. Shrugging, I reached into the table's pockets and tossed the balls onto the felt. "Nothing. It wasn't worth fighting over." I tried to pretend it wasn't a big deal, but something happened in that flash of connection, and it wasn't good.

"I wish I had a camera. Didn't think Dirk was capable of looking so confused." Justin rounded the table and grabbed the rack. "One more game?"

I shook my head. I really needed to do something else. "No. Let's go eat. I'm hungry." Before we reached the table where Dani and her mom sat, I knew something was wrong. Justin bumped into the back of me when I stopped.

Dani sat across from her mom, Janice, at a table in the middle of the restaurant. I couldn't see Dani's face, but her mom kept looking over her shoulder at three men sitting next to each other at the bar. She wasn't smiling.

"What's up?" I asked when Justin and I reached their table.

Dani and her mom straightened up.

"Oh, hey! Who won the pool game?" Janice asked.

I stared at the men at the bar. Nothing seemed out of the ordinary. They were just hanging out, drinking beer. But then I saw that the one in the middle kept looking over his shoulder at Dani's mom. He wasn't looking at her like maybe he was interested in her, but like he was a predator looking at his prey. Not cool.

"Who's that?" I said, jerking my chin toward the bar.

Dani's eyes flashed to the men for a moment. "He lives a couple of streets over from us." She scooted over to make room for me and Justin.

I settled next to her and grabbed her hand.

Leaning closer, she whispered, "I think he likes my mom, but he's really creepy."

"Dani." Her mom frowned and shook her head. "It's okay."

Janice's smile was weak, different from the confident smile she usually had. She was attractive, in a mom kind of way. Her hair was dark, like Dani's, but her eyes were brown. And, like Dani, she was always decisive and totally together; probably another reason men found her attractive. But this guy's staring had Janice wringing her hands together until her knuckles were white. Her smile didn't cover what she felt—what I *knew* she felt—underneath. She wasn't okay. And neither was Dani.

It didn't take long for Maksim to start talking.

See how upset your woman is? You can protect her.

Letting go of Dani, I grabbed a couple of French fries and shoved them in my mouth.

Protect her, huh? How? I asked.

The guy turned all the way around on his stool to face us and leaned his elbows against the bar.

What he really needed was to be taught some manners, I thought.

Let me do it. There was a smile in Maksim's voice. *Better yet, let us do it together.*

Okay, I was down with that.

We have power, he breathed. *We could... persuade him to leave.*

Yeah, I was definitely down with that. *But how?*

I got my answer before I finished my question. Heat surged through my veins and shadows raced behind my eyes with horrible force. As much as I wanted to close my eyes to the pain, I didn't look away from the jerk at the bar.

The guy stood up and took a step towards us at the same time I stood up. Every head in the room turned to the man when he fell back against the bar stool, choking on his beer, sending a spray of foam onto the peanut shell-covered floor, his eyes wide with disbelief. He didn't know what had hit him.

Our eyes locked.

Then he pissed his pants.

"Hey, Mac. You've had one too many, huh?" The bartender reached over and took away his glass.

The man said something, but whatever it was, was drowned by everyone's laughter. He scrubbed his face with his hand, grabbed his coat, and hurried out without looking back.

Freakin' A, Maksim! That was unreal!

As you wished. Protection for your woman and her mother.

"Serves him right for creeping out my mom," Dani said.

I sat back down and put my arm around Dani and pulled her close. Her hair was smooth under my lips. "I love you," I whispered. "Sometimes I can't believe how lucky I am to have you."

Dani's arms wrapped around my waist and she gave a tight squeeze. "I feel the same way," she whispered back.

The buzz of conversation started back up again as soon as the guy walked out the door, but the rush of power lingered underneath my skin, crouched and ready to go again. Everyone had seen *what* happened, but no one knew *how*. Then I noticed Dirk sitting a couple of tables over from us. Our eyes locked and the rush of adrenaline fired up again.

"Let's get out of here," I said to Dani and Justin, breaking the stare. I pulled out a ten from my pocket and dropped it on the table. "We're going to walk down to City Beach." I said to Janice, shrugging on my jacket.

"Oh, okay. I'm ready to head home anyway," Janice said, gathering up her jacket and purse.

I grabbed Dani's hand and pulled her toward the front door.

"Thompson!"

There wasn't any reason for me to respond to Dirk's challenging call. I had nothing to say to him. What I needed was distance. A lot of it.

Chapter 10

Already I grow tired of the games. I am restless, a caged animal, needing release.
~ Maksim

I shrugged my shoulders, trying to get the suit jacket to fit right. My shoulders and arms had gotten so much bigger over the past few weeks that if I pulled my elbows out in front of me, the suit stretched tight across my back. It'd have to do, though.

Things were really starting to happen for me, now that I had Maksim tooling around inside. Everything he was showing me, letting me do, was way, way cool. Things I had wanted to do, like being able to protect Dani and make her melt when I kissed her, were awesome. But even better were those skills, like not getting burned and stopping a few moments of time—though I still had to wrap my head around that last one. And he said there was so much more and to be prepared. So, yeah. I felt pretty good.

I was actually looking forward to tonight's Winter Dance. Dani had probably spent all afternoon getting ready, and I was going to make sure the night was perfect for her. And with my angel's help, I had the power to do that.

My truck's engine purred to life, humming smugly as I backed out of the driveway and headed out to pick up Dani. I truly did have it all. I was totally stoked that I'd made that auction purchase because now I had no problem believing that I had what it took to keep Dani forever.

Standing outside of Dani's front door, I straightened my tie and suit jacket.

"Oh, hey, Mrs. Parsons," I said as the door swung open. "How are you doing?"

"Hi, Seth! I saw you pull up." Dani's mother stepped back to let me in. "Well, well, don't you look handsome?"

"Thanks," I said, flushing a little as I stepped past her into the house. I was never very comfortable with compliments.

"Leave Seth alone, Mom," Dani called from the other room. "You're embarrassing him." She appeared from the hallway leading to the bedroom and came straight to hug me. "He has no idea how cute he is!" With the top of her head barely reaching my chin, she had to stand on her tip-toes to give me a quick kiss. "One of the reasons why I love him so much."

I held her at arms' length so I could get a better look at her. "Wow, you look great!"

Dani stepped back and twirled around. The green sequins that made up the top of her strapless dress matched perfectly with her eyes and the rest of the skirt layered down in waves to stop just above her knees. It showed off her beautiful long legs.

"Thanks, babe!" she smiled.

"Let me get my camera," Janice said. "That's a great shot."

"Hey." I pulled Dani against me again and rested my forehead against hers. "Thanks for going with me tonight."

"I don't know why you thought I wouldn't." Dani leaned back and searched my face. "Is everything okay?"

"Yeah, definitely." This night was going to be great. "I love you," I said.

"Me, too."

I cupped her face, pulling her close enough to brush my lips against hers, closing my eyes to shut out everything that could possibly distract me from this moment. The dark behind my eyes became darker before it flared, and stopped me mid-kiss. Something didn't feel right.

"What's wrong?" Dani frowned.

"Your mom's coming." Perfect timing, because I couldn't explain what was wrong, just that something felt off, as if something bad was about to happen.

Janice appeared in the doorway. "Sorry I took so long. I had to replace the batteries. This darn thing uses them up so quickly. Okay. Get closer," she said, sweeping her hand through the air, motioning us to get closer.

I draped my arm around Dani and pressed my cheek against her hair, smiling at the lens.

In the split second after the flash went off, I blinked and in that split second of darkness, I saw *it*.

What the HELL?! Maksim?!

I focused on Dani, squeezing her shoulder and pulling her closer still. I wasn't feeling so good anymore. "Thanks, Mrs. Parsons," I managed to say. "I think we'd better go, Dani. Justin is probably waiting for us." But there was nowhere I could run to hide from what I had seen. And it was more than seeing; it was suddenly knowing the truth. Knowing I had been duped.

I took a deep breath, causing a tremor in my chest. The voice had a face. Freakin' A. He had a face.

And that face told me that Maksim was no angel.

~ ~ ~

The music was already blasting from inside the Sandpoint Event Center, getting louder each time the doors opened, dulling to a pulse when they closed.

Justin stood outside the doors of the entryway with his hands shoved in his pockets, making sure there was a little space between him and his date. He looked uncomfortable in his suit, like the collar was making it hard for him to turn his head. His face broke into a relieved smile when Dani and I walked in.

Justin had told me yesterday he'd just asked the small blonde from Dub's to go to the dance that morning. Her dress, a fire-engine-red halter dress, hitting at about mid-thigh, matched Justin's red tie. I wondered if she'd asked him to wear red. Justin would do it for her to be nice, but he'd be hating it all night long.

"Hey, you guys!" Dani smiled at them.

"Took you long enough to get here," said Justin.

"Yeah, well, we had to have pictures taken." I shrugged. "You know how Dani's mom is with that." I forced a smile, hoping my voice was steadier than I felt. I still hadn't been able to fully digest what I had seen at Dani's house. I wasn't sure what the hell it was, but I knew it wasn't Casper the Friendly Ghost. Maksim's random silence was getting on my nerves. He put me in situations, showed me how to do things, helped me out sometimes, but then disappeared. What the hell? Was he toying with me? Was he *trying* to freak me out?

Dani pretended to look offended at my comment about the camera. "Hey, it wasn't…" her voiced faded when she looked into my eyes. "… that… bad."

Shit! I blinked and looked away, towards the entrance to the dance, so she couldn't look into my eyes anymore. Because, yeah, I was thinking it *was* that bad.

"Come on. Let's go in." I led the way to the door. After handing in our tickets, we made our way onto the dance floor, where white lights were strung across the rails above us to look like stars. Tables crowded the back of the room and along the sides, leaving a huge space for dancing. At the far end of the room, the DJ had set up camp.

"I'm going to use the bathroom." Squeezing her hand, I left Dani there with a question forming on her lips. *Not now*, I thought.

The bathroom was quiet. Turning on the faucet, I let it run for a few seconds before splashing the cold water on my face. I wasn't ready yet to look at my reflection, and when I finally did, there was nothing. Even inches from the mirror, my eyes were the same shade of brown they'd always been. Maybe I'd imagined the shadows, but the way Dani looked at me, I wasn't so sure.

"Maksim?" I hated the way my voice quivered.

There was no answer. No noise except for the music filtering through the walls.

Shoving my hands though my hair, I headed to the door and out onto the dance floor. I didn't want to leave Dani by herself any longer.

The music throbbed through my skin, straight to my bones. But there was something else getting through to me. What, though? I scanned the room. Strobes of light hit the floor and walls at different angles, flashing in time to the music. It was difficult to see clearly through all the bodies dancing, but I felt *someone*. And there she was. Goth Girl was leaning against the wall next to the DJ set up. I turned my back to her before she could see me and headed toward Dani.

"Oh! I love this song!" Dani grabbed my arm. "Let's dance!" She raised her voice to be heard.

Justin's date pulled at him.

Dani dragged me towards the dance floor until we had been swallowed up by the crowd. For about half the song I was so caught up in dancing, trying to focus on having a good time for Dani's sake, that I hadn't noticed Dirk and Jessica had appeared beside us on the dance floor. Yeah, my radar was all off.

"Hi, Seth! Hi, Dani!" Jessica shouted. "Great dress!"

I couldn't ignore the way Dirk's eyes raked over Dani's body, and neither could Jessica. Dani was apparently oblivious. She just waved at Jessica and said, "Thanks! I like yours, too!"

"Yeah. *Really* great dress, Danika," Dirk smirked.

Dani narrowed her eyes at him. "Yeah? Thanks." She turned her back to Dirk, but to me she flashed a beautiful smile.

The next song started right away and Dani didn't miss a beat. As for me, I wanted to lose myself in the energy of the music and the flash of the lights. I wanted to forget the sinking feeling in the pit of my stomach.

The song wasn't over when heat began pressing on the sides of my face, shoulders, arms, and legs. I knew only too well what that meant. Not only was Maksim around, but Dirk and Jessica were getting close again. Jessica kept shifting her position, trying to block Dirk's movement across the floor, but he kept on his slow progression until he was beside us.

"Hey, Jessie," Dirk spoke loud enough to be heard over the music, "why don't you dance with Seth and I'll dance with Dani?"

Jessica glared at Dirk before she turned, looked at me up and down, and smiled, suddenly okay with the idea.

Dirk reached out to grab Dani's arm, his teeth gleaming in a predatory smile.

Use me.

I flinched at the voice. I didn't want to hear him, not right now. But this wasn't a request, it was a command. A low growl rumbled in my chest, and I put my palms out in front of me, pressing against the air between me and Dirk.

He stopped and stepped backwards, a frown wiping away his smile. He started to step toward Dani again, but stopped.

My fingers tingled and burned with a searing heat, but this time I didn't even try to stop it.

Dirk leaned in again just a little, then his eyes narrowed, and, with his hands held up in surrender, he backed off. "Maybe another time, then." He slung his arm around Jessica's shoulders and gave her a hard kiss. "Let's go."

"What just happened?" Dani asked, looking at Dirk and Jessica as they disappeared.

With each step that separated Dirk from me, the pressure inside my body faded and the tingling settled down to a hum. I shoved my hands into my pockets to hide the fact that they were shaking. I was coming to the realization that what I'd bought on eSouled—what I'd bought for one dollar, power and control—I'd paid for with more than my debit card. I had let something in and had given it a home. And if it was an angel, it was not the good kind that you read about, glowing white, flying around with a halo over its head. No, if this was an angel, it had fallen. Big time.

I looked at Dani and shrugged my shoulders. "I guess Dirk finally figured out you're off limits."

From across the room, even with so many bodies between us, I could feel Dirk's stare. But when I turned my back on him, whatever it was that connected us, snapped.

"Dude." Justin appeared. "Everything okay?"

"Yeah. No problem," I looked over my shoulder one last time at Dirk, but instead found myself locking stares with Goth. And her eyes didn't leave mine.

"I didn't want to miss out on any of the fun," Justin said. "I'll take *any* reason to kick that guy's ass!"

"Come *on*. We're supposed to be *dancing*." Dani pulled impatiently on my hands.

I broke away from Goth Girl's stare and looked down at Dani's face. For the second time in my life, I was scared. The first time was when Dad and I had found out Mom was sick and that the doctors gave her no chance of recovering. I wondered what I would lose *this* time around. My mind? Or would it be Dani? What the *hell* had I gotten myself into?

"Hello?" Dani took in a short, quick breath as she looked into my eyes. "Where are you?"

I gripped her hands tighter and quickly pulled her close, breathing in the flowery scent of her hair. "I love you, Dani," I whispered in her ear.

Our arms slipped around each other and I held on.

The music slowed and I pulled her even closer. Over her head, I saw Dirk across the dance floor, his eyes focused on me. Against the wall, Goth still watched. I shut them out, shut everyone out, and lost myself to Dani's voice as she sang the words of the song.

Justin and his date were dancing pretty close, too. Justin glanced at Dani, then realized I was watching him. He gave me a quick *s'up* nod before burying his face against his date's hair.

I didn't want to know what Justin was feeling, I didn't want to sense Dirk's anger, or the Goth's damn curiosity, and I didn't want this freakish thing I was becoming. All I wanted was to enjoy this dance, and to remember how it felt to have Dani's body against mine.

Because I had an awful feeling I might not have the chance to dance with her this way again.

~ ~ ~

Women found Maksim compelling and attractive—a fact Silura tried to ignore. And his powers of seduction were increasing with each lesson she gave him.

Her heart clenched at the thought that he touched other women with his energy. When she herself reached out to the women in the village, she felt their lust for Maksim.

He was merely attempting to perfect his skills, he insisted to her. These women meant nothing to him.

She understood... to a point. Maksim needed to practice energy transfer on unknowing men and women. Still, she would have preferred that he practiced only *on men.*

She leaned against the thatched hut of the herbalist, watching her lover across the square. Her smile held both pride and jealousy. He was a glorious man, in a position that suited him well.

He had just released his hold on one of the village girls, leaving her weak-kneed and speechless. Backing away a few paces and stepping slowly so that his body turned in a circle, he spread his arms wide in a welcoming gesture. His body quivered slightly as he gathered the energy of those around him, searching, feeling, and learning.

Whispers of the arrangement between Maksim and her had undoubtedly passed through the village. Despite this—or perhaps because of it—people were drawn to him like bees to a hive. But they knew better than to get too close.

How ironic, she thought, bitterness pulling her lips into a straight line. She had chosen to love the one man she now knew would never be tamed, whose lusty appetite for women would only be enhanced by what she taught him. It was an appetite she wished she could control, that she alone wished to satisfy... and perhaps, even turn to love.

Love. It was something she had never felt. Until now. It consumed her every thought. She would turn her eyes away from his infidelities. She would continue to train him to be a great sorcerer. And yes, she freely admitted to herself, she would die for him. Is that not what true love was? The willingness to give one's life for another? She doubted he was capable of such depth, but she still loved the arrogant bastard.

The circle of women closed around him, twittering eagerly.

She sighed. A touch was all she craved from him, and like a beacon, he answered.

Over the heads of his admirers, he glanced in her direction and snared the energy that she stretched out to him.

Her breath caught.

He winked.She blushed.

Yes. She would die for him. And perhaps, even kill.

Love. It was a deadly emotion, indeed.

~ ~ ~

Chapter 11

I am no demon, but a curse. And the curse is me.
~ Maksim

"May I help you?"

The clerk behind the counter started to put down a spray bottle and a rag when I came into the jewelry store, but I put up my hand and shook my head.

"I'm just looking, thanks."

She looked at me a long second before going back to wiping down the glass cases, but she kept an eye on me as I walked down the short length of the counter. On the far end of the case, the selection of earrings sparkled under the lights. I leaned over the glass to get a better look. There were quite a few sizes and shapes to choose from, but the only pair that was in the price range Dad and I had agreed upon were the one-quarter carat studs. They were dwarfed compared to the one- and two-carat diamonds that sat next to them in their black boxes, but the heart-shaped earrings would be perfect for Dani. Man, what I wouldn't do to be able to give Dani the bigger cuts of diamonds, especially the two-carat solitaire pair that sat higher up on a display box. They would look great on Dani. Someday, I thought. Someday.

I traced the outline of the square diamonds on the glass above it. Maybe I could get a part-time job on the weekends that wouldn't interfere with school or wrestling. Then I could...

The glass beneath my finger heated a little before giving way under the slight pressure of my finger.

The diamonds looked distorted where the glass shimmied under my touch.

Take them.

I yanked my hand back and the glass shifted back. I gripped the edge of the glass case until my knuckles ached. A grunt slipped out as pain shot through the middle of my chest. *Are you freakin' serious?* I was *not* a thief.

"Did you find something you liked?" The short, dark-haired young woman stood behind the counter, her eyes sweeping my face and body.

Startled, I stepped back two steps and swallowed hard.

She raised her brows.

"Those." I stepped close again and tapped the glass over the smaller earrings, then pulled my hand away, afraid the glass would melt under my fingers again.

She smiled as she pulled the keys out of her pocket to unlock the case. "Lucky girl," she said under her breath. "Perfect timing," she said louder. "They're on sale this week."

"Yeah, I heard your ad on the radio," I said.

I slid my credit card over the glass.

She picked it up and studied it. Looking up at me, she smiled. "May I see some ID?" Her tongue slid across her lips and desire rolled off her like a tidal wave.

I was drawing her in. *He* was drawing her in. Her raw lust flowed through my veins. I held her stare until she staggered under the weight of it.

Ahh... Just like it used to be.

What was I doing? What was Maksim doing? I needed to get out of there. I clenched my jaw hard. Whatever he was up to, I wouldn't give in. I wasn't a thief and I wasn't going to screw around on Dani. I flashed my license, and with a long glance from the license to me, she took the credit card and earrings and walked to the other end of the store.

"Can you put a ribbon or something on the box?" I called to her. I took another step back. The farther away the better.

"Absolutely. No problem."

I turned and leaned against the glass, keeping my back to the sales girl while she rang up the sale.

"Here you go," she purred a few minutes later. She held up the small white box with a gold ribbon wrapped around it. Then she carefully placed it in a small bag and handed it to me.

"Thanks," I said, taking the bag from her, and backing away.

"You are *very* welcome," the girl sighed. "Do come back… soon."

Outside of the store, I pulled my collar up and my beanie down against the cold. I climbed into the truck and glanced at my watch. There was still time to get to Dani's. I took the box out of the bag and held it.

It would have been so easy to take it.

I gripped the box tighter. No way. I hadn't lost myself completely. Still… put my hand through glass? The temptation was getting to me.

"Show me," I challenged.

Touch the windshield.

I reached out and gently touched the glass. It was cool under my fingertips and solid, of course… until it quivered like Jell-O, before hardening again. I curled my hand into a fist, staring at it. I closed my eyes, not wanting to believe what I saw, but that didn't keep my heart from thumping against my chest or the voice from speaking in my head.

Why do you fight me? You have so much more to learn.

The space underneath my ribs came alive with shards of pain as I shoved the keys into the ignition, turning the motor over. I gunned it and headed for home.

Dani's box now lay on the seat next to me, the gold bow crushed. I wasn't ready to see Dani. This was bad. I couldn't remember one time in the last two years that I'd purposely stayed away from her.

It was a feeling I didn't like at all.

Chapter 12

He cannot resist much longer, for the desire to
have it all will overtake him.
~ Maksim

The full moon glowed over Schweitzer Mountain
and Scotchman's Peak with the pearly shades of the
pre-dawn morning. I was vaguely aware of the few
cars that sped by on the road behind me. Sleep had
evaded me, so with three more hours until school, I'd
driven around and ended up parking my truck at the
restaurant on the south end of the Long Bridge, the
bridge that stretched over the water between
Sandpoint and Sagle.

In the two hours that I sat in my truck, I was
schooled by Maksim in Fire 101. It wasn't so hard,
lighting matches without the striking them on
anything, but then again, I wasn't sure I had anything
to do with it.

The tip of the match that I held popped to life
with nothing more than a brush of my finger, and now
it seemed to burn endlessly. Bored, I snuffed the
flame and put the match in the ashtray along with a
dozen or so others. Since the dance, since stopping
Dirk from getting near Dani, I'd begun to wonder
what else I could do, what else *Maksim* could do. The
constant temptation was too much for me. Besides,
each time I tried to resist, the pain in my stomach and
chest would get worse. Like I was being punished if I
disobeyed.

Shouldering open the door, I stepped out of the truck and made my way to the bridge. I walked slowly, my steps mirroring my breath that materialized as silvery-white apparitions before dissipating into the cold air. I took the undercrossing path to avoid being seen by the cars on the bridge, walking until I stood directly under it. The water level was still low, exposing the rocks along the edge of the lake.

I stared into the water that rippled lazily against the columns of the bridge. The hollow roar of the cars seemed distant as I focused on the inky depths just beyond the railing. Why *was* I fighting this? Grabbing keys and forks, protecting my girl, lighting matches. Was that so bad? Hell, Sandpoint was filled with metaphysical groupies. I'd fit right in. Yeah. I could probably teach them a thing or two.

I spread my arms and welcomed the cold morning air. If I just let go, Maksim's energy would flow through me, as if I were a human conduit. It was like... I don't know... like I was riding the crest of a wave and the momentum was pushing me forward.

Allow me to guide you now.

Do I have a choice? I asked him.

There is always a choice. But the choices we make will not always bode well for us.

I was still trying to figure out where the switch was to turn him off, but I didn't want to turn his power off right now. I wanted to feel the power of doing something extraordinary, something no one else could do. So I closed my eyes and let Maksim guide me.

Your core is everything. It is where your energy radiates from. It is a pulsating sphere waiting to expand. Release it.

I found it, right below my ribs, sitting above my stomach: the solar plexus. My core pulsed, all right, mimicking the beat of my heart, which had suddenly sped up. I imagined a snowball that melted away as the edges bled outward. The consistent warmth and pressure pulsed its way around my muscles and bones before escaping the confines of my skin and losing itself in the space around me. I wasn't a solitary entity anymore. I was blending with the energy of the air and water, mixing my energy with theirs.

Become the water. As if the water is in you, and you in it.

The two-thirds of my body that consisted of water found its counterpart in the lake and connected us on a deep level. The connection was like a key into a lock, and it fit perfectly.

Push it. Pull it. Manipulate the stream of energy.

I opened my eyes to let in the full spectrum of the water's energy. A wet breath caught at my lungs, but there was no pain, no drowning, just infusion of the added energy from this element.

As the water shifted below me, I brought my hands down over the railing, to redirect the flow of energy back away from me, back down upon the water, and created an indentation on its surface. Multiple ripples slid outward, without a sound, in endless succession.

Now!

My hands came together and lifted. The water drew up in response, gathering in a thin column, seeming as solid as the concrete pillars that held up the bridge. The top of the water crept higher and higher until it was almost level to my face. Fatigue took hold of my muscles, but I couldn't let go and, despite my shaking arms, the water didn't waver.

Enough.

Air rushed out of my lungs at the same time that my muscles released the pent-up energy, and the water collapsed onto itself with a shattering splash.

Satisfaction spread through me like warm liquid. I felt like I was being given a pat on the back, like my teacher was pleased. Or like I was a ventriloquist's dummy.

Something inside me was changing. I felt it every time I stopped resisting Maksim. My mind and soul felt somehow tougher, their edges rougher.

Now, with my energy spent, the cold bit hard into my skin. I brushed it away as I made my way back to my truck. It was still early in the morning, but Dani would be up by now. I needed to see her, needed to feel like things were normal. Like *I* was normal, even though I knew I wasn't. Not anymore.

~ ~ ~

Through the curtains of Dani's kitchen window I could see someone moving around. I pulled out my cell phone and sent her a text.

You up?

Yep.

I'm outside.

Dani's face appeared at the window and she peered out into the still-quiet street. Seeing my truck, she waved at me.

The front door opened noiselessly and Dani stepped back to let me in. "What are you doing here so early?" She rubbed her arms at the cold that followed me.

"I couldn't wait to see you." I shrugged, trying for a light tone. "Your mom still asleep?"

Dani nodded and motioned for me to follow her into the living room. "Is everything okay?" She kept her voice low.

"I wanted to give you your birthday present."

She caught her breath at the sight of the small white box, and when she opened it, her mouth opened in surprise.

"Seth! This is too much," she protested, but her eyes gleamed.

"Happy birthday."

Dani looked at me for a moment before walking over to the mirror that hung over the fireplace mantle. She took out the silver hoops she already had on and replaced them with the diamonds, tucking her hair behind her ears.

"Oh, my God, Seth!" she gasped. "They're beautiful!"

I stood behind her and smiled at her reflection. "*You're* beautiful," I murmured.

"Really, Seth. You didn't have to—"

"Shhh," I said softly, holding her shoulders and turning her to face me. I wanted this moment to last. She looked at me with so much love in her eyes, so much trust. My hands tightened on her shoulders.

Possess her. All of her.

Dani went perfectly still, her gazed fixed on my face. She must have noticed the way I was shaking, how tightly I gripped her shoulders.

I looked up. *The clock had stopped ticking.* I looked back at Dani's upturned face, and I breathed in the stillness.

Yes.

This moment was mine.

My hands slid down the length of her arms and gripped her hands. When she didn't grip back, I stepped back and looked around.

Impressed? laughed Maksim.

I ignored him. I was too busy being caught up in the power surging through me. I studied Dani's face and looked at her in a way I'd dared only in my dreams. Leaning closer, I caught the scent of her freshly-washed hair. Even her skin smelled like flowers. I nuzzled the soft spot behind her ear and nibbled on the lobe. Her skin was smooth beneath my fingers as I trailed a line down her neck, across her collarbone, to the hollow of her throat, feeling the pulse of her heart. Cradling her face in my hands, I brushed my tongue lightly over her lips, flicking the corners of her slightly-parted mouth.

I smiled against her lips. I needed to seduce and control her because…

She is mine.

No! She's mine! I warned.

That is what I said. She's yours.

But the moment was lost as I started to second guess what I heard.

I felt Dani flinch at my kiss, and at her own eagerness. But it was only a moment before she pushed me away, breathless, blinking in surprise.

"Wow! You have a way of making me forget everything when you kiss me like that!"

I leaned in again. I wasn't done. I wanted that moment back again.

Dani pressed her hand against my chest. "I think I hear my mom," she whispered. Her reflection in the mirror stopped her before she turned around. She gently touched her ears and her eyes met mine. "Thank you, Seth. They're beautiful." Her smile dissolved into a gasp and she spun around, staring at my eyes. She looked behind me, then at my eyes again.

"What's the matter?" I asked her.

120

She shook her head. "Um… nothing. I thought I saw… It must have been a reflection… or something."

"Good morning, Seth! What are you doing here so early?" Janice made her way down the stairs and headed towards the kitchen.

Dani squeezed my hand as she stepped around me to follow her mother. "Mom, look at what Seth gave me for my birthday!"

I spun around and faced the mirror. The skin under my eyes was shadowed from lack of sleep, and my eyes, usually light brown, glared back at me, piercing, dark, and glassy. *Not mine.* The edges wavered and a wave of darkness passed through my eyes, like a silhouette passing by a window. Instinctively, I backed up, as if distancing myself from my reflection would somehow separate me from Maksim. Shaking off the image, I headed toward the kitchen.

"They're gorgeous earrings, Seth," Janice said.

I tucked Dani's hair behind her ears, grazing her lobes with my fingers, pushing away a feeling of dread. I felt a strange mix of strength and anger when I touched her. "It's all Dani, Mrs. Parsons," I said. "*She* makes them beautiful." And I meant that. Dani was more than pretty. She was beautiful on the inside, too. Curling my fingers into my palm, I backed off. "I need to do something before school. I'll see you there, okay?"

"Yeah, okay." Dani nodded. She took a step to follow me but I shook my head.

"You get ready and I'll meet you in first period." I left, not wanting to give her a chance to say anything.

~ ~ ~

"So, how'd you do it?"

"Do what?" I returned Dirk's stony gaze and rubbed my shoulder. He'd purposely bumped into me in the hall. I wanted to back away, to get some space between us, but our energies locked and I stopped. I cleared my head of any thoughts, hoping that might stop the connection, and it did, to an extent. But not enough, because Dirk wasn't going away.

He stared, his lip curling. "At the dance. I felt it. I couldn't see it, but I felt it."

"I don't know what you're talking about," I told him. I started to walk around him, but he grabbed my arm.

"Like hell you don't," he hissed.

I shook him off and pushed past him, hoping he wouldn't follow.

He isn't so bad.

He is bad, I thought back to Maksim.

Just because he wants your woman?

"Isn't that bad enough?" I muttered.

You forget an important tactic in battle, my friend: Keep your friends close, and your enemies closer.

~ ~ ~

Not far from where Justin, Dani, and I stood in front of the school, a few feet from where the students were loading up on the buses, were two starkly contrasting people. A tall, lanky guy, dressed head-to-toe in black, his wool coat buttoned up tight against the afternoon air, kept his gaze fixed on Travis, a stocky tackle on the football team. Travis shifted from one foot to the other, looking around with his hands tucked under his armpits. It seemed as if Travis wanted to be anywhere but standing in front of this guy.

Tall dude's lips moved silently. I couldn't hear him, but his face was devoid of any expression. Travis' eyes narrowed for a moment, then he burst out laughing.

"You're kidding, right?" I heard Travis say.

Tall dude didn't react.

"Yeah, sure. Why the hell not?" Travis shrugged and put his hand out. The other guy handed over some money, which Travis grabbed and shoved into his pocket. Then he walked away, laughing.

"What was that all about?" Justin asked me.

I shrugged. "Who knows?" I didn't really care. I was more interested in the group of Goths who huddled together talking.

Though I couldn't put my finger on why, uneasiness crept up my spine when I singled out Goth Girl from the group. She was leaning back just far enough to be able to look around the shoulder of the tall guy. Her gaze sank deep into me.

"Isn't that the girl from your math class?" I asked Dani.

"Huh?" She stopped her texting and looked up. "Who?"

"Over there." I tilted my chin in the girl's direction, but by the time Dani figured out where I was looking, Goth had stepped out of sight.

"Chicken," I said, under my breath.

"What?" Justin and Dani asked me in unison.

"Nothing." I muttered.

Dani shoved her phone inside her pack and pulled out some pictures. "Look. My mom had these printed up." She flipped through a few pictures before she found the one she wanted. "Not bad, but your eyes are a little dark." She stared at my eyes. "They're not really that dark, are they?" She looked back at the picture. "Or maybe the whole picture is off. I told you Mom needs a new camera."

Justin and I leaned in to look. There was no mistaking the blackness of my eyes. The feeling of complete dread rolled my stomach again. I felt like the star of some freaky reality show.

"Yeah, she definitely needs a new one," I said, straightening up. I shot a glance back at the Goth group, but they had left. Why did that girl irritate me so damn much?

Dani nudged her shoulder into my arm. "Want to go with me to the library? I need to get some books on ancient civilizations."

"How about if I drive you?" I said, hooking my fingers in her belt loop and guiding her toward the parking lot.

She shrugged. "Sure." She turned to Justin. "Do you have your notes already?"

"No. I guess I should go, too."

I tried to kick the image of the Goth girl's face out of my mind, but I couldn't. I didn't trust her. There was just something about the way she looked at me, as if she knew something I didn't know. I felt like I knew her from somewhere. Somewhere other than Sandpoint. That had to have been it. Someone like her, here in my little town, would be hard to forget.

~ ~ ~

As soon as we walked into the library, Justin headed to the history section and Dani and I went the other direction, to the library's catalog computers.

"This won't take long," Dani said.

"Take your time." Leaning up against the counter, I waited until she scribbled numbers on a piece of paper.

When she was done, I followed her close enough to nibble on her neck. She laughed and walked faster, then ducked into one of the aisles.

"Not now, Seth! I'm trying to be serious," she scolded me, running her fingers along the book spines. "Here it is," she said, stopping at a thin book.

"I'm trying to be serious, too." I slipped my arms around her waist, using her shoulder to rest my chin on. As she flipped through the pages, something caught my eye.

"Hey, let me see that," I said, grabbing the book from her. "That was cool."

"Seth, *I* was looking at that!"

"Hang on a second." I leafed back through the pages. "There it is," I muttered. A snake, or maybe a snake and a sun, but definitely inside a labyrinth. Huh. I'd remembered reading somewhere that the sun is a symbol of energy; the snake is an ancient dual expression of good and evil, rebirth and immortality. My finger traced the snake's body. It was contorted into the *shape* of a labyrinth, with the pattern on its back forming the sun. The red jewel set at the center of the snake's head screamed power and control.

You know what you need to do.

Yeah, I did.

"Where are you going, Seth?" Dani whispered.

"I'll be right back," I said over my shoulder, taking the book with me. I went straight to the copy machine and dug some change out of my pocket. It was important that I have this picture. Permanently. We—Maksim and I—agreed that the symbol would make a very cool tattoo.

~ ~ ~

The spark spun itself in a small inferno that licked the skin of Maksim's palm. It was marvelous! Had he not conjured this himself, he would have sworn the spark was sent from the sun god himself. But, no, it was Maksim who had plucked the energy from the cool evening air, weaving it tightly until it burst into flame. The power that emanated from the flame was intoxicating. As easy as it had been to create the fire sphere, he could just as easily destroy it, but there was something he would try before the flame's demise.

His latest skill promised to be quite useful. It was a skill he had been perfecting for the past two days. He closed his eyes and withdrew, pulling with him the moments that followed. Time filled every space within his mind and the seconds stopped, for they no longer had anywhere to flow. The sudden hush around him was palpable.

Raising his eyes to the flame, his smile grew. It had worked. The tips of the flame danced no more. Instead, the edges of the fiery fingers curved in graceful arcs, then into pinnacles that reached high, frozen in motion, before sliding back into the pool of heat in his palm.

Time. It was now his to command.

~ ~ ~

Chapter 13

He hesitates between our two worlds now. No longer the eager student, he reluctantly opens the door, allowing me to slip into his mind. He feels my darkness, acknowledging it as his own.
~ Maksim

I reached out again to everyone around me. I couldn't stop myself. Or maybe I didn't want to stop. As I walked down the school halls, every girl I touched with my energy was compelled to look at me. I was a magnet, and I pulled in their thoughts and feelings—interest, curiosity, desire, and lust. Until Dani slapped me on the arm.

"Hey!" I frowned at her and shielded my shoulder with my hand. The skin felt raw underneath my sleeve where my newly-inked tattoo was healing. Almost twelve hours old, the mark was settling into the cells of my skin, sinking deep.

"I was *talking* to you," Dani said. She grabbed my hand. "What's the matter with your shoulder?"

"It's nothing."

She pried my hand away—not that it took much effort—and pushed my sleeve up. Her eyes widened with a little bit of shock and a lot of surprise when she saw my tattoo. "You didn't tell me you were going to do that."

I shrugged. "It was a spontaneous thing."

She cocked her head to the side. "What is it?" she asked.

Lowering my voice and leaning close to her ear, I told her. "It's an Egyptian symbol of power."

"Oookaaay." She raised an eyebrow, looked at the tattoo a few seconds longer, and pulled my sleeve back down. "I just didn't expect it, that's all," she smiled up at me and glanced away, then snapped her head back to my face, her jaw dropping. "Seth?"

"What?" I asked innocently.

"What... your eyes! It was like there was smoke... behind them..." she sounded confused.

That wasn't good. I didn't want her looking that closely.

The door to our next class was right beside us. Perfect timing. "Oops! Don't want to be late." I pulled her inside, looking anywhere but her face, and we sat down. The teacher started right away and there was no more time to talk.

~ ~ ~

The yapping of the dogs, all fifteen of them, rose to a level I wouldn't have thought possible.

"Starved for attention, I guess," Dani muttered before setting off on her routine check.

I flinched from the intensity of energy the animals were shooting off; confused, nervous, and defensive. I hung back by the door, behind a rack of aprons and towels, and started blocking off the assault of energy in my mind, dog by dog. This was getting a little out of control. Out of *my* control.

Max's cage, in the middle of the kennel, was the only quiet one. The Labrador stood firm, his haunches splayed in a defensive stance, his nose frantically sniffing the air.

At the end of the row, Dani knelt in front of the new dog's cage and stuck her fingers through the wire. The Schnauzer crept towards her, slowly putting one paw in front of the other, and let his nose graze her fingers. His eyes darted in my direction and after a quick flick of his tongue on Dani's fingers, he backed away. She let out a huge breath, leaning her forehead against the criss-cross of the cage.

I walked to the Schnauzer's cage, making sure my steps were slow. Standing behind Dani, I leaned over and smiled.

The dog bared his teeth and took a few steps back.

"What do you think is wrong?" she asked me. It killed me to hear her so confused and desperate for answers.

But I knew. I knew *exactly* why they were reacting this way. My smile faded. I couldn't tell her why, so I gave her the next best answer. "He's just never liked me."

Then Dani's eyes widened as she took in the chest-deep growls, the threatening barks, the high-pitched whines of every dog in the kennel. "What's going on with all the dogs?"

I straightened up. Hot, dry prickles spread over the back of my neck. Fear. Mine? The dogs? Dani's? This guest I had riding on my back was quickly wearing out his welcome. I could shield myself from energy coming in, but I obviously had no control over what was going out. I turned to Max, sure that he would recognize me. I crouched down in front of his cage, trying to seem less intimidating. "Hey, buddy."

One sniff was all it took. A sharp ridge of fur rose high on his spine and a slow whine vibrated in his throat.

"It's me, boy. Don't be afraid," I pleaded.

Max's ears perked up and he took a cautious step toward me. He stretched his neck, standing as far away as possible and sniffed my fingers that I had shoved through the cage. Then he stood still, staring at my fingers as if undecided.

I whispered in a quiet, crooning tone until Max crept closer, trembling on unsteady legs. He wouldn't look directly at me, only stealing glances out of the corners of his eyes.

I shifted my weight a little, and when I did, Max bolted out of reach, flattening himself into the corner.

"Maybe it's your coat?" Gracie stood at the door, watching me.

I took a quick glance at the black long rider coat I wore. I put on a polished smile, replacing the scowl that pulled at my face. "Hey, I bought this next door, at the shelter's thrift store. You know, trying to help the cause." I faced her, my hands away from my body. "Don't you like it?"

A tremor shifted close to the surface of my skin, making the muscles in my neck and back twitch, but I made sure my smile never wavered. I was going to beat Maksim down. I wanted my control back.

Gracie shrugged. "Seth, I have an idea. Why don't you come up front and help me with some paperwork? Or you can help Ron out in the back with the dog food donations."

I know Gracie was trying to be nice, but I had a feeling I was just demoted from my volunteer job. I looked at Dani. My excuse of a smile didn't wipe away how sad she looked. How much worse could this get?

~ ~ ~

"Hey, why are you still up?" Dad stood in the doorway, tucking his robe tighter across his chest.

He'd pulled in a few hours earlier. He told me he was too tired to even eat so he'd gone straight to bed.

I'd thought he'd been asleep, but still I'd tried to keep the weights quiet. I just didn't want to worry him. I didn't want him to start asking questions, but I guess it didn't really matter what I wanted anymore.

I eased down the bar that I had been curling and put it on the floor. Even though I had been upping the weights almost every day, lifting was only getting easier. Working out hard used to exhaust me, but now it seemed to just feed the intense energy simmering under my skin, in my chest and in my head. Kind of like revving up the engine of a Mustang, I felt ready to peel out at any second. I knew sleep would help, if only I could get to that point. Every time I lay down to rest, my eyes would follow the shadows that raced behind my lids and around my mind like a silver ball in a pinball machine. I dreaded closing my eyes.

Shoving my hands through my hair, I looked up at Dad. "I couldn't sleep." I gestured to the weights. "Thought this might help tire me out."

Dad nodded, but raised his brows when he noticed the plates on the bar. "You're lifting a lot heavier."

My cell phone beeped. I snatched it up from the bench behind me, grateful for the distraction. I answered the text, my thumbs quickly moving over the keypad. "Dani," I explained, looking up at him.

Dad leaned against the door jam and folded his arms across his chest. Normally so easy-going and seemingly oblivious to the details around him, he now scrutinized me a little too closely.

My shirts had become tighter around my biceps and shoulders, and across my back, and I'd let my hair get shaggier, and Dad noticed it all. Pushing himself away from the door, he slowly closed the gap between us and stopped right in front of me.

I looked down at his bare feet, the safest place I could think of, but he wouldn't have it.

"Look at me, Seth."

I didn't want to.

The seconds ticked by.

"Are you doing drugs?" he finally asked.

A laugh busted out before I could stop it. If only it were that simple! Drugs I could kick. Drugs I could get help for. Drugs could end. For what I had gotten involved in, there was no remedy that I knew of. It was like a disease that had no cure. I didn't even know what the hell it was, only that it seemed to be charring me from the inside out, transforming me in ways I didn't understand.

"You think this is funny?" He frowned.

"No, I don't, Dad. It is just such a crazy thought, is all." I shook my head. "No drugs. Just stuff with Dani and school."

Relief softened the lines on his face. "Well, good. I'm really glad to hear that. I have to admit, I was kind of worried." He sighed. "I know I'm not here a lot, but I'll do whatever I can, and someday, when I can get off the road..."

"Hey, it's okay, Dad. Don't worry." I smiled at him, but cringed at the irony of all of this. Getting him off the road was one of the reasons I bought the damn soul, and it was all I could do to try to keep it caged in.

Dad reached out and ruffled my hair, just like he did when I was younger.

"I love you, Seth."

Love! Maksim's anger billowed. *He does not understand love.*

Shadows swirled behind my eyes, making it hard to see, but the love of my dad that covered me was too strong for the... demon. I knew that he was no angel, and I didn't know how else to think of him.

Maksim fell back, and I was finally able to relax.

132

Chapter 14

There is the other girl, the one in black. She is of a bloodline that haunts me, but from which one, I cannot be sure. Her darkened eyes hide her well as does the shield she has surrounded herself with. Her curiosity is strong. But then again, so am I.
~ Maksim

While the wrestling team practiced at the upper level of the gym—prepping for the state championships—the basketball team was running drills down below on the court. No one seemed to notice how thick the tension was on the practice mat.

Except me. While everyone stepped in it, over it, around it, I lived it. I was battling for balance, always straddling the line between sanity and insanity, light and dark.

Light and Dark.

I glanced in Dani's direction. She sat on the extra mats stacked along the wall, with a book open next to her and a pad of paper on her lap. Light.

The Goth girl stood against the wall in her usual spot, wearing a calf-length black skirt with black tights that disappeared into black Doc Martens. An oversized black messenger bag, slung across her body, rested against her hip. Charcoal-lined blue eyes, peering out from under spikes of black bangs, pierced me. Dark.

She looked at me, or rather, looked *through* me, in a way that made my muscles tighten up in knots. It wasn't like she was trying to hit on me. *That* I could handle. This one looked at me with fascination. Like a little kid discovering a caterpillar for the first time, or a scientist stumbling upon an interesting find.

What exactly *did* she see? Was it possible she could see the soul that swam shark-like beneath my skin?

A low vibration hummed in my chest and I turned to my next opponent. Unfortunately it was Dirk.

"Your latest groupie, Thompson?" he sneered, looking in Goth's direction. "Not too selective these days, are you?"

I ignored the barb and instead planted my feet firmly into the mat, crouching low in ready-stance. I could take him easy. I was stronger now, faster, and meaner.

At the coach's signal, Dirk and I tried to tie up, but we kept knocking each other's arm away.

Prove to him who is stronger now.

A fire blazed inside of me so fast, I couldn't stop it, but the rush was incredible. My solar plexus burned as my core energy burst out of my chest and pulled on the threads shooting out from Dirk and tied them tight with mine. I fought it, trying to block off the pathway, trying to use what Maksim had taught me, but this was different, something he didn't bother to teach me. It wasn't like shutting down everyone's emotions. It was as if I were hanging on like a leach, drawing on Dirk's energy to fuel my own, making it like a life force, a tool of survival. And I couldn't shut it off any more than I could shut off my breath.

I dug in and circled to bring Dirk's foot forward. Shooting down onto both of my knees, I grabbed his leg and held onto his arm. I was quick to hit my hip and flip him over, throwing my arm over him. My arm slid around his arm and head and I locked my hands behind his head, pulling in tight.

Though I had pinned Dirk again, it didn't seem to bother him at all. In fact, he was hardly put up a fight and... he was smiling at me? What the hell?

He looked at me like he was high or something. That was just creepy. A hard shake of my head cleared my thoughts for the next round. We switched opponents. This time it was Troy, a guy who weighed about twenty pounds less than I did. I dug my feet in again. It would've been an easy pin—had I not been distracted.

A second before the coach had given the signal, Goth Girl had headed towards Dani and stood next to her. I couldn't tell what Goth was saying because that was when I hit the mat. All I saw were her lips moving and Dani looking up, saying something back to her.

Troy took advantage of my distraction. He snapped my head down, put it under his arm, and leaned down. I was still trying to focus when the pain hit. Troy's shoulder was pressed into mine and he had my arm stretched out so far it felt like it was slipping out of its socket. He held me in a headlock and wouldn't let up. With my forehead and nose smashed against the mat, I still managed to look at the girls from beneath his arm. Goth Girl leaned over, talking to Dani. Both girls glanced at me; Dani looked confused, Goth Girl looked intrigued.

Not good. I didn't trust the girl in black. I needed to break up their little chat.

In a smooth motion, I reached around to wrap my arm around Troy's neck. I rolled fast, leaning back and pinning him.

But I was too late. Goth walked away, headed down the stairs that led to the gym below, looking at me over her shoulder, with Dani following.

I didn't like the way Goth had stared at me so intently. I tried sensing what she was thinking, but there was nothing. Not one shred of emotion coming off her, no thoughts, nothing. I didn't understand. There was no way someone could be that intense and not be shooting off vibes like missiles.

I had to see for myself what Dani and the Goth Girl were up to, so I quickly pinned the next guy, James, a scrawny kid. I probably was a little too harsh on him, but I didn't have time to mess around. I sprinted to the wall and looked over the top of the railing.

~ ~ ~

"You have no love for me?" Silura demanded.

He placed his hands on her shoulders and sent out a gentle wave of heat through her, spreading it across her collarbone, to the hollow below her throat.

Any other time she would have welcomed such seduction, but not now. She would have his answer to her question! Though she could delay the progress of aging, one day her raven hair would be streaked with gray and her senses would dim. So, while she was young, she wanted—no, needed—to feel cherished and loved unconditionally by this man.

"I have much affection and gratitude for you," he said, glancing away.

"Those are not the same as love."

When he did not respond, she pushed for an answer. "What is it you fear about love?" She gave a little nudge into his mind. She knew he would feel her invasion, but she did not care.

"I fear love will end." He frowned. "And I think I would go mad if it did."

"So you take no chances?" she demanded. "Is the joy of being in love not worth risking all?"

He shook his head. "There could never be enough joy to counter the possibility of pain."

Her spirits lifted a little. So, it was love he opposed, not her. She smiled at him. That was the difference between men and women, she thought. Women had foolish hearts and men... well, they were just foolish. She could change his mind. She knew she could.

~ ~ ~

Chapter 15

This girl, the one who favors darkness, is quickly becoming a nuisance. She could destroy me and the boy. She seeks to hide from me, but by karmic souls, there is no place she cannot be found.
~ Maksim

By the time Dani reached the bottom of the stairs, Goth was halfway across the gym, headed towards the Commons, her shoes thudding against the polished floor.

"Alyx! Wait up!" I heard Dani yell to the girl.

She stopped and turned to face Dani.

They both stood, Goth looking bored and Dani standing defensively as if she were confronting the girl with something. Goth had obviously said something to Dani before she had gone down the stairs and knowing Dani, she wasn't going to let it go until she got some answers, whatever they were.

The way Dani shifted her weight on her feet, the way she bounced between speaking animatedly with her hands and crossing her arms over her chest, I could see she wasn't getting those answers.

They should not be together. Maksim whispered.

I know. I answered. *I have my reasons, but what about you? What do you have against Goth?*

He was silent, but pressure built up against my eyes, like he was watching her through mine.

This entire time, Goth's face was a clean slate, free of emotion, but she stood still, seeming to listen intently to what Dani was saying. Then her eyes got wide and her mouth opened and quickly closed like she started to say something, but changed her mind. Her eyes drifted up past Dani's shoulder and found me where I stood upstairs at the railing. I knew the second she registered it was me, because her mask of boredom slid into place.

Dani turned and followed her gaze, and once she saw it was me, she quickly turned back to Alyx.

A second or two passed before Goth turned on her heel and walked from the gym, letting the door slam behind her.

I'd stepped back from the railing just as Dani began to turn around. I found a partner and began doing drills with the others, keeping an eye on the top of the stairs.

A couple minutes later, Dani stepped through the door of the wrestling area and walked to the book and papers she'd left laying on the floor. Scooping them up, she shoved them into her backpack and zipped it up. On her way back to the stairs, she waved and then made the telephone sign to me, telling me to call her. She didn't look back as she disappeared down the stairwell.

I made a snap decision to follow her. Running off the mat, I grabbed my sweats and threw them on, leaving my gym bag behind as I bolted across the wrestling floor.

"Hey, Thompson!" the coach called to me. "Where do you think you're going?"

"I've gotta take care of something, Coach," I yelled over my shoulder.

I got a few looks with that answer because nobody ever just took off like I was, but there was no way I was going to be able to concentrate anyway, so... yeah. Whatever. I passed Justin on the way out. "Hey, grab my bag, will you?" I asked him. "I'll pick it up from you later." I didn't wait for an answer and instead picked up my pace.

I reached the bottom of the stairs just as Dani slipped out the gym doors. I had a pretty good guess what she was up to, but I needed to be sure.

~ ~ ~

War Memorial Field, the community field where most of the town's school sports and special events were held, was hardly the first place I would've chosen to meet someone. The field was tucked out of the way, next to the lake, and during the winter months, it was cold and uninviting. Personally I would've been a lot happier at Dub's, but then again, the Goth Girl isn't me.

It hadn't been difficult to follow Dani from the school unnoticed. She'd probably thought I was still at practice so she had no reason to be going stealth. I'd sort of hoped she would see me. If she had, maybe she would've given up on whatever it was she was trying so hard to find out from Goth. There was no chance, though. The residue of curiosity that lingered in her wake when she left the school was strong and confrontation with Goth would be the only way to satisfy her curiosity.

From where I had pulled my truck over at Lakeview Park, I watched Dani push on the fence surrounding the field, duck under the chain that held the gate together, and walk toward the bleachers. She didn't even look back. Yeah, she was definitely on a mission.

Quietly getting out of my truck, I jogged through the park behind the bleachers, climbed over and dropped down the other side of the fence. Unless they were looking over the top of the wall that enclosed the bleachers, they wouldn't know I was there. Then again, I really didn't care if they did, but if I could hear what they were saying, that would be all the better.

I walked close to the wall around the side of the bleachers and peeked around the corner to see where they were sitting. It was too bad I didn't have super Batman ears or something because the girls were too far up the bleachers for me to hear.

My options were limited. In fact, I had none. I wasn't about to leave them alone to talk about God knows what, and since I couldn't hear them, I decided it was time to make an appearance.

The air around the bleachers suddenly became quiet as I made my way up the stairs and stepped into view.

Chapter 16

The girl in black with the blue eyes. I have seen her kind before. Light seekers, they call themselves. Witch-hunters, in truth. They only seek to destroy, to rid the world of our kind. But the only truth to be had, the only one that matters is this: I cannot be destroyed.
~ Maksim

Dani's face turned pale when she saw me standing at the bottom of the bleachers. By the way Dani had been standing, with her arms crossed over her chest, totally closing herself up, it would be my guess that they weren't having a cozy conversation. Especially since Goth had been writing in her notebook. Undoubtedly things about me, because as soon as she saw me, she'd slipped the pad into her bag and buckled it shut.

Though I took the steps two at a time, closing the gap between us faster, Goth was hardly intimidated. She sat calmly, her chin resting in one hand, a cigarette in the other, with her eyes fixed on my face.

Dani was the first to break the silence. "Hey, babe!" She wrapped an arm around my waist. "How'd you know I'd be here?"

I shrugged away her question. "Aren't you going to introduce us?" I tipped my chin at Goth.

The girl took hit from her cigarette and blew the smoke in my direction, her eyes never leaving mine.

Dani looked from me to Goth and back again. "Seth, this is Alyx. Alyx, this is Seth."

I managed a small smile. "How's it going?" I asked. Not like I cared or anything. I was being nice for Dani's sake. My core exploded in its rush to punch through Goth's space and feel her energy, to figure out why she insisted on hanging out with Dani, but not only did I get blocked, I was pushed back, and instinctively my walls went up, protecting my own thoughts. What the hell?

She is searching, looking for her own answers, Maksim's voice echoed in my head

Really. I hardly needed you to tell me that.

"Nice to finally meet you," Alyx said to me with a hint of sarcasm. She glanced at Dani. "I've gotta go. We'll talk later."

"Okay. Yeah, sure," Dani said.

Alyx slung her bag over her shoulder and clomped down the stairs.

"What were you two talking about?" I asked when Goth was out of earshot.

"Not much." Dani wrapped her arms tighter around me, shivering a little.

It was cold here. Bone-chilling cold. "This is a strange place to not talk about much," I said.

She's hiding something. The voice whispered.

Well, that much was obvious.

"Hey, I'm cold," Dani said. "Let's go get some hot chocolate, okay?" She reached for her backpack, and for the first time, she avoided looking into my eyes.

~ ~ ~

"Really, what Alyx and I were talking about wasn't a big deal. You know. Just girl talk." Dani's hands were wrapped tightly around her cup of hot chocolate. Bringing it to her lips, she blew over the

top of it before taking a sip. "Oh, that tastes good."
She leaned back against the booth in our usual seat at
Dub's, with me next to her on the bench.

It was quiet during the lull between the high-
schoolers' after-school meal and the dinner crowd.
Only a few people drifted in and out with ice cream
or burgers in hand.

I'd been mostly silent since we arrived, looking at
Dani with the patience of a police interrogator,
knowing that my subject was about to crack.

"She really is an interesting person. Not at all like
I thought," Dani volunteered.

"So interesting that you had to meet her at the
field? What's the matter? Are you embarrassed to be
seen with her or something?" I grazed her jaw with
my fingertips, intentionally spreading warmth to her
cheeks.

She leaned into my touch for a moment before
jerking back. "I thought she might be interested in
you, so I was going to talk to her, okay?"

She won't look at you. She's lying, the voice
hissed.

I reached a hand behind her neck to massage her
muscles. Without guilt, without thinking, I used
Maksim's power to get her to talk.

Rubbing her neck, I pushed waves of ecstasy up
and down her spine. I leaned in close and brushed her
lips with mine, teasing the corners of her mouth with
the tip of my tongue before kissing her, wrapping her
up with enough heat to make her melt against me.

And her lips moved with mine in perfect
compliance.

As it should be, Maksim breathed her in.

"What did she say to you?" I whispered against
her mouth.

145

"Alyx said… you have it bad," Dani said breathlessly, pulling back slightly. She brought her hand up to my face and gently touched my cheek. "You take my breath away when you kiss me like that, Seth," she sighed, "and my mind along with it."

This Alyx, what else does she say?

Back off, Maksim.

I didn't care. I'd heard enough. If Goth was telling Dani things that would turn her against me… I couldn't let that happen.

"Don't hang around with her. She's trouble." It was then that I realized how serious I was about that. I didn't yet know why, but Goth could make things a lot worse for us. I didn't want to lose Dani. Especially not now. I drew a deep breath and let it out. "Please don't leave me, Dani."

She laughed. "But I have to go home sometime, Seth" she said.

"Do homework at my house tonight," I said, resting my forehead against hers.

"Seth?"

"Yeah?" I closed my eyes.

"I love you. I would do anything for you. You know that, right?"

I did know, but would she still say that knowing what I've done? Would she want to be with me if she found out I have another soul looking over my shoulder all day every day? One day when she looked at me, would she see *him*? *Shit.* I really screwed up this time. I could only nod my head, afraid my voice would give me away.

Chapter 17

*This is how it should have been from the moment
he bought me. We move as one. He depends on me
and I on him.*
~ Maksim

I closed my eyes and focused on the energy
pooling in my thighs, my chest, and my arms. With
my strength and speed, and my ability to cripple my
opponent by simply reaching out and choking off his
spirit, it was easy to dominate the mat.

Here at the state championships I knew it was
wrong and totally unfair to use Maksim's power on
my opponents. And I finally realized that's all it
really was—Maksim's power. But he *did* promise me
that, and I *did* want to win the championship. So I
played nice.

I felt like a freakin' child, and Maksim was the
parent, so like a rebel teenager, I'd been trying to do a
little control on my own, trying to control what he did
through me, but I ended up with major headaches and
stomach pains as punishment. I was completely
helpless against him. The bastard seemed to get a kick
out of infusing his power into my veins, spreading the
euphoric feeling, and destroying every reason I had
for fighting him.

Like now.

The sounds of the other wrestling matches around
me intensified—grunts, expelled breaths, and the
scrambling of feet. I opened my eyes and studied my
opponent. He was taller by about two inches, with a

strong frame, huge shoulders, and determination burned in his eyes. Until, that is, he looked into *my* eyes. I smiled at him as a shudder rolled through his thick shoulder muscles and his eyes became a little unfocused.

"Nail him, Seth!" Dirk encouraged from the sidelines.

I glanced over at him and the rest of the team who sat in chairs along the edge of the mat. Justin said something to Dirk and Dirk shrugged it off, never taking his eyes from me.

I shut them both out and wrapped myself up in my own internal battle cry.

"Come on, Seth," Justin called out.

At the referee's signal, I faked a tie up, dropped down, and instead of driving my shoulder into my opponent, I lifted and then slammed him onto the mat. He coughed out a breath when his head slammed back.

"Take it easy, Sandpoint," the referee warned.

We stood to face each other again.

I couldn't take it easy. My blood was pumping faster than my heart could keep up. I was going to finish this right now. After shaking my opponent's hand to start up again, I put him into a headlock, put my hand under his arm and across his back, twisted, and fell on top of him—hard—until his shoulders hit. Easy pin. The combination of adrenaline and darkness shot through me, leaving me feeling high. This time, I'd be the state champion.

Dirk jumped up off the chair and met me as I came off the mat.

I avoided his high five.

"That was *sah-weet!*" Dirk laughed, slapping my shoulder instead.

"Yeah, whatever, dickhead." I shrugged off his hand. Why was he all of a sudden so nice? I grabbed a towel out of my bag and sat down, wiping my face. Dirk took the chair next to me. He had a stupid grin on his face, like all of a sudden we were friends or something. I needed space from him, so I slid my chair away. I was starting to feel like Siamese twins or something when I was close to him.

"You nailed that one!" Justin grinned.

"Thanks, man," I said.

Soft lips kissed my shoulder and a shower of hair slipped down my arm. The touch totally raked my nerves. *His* nerves. Without thinking, I pushed it off.

"Hey!" Dani straightened up, clearly hurt by my reaction.

"How ya doing, Dani?" Dirk looked over his shoulder with a leering smile.

I punched his arm.

"Danika." She sneered.

"Oh yeah. I forgot," laughed Dirk.

Reaching for her hand, I pulled Dani to me. "Sorry. I was getting a little intense."

"A little?" She said. "That's putting it mildly."

"Come here." I twisted in my chair and wrapped my arm around her waist, pulling her close. "Sorry," I said again.

Her hand grabbed my jaw and she forced me to look at her. Her lips, with a blush of color on them, were pressed into a determined and very serious line. Her eyes bore into mine as if she were looking for something very specific.

Maybe if I held my breath, it might stop Maksim from moving. And if he didn't move, then Dani couldn't see him.

After a long minute, her mouth softened and her eyes lightened. Her arms went around my shoulders and she hugged me tight against her, resting her cheek against my hair.

I melted against her. That was too close, I thought.

Too much light. She hurts us.

How can she hurt us? Wait a minute… there is no "us."

I gripped Dani tighter and hid my face in the folds of her jackets. My teeth ached from gritting them. No. I. Won't. Lose. Her.

It was a promise to me. And to Maksim.

~ ~ ~

"Why is it that I can read the emotions of anyone I choose and know their thoughts…" He paused, closing his eyes to try one more time.

She felt the push against her mind. She would reveal nothing. Not even a ripple of emotion.

"But you," he said, "I cannot feel. Why?"

She turned her face from his gaze. The shield she had built around herself protected her thoughts from him. She loved him, but did not trust him, for she knew he could, and would, use those thoughts against her.

She never had any intention of teaching him the spell for the shield. If he used it, she would not be privy to his mind's workings. In time, she knew, it would become a necessity, for she would not see him harmed. The spell of the shield would protect both his body and his mind from his rapidly growing list of enemies. It would create a wall between him and everyone else.

Including her.

~ ~ ~

Chapter 18

There will always be keepers of secrets. Saviors with gilded swords. The knowledge, woven into the fiber of their souls, is passed on through the bloodlines. They know they are gifted, but they do not always realize how much power they really have. I thought she was merely a Light-Seeker, but this Girl in Black, with her startling blue eyes... she may be of such a bloodline. I will watch her. I will tolerate no threats.
~Maksim

The thick ceiling of gray sky squashed any hope of relief from the dampness. The clouds seemed to press down on the town, which was already soaked from the downpour of the last two days. Another storm was coming.

But that didn't stop everyone at school from hanging around outside the buildings, huddled in their groups. Some were blowing the first layer of heat from their coffees and mochas. Most of them were glum-faced, matching the mood of the sky.

Like the Goth group, an island of black floating in the sea of gray. They came together because of their similarities to each other, or maybe because of their differences from the others.

Suspicion flowed like a river through them. Their eyes flitted about, like gazelles ready to flee when stalked by a lion.

The Goths are nervous, I thought, *but not Alyx.* She kept her face passive, though she knew Dirk and I were watching her. She kept herself hidden behind others in the group, but they kept shifting, mimicking the unrest in the air and when her cover moved, she found someone else to hide behind.

I glanced at Dirk, whom I just couldn't seem to shake anymore. But after two years of him constantly at my back, taking digs, trying to undermine everything I did, I had to admit I was enjoying having an edge over him. Through Maksim and because of Maksim, we were connected. I didn't know what Maksim wanted with Dirk, but I did know what Dirk wanted from me: power. He probably sensed it, just like the dogs at the kennel, like the girls here at school. Power is power. Everyone gravitates to it. And I had it in spades.

"Wait here," I told him.

I closed the gap between me and Alyx, and the herd of Goth kids scattered like frightened animals, leaving her alone.

Pathetic.

Not Goth. No, she was anything but. She met my eyes straight on, even tilted her chin in defiance, daring me to come closer.

And I did. Right up to her toes.

"Hey," she said, backing up two steps. "Respect my personal space."

A black crocheted beanie, shot through with sparks of red, covered her inky black hair and pressed it against the sides of her face, as if trying to keep her thoughts corralled. An amulet of yellow citrine, wrapped with a wire, dangled from a thin, black cord, protecting her heart. The set of her jaw showed she was determined not to let me intimidate her. I hated to admit it, but I liked the fact that she endured my scrutiny without flinching, without a hint of fear.

I probed her thoughts and tried to read her. I searched for the sound, the voice, but heard nothing.

154

Why can't I pick up anything? What *is* it with this chick? I looked towards the parking lot. There. That girl. Yeah, I could read her with no problem. But this one, this Goth... there was a cold wall—a definite block in my face. None of her emotions were getting out and nothing was getting in. She was on permanent vibrational lockdown.

Maksim and I gave up on the poking and prodding and tried something a little more dramatic. Wrapping my energy around her, I squeezed, slowly at first, then harder. I laughed when her black-lipstick lips parted slightly and she gasped.

I took a step closer. "Dani tells me you're filling her head with lies? I can't let you get away with that... now can I?"

She squared her shoulders and took a step back, touching her amulet as if to make sure it was still there. "Nice try. Your voodoo doesn't work on me."

I let out a snort. "What? A piece of glass is supposed to stop me?" Looking around to see if anyone was watching, I leaned in close, and whispered in her ear, "I don't think you realize just who you're messing with. I'd be careful if I were you."

Straightening up, I took the amulet in my hand, purposely grazing her skin with my fingers. I grinned when her eyes fluttered and she sucked in a quick breath.

Amulets mean nothing. They are merely false promises of protection. Pretty little trinkets.

"You know," I said, "citrine is supposed to open your mind, so this actually calls me to you."

For a fleeting moment, uncertainty clouded her face, but then she steeled herself and the mask of defiance slid back into place. She was good.

Her sudden smile was nothing more than a mask to hide her sarcasm. "Good. Then I'll always know where to find you… and I'm. Not. A bit. Scared. Jock Boy."

Fire and darkness both swirled behind my eyes, making them burn. I let go of the amulet and stepped back. I was angry. *Maksim* was angry. I wasn't sure anymore where I ended and the other began. My anger was *his* anger. Or was it the other way around? Who was feeding who?

I clenched my jaw and stared down at Goth. "Stay away from Dani." Her face gave nothing away, but I watched the pulse in her throat beat quickly. Ah, a little truth revealed. I smiled and whispered, "Not afraid you say? Then why can I see your heart beating like a scared little rabbit?"

I turned around and headed to Dani.

"Dude!" Dirk laughed, pointing at the girl. "I think you made her cry."

"Shut up," I said.

Dirk grinned stupidly as I brushed past him and went straight to Dani's side. Good, God. It was almost sad what he'd turn into. Almost.

"What was that all about?" Dani watched Goth disappear into the building.

"Nothing much, but she's a mental case. You definitely need to stay away from her."

Dani raised a brow and didn't say a word.

"Come on. Let's go." Lacing my fingers with Dani's, and holding on tight, I looked over my shoulder at Dirk. "Catch ya at practice."

"Since when are you so nice to him?" Dani asked as we walked away.

I shrugged because I couldn't tell her it wasn't my choice to make. "He's really not that bad once you get to know him."

156

Chapter 19

Drawing on the dark one's energy, the only source I seemed to have, I howl with rage. How dare the boy continue to box me in. Me! The most powerful sorcerer who ever walked the earth!
~ Maksim

"I don't know, Seth." Dani chewed on her bottom lip, looking at the cars lined up to leave the school parking lot. "I can't. I have to go to the Prestons' tonight. I'm babysitting."

And there it was. Dani's third excuse this week to not see me.

You need to be alone with her.

I know, I know. It sounds like Goth had said something to her after all. But what? What could she possibly know?

Dani pressed her forehead to my chest.

"Dani?" I backed up a little bit, trying to get her to look at me. "Can I see you later, after you're done babysitting?"

Her silence drew out. She finally looked straight into my eyes, and whispered. "I don't think so."

My lungs tightened up and my breaths came out in short huffs, just like a bull facing the red flag. The demon—that was what he was becoming to me—was not happy, and he was trying to make me feel it with him. But I wouldn't. I wouldn't let this come between Dani and me. I'd figure out a way to get through to her. For now, though, this was not my anger, not my problem. *Back up, Maksim.*

As you wish. For now.

Huh? I immediately got my breath back under control. That was it? That's all I had to do? Tell him to back up and he would do it? Something wasn't right. That was too easy.

Justin and Dirk stood by my truck a few feet away, talking, and I caught Dirk's eye. If my smile came off half as wicked as it suddenly felt, then there was no wonder why Dirk tagged Justin's chest and pointed my way.

Cradling Dani's face in my palms, I planted light kisses on her lips and waited for her to give in. This was what I wanted. I wanted Dani and me to be okay... but then I made the mistake of sliding my hands down her back and over her back pockets, but I couldn't—didn't want to—stop myself.

"Seth, not here." She grabbed at my wrists, pulling them off her.

"Come on, Dani," I whispered. The scent of her hair was putting me over the edge. I leaned closer, but she pushed me away and managed to get some distance between us.

"Why are you doing that?" She glared at Justin and Dirk. "Are you trying to impress them?" She pointed an accusing finger at Justin and Dirk. "Is that it?" She raised her voice so they could hear. "I hope you enjoyed the show, boys."

Maksim's energy exploded without warning and I pulled Dani against my chest with such force, she gasped. A deep laugh that was not my own rumbled up my throat. I kissed her, planting one hard on her mouth and worked my way down her neck.

Take her! She wants you to. All women do. Maksim's voice echoed in my head.

Her hands pushed against my chest. "Seth! Stop!"

You want her. You always have.

I muffled her words with my lips over her mouth and pressed harder and pulled her closer. I knew I should stop, I knew this was wrong. but at the same time, something inside me snapped and I wanted more. I just wanted her to respond.

She responded all right.

"Ow!" I backed up, holding my bleeding lip where she had bitten me. "What was that for, *Danika*?"

Her eyes widened at the way I said her name, then they narrowed. "What is *wrong* with you?" She took a step forward, slamming her palms into my chest, knocking me off balance. "Are you trying to show off to your friends or something? What's gotten into you?"

"Dude! Take it easy!" Justin rounded the front of my truck, his fists balled up.

Dirk laughed.

"What the hell are *you* laughing at, Dirk?" Justin shot him a disgusted look and then turned his anger on me.

"What's up with that look, Justin?" I snarled. "You got a problem with me?"

Justin glared between Dani and me. The energy flowing off Justin was practically shouting at me—frustration, loyalty, anger, and… yeah, definitely love. And the love certainly wasn't for me. So, he cared for Dani as much as I had suspected.

"Ugh!" Dani blinked back her tears. "I don't even know who you are anymore, Seth!" She backed up a couple steps, her breaths coming out fast. Dani fisted her hands and stomped towards her car.

Justin turned, his hands out to his sides. "What the hell was that all about?"

The tension in my muscles faded quickly, taking Maksim's laughing with it into the recesses of my mind.

I don't *know* what the hell that was all about.

I only helped you see what was in your heart... lust.

No! I screamed at him in my mind. *Not lust! I love her! You made me do that! You made me hurt her!*

Love is never a good choice. It only leads to a broken heart, a broken body.

What? I spun around, hoping to catch a glimpse of Dani, but she was gone. *What did you mean by that?* My stomach dropped. I finally did something to screw us up. And with Justin glaring at me over here, I knew I was about to mess things up between us, too. I looked around again, hoping to see Dani. I wanted to follow her and try to explain that it wasn't me who did that, that I was sorry, but I knew that she wasn't safe around me anymore. Maksim didn't seem to have any problem making himself known. No, she definitely wasn't safe around me—at least not until I could figure out what to do about this demon.

"Let her go, man," Dirk said from behind me. "She's not worth it. There are plenty of other willing girls." His hand came up to slap my back, but I knocked it away.

"Come on, Justin," I said. "I'll give you a ride home."

"No thanks," he said, grabbing his backpack and slinging it over his shoulder. "I'd rather walk."

~ ~ ~

I sat at my desk with my feet propped up on the edge and the chair tipped back when the front door of my house slammed, shaking the walls.

160

Right on time.

Justin appeared in the doorway, his hair plastered to his head, soaked from the rain. "What the *hell* is wrong with you?" he demanded.

Justin has been my best friend since we were five. Backyard barbecues, camping trips, jet-skiing, Fourth of July at City Beach – we had a long history together, so even as he stood there, fists clenched, looking ready to take me down, I was willing to cut him a little slack.

"What do you mean?" I said, though I knew exactly what he was talking about.

"First of all, to *treat* her like that, and in front of everyone? You've always respected Dani, now all of a sudden you're grabbing her ass in front of Dirk? Come on! That was bullshit!" He landed a clean punch to my door without flinching.

But I did flinch. He was right. I closed my eyes and relived Dani's humiliation and anger. It nearly killed me. She deserved so much better. But I couldn't seem to help myself.

"Speaking of which," he kept talking. "Why are you friends with Dirk? You used to hate him and now you're buddies? I think Dani was right about you trying to impress him."

"Let's go for a ride." I kicked my feet off the desk, easily catching Dani's picture that I'd knocked off in the process. Without stopping to look at Justin, I pushed past him into the hallway. "Come on."

"We're not done talking, Seth."

"We'll talk in the car," I said over my shoulder. "I want to show you how well the truck is running."

"You've got to be freakin' kidding me!" he shouted from the doorway.

I kept walking, out the front door, down to the sidewalk. I knew he'd follow.

"Where are we going?" Justin asked, trailing behind, still fuming.

"Nowhere, really. I just want to get out." We got into my truck and I eased it into the street, heading south, towards Sagle.

We were both quiet in the few minutes it took to drive through town. The silence was punctuated by the rhythmic *whoosh* of the windshield wipers and the slosh of the tires against the wet pavement. The water on either side of the Long Bridge had taken on the murky brown color it usually did during rain storms.

"It's been a long time since we've just hung out, just the two of us," I explained.

Justin cast a look in my direction. "Are you doing drugs, Seth? Because, man, you have really changed."

I glanced at him for a second. "Nope. No drugs. Things just have a way of changing before we realize it." I lifted a shoulder, at a loss for words. "I just want to make sure we're still good." That was only partially true. I also needed something from him.

I turned onto the road leading past the beer plant and headed over the train tracks.

"Are you going to answer me?" Justin wasn't going to let it go. "What the hell happened today with Dani?"

I accelerated out of the first turn before I responded. "Do you notice how the truck runs better now?" I leaned up and patted the dashboard. "I've gotten her tuned up so she's faster and quieter."

"I get it, Seth. Now slow down," Justin muttered.

I laughed and pressed on the gas pedal.

"Dani's fine," I said. "She's been a little sensitive lately, that's all."

"I've never seen you treat her like that." Justin's eyes darted to the road twisting in front of us.

I took the car into a sliding turn, feeling some satisfaction when Justin's head thumped against the side window.

"You humiliated her!" His voice had a slight tremble to it. "What did she do to deserve that?" He gripped the door handle.

I hit the brakes right before a hairpin curve and floored the gas to fly around the rest of the turn.

So your best friend... he has an interest in your woman. Everyone is after your woman.

"What do you care?" I asked quietly. "She's *my* girlfriend. *My* business." The truck eased into the next turn. "I thought we were best friends. You should be backing me," I said.

"Not this time." Justin sucked in air as I drove too close to the edge of the road where a sharp incline led straight into the water.

I pushed the truck faster.

"Say it."

"Say what?" Justin's eyes left the road for a second to look at me.

"Admit it!" I yelled. How could I have missed his feelings for her? They were so obvious to me now. "Admit how you feel about Dani!"

When Justin stayed silent, I careened around another corner, sliding the back end of the truck into a mailbox, splintering the post, sending the box sliding into the street.

"Okay! Okay! I love her! I love Dani!" he shouted.

Our seat belts caught hard and bit into our chests as I slammed on the brakes. My heart pounded in my ears, but not loud enough to drown out Justin's words that replayed over and over in my mind. I think I'd known about how he'd felt about her all along, but didn't want to believe it.

I released the brake and eased the car to the side of the road. Turning off the ignition, I shouldered open the door and walked across the road to look out over the water, ignoring the cold rain dripping down the back of my jacket; it wasn't anything nearly as cold as what was consuming me.

Even though I felt betrayed, I knew Justin would never take his feelings for Dani any further. But just knowing he loved her… that tore me up.

"Are you happy now?" Justin had followed me.

"Not really," I said. "But I understand. I mean, how could you *not* love her?"

"You know I'd never…"

"I know, man. I know." I nodded.

Justin toed at some rocks in front of him and kicked them over the edge. "She didn't deserve how you treated her."

"She won't answer my calls or texts."

"Do you blame her?" he asked.

"How long?" I gritted.

"How long what?"

"When did you realize you loved her?"

Justin ran his fingers through his wet hair and let out his breath. "I don't know. Awhile ago, I guess."

More rocks fell over the edge.

"Well, *I* know the exact moment when I fell in love with her." It was two years ago, but I remembered it perfectly. "Do you remember that day when the dog got hit in front of the school? We all stood around and watched her wrap it up in her jacket."

Justin smiled. "She told you to stop staring and go get help."

"That was the moment." I sighed. "I know I don't deserve her, Justin. She's so good. Pure angel material." A deep breath rattled my chest. "I'm bad

164

for her. There are things about me…" I stopped when Justin cut me a sharp glance. "You know what? I'm glad you love her. She'd be better off with you. I want you to take care of her."

"What? What are you talking about? What's wrong with you, Seth?"

"I don't want to hurt her anymore."

"So don't. Just apologize and don't do it again."

"It's not that simple, man." Not simple at all. I waited for Maksim to say something, but he was too quiet, like he was listening.

"Why don't you explain it to her then?" Justin said. "She'll understand. She always does."

"I want you to take care of her for me." I said again.

"Dude! You're my best friend. I'm not making any moves on her."

"Please, Justin." I turned and walked towards my truck. "Just promise me you'll watch out for her."

"Don't you think she has anything to say about this? Don't you think she has a choice?" Justin yelled after me.

With my toes hugging the side of the road, I stared into the windshield of an approaching car. I didn't bother to step back, making the driver slow down to a crawl and inch his way between me and my truck. My response to him laying on the horn? Simple. I flipped him a double bird

"Maybe she doesn't," I answered as I watched the car pick up speed. Looking over my shoulder, I said, "Get in. I'll take you home."

Justin followed me across the road. "I just don't get you, Seth. I really don't."

It's not me, I thought. *It's the thing inside me.*

I had to protect Dani from Maksim.

~ ~ ~

His hands caressed the ivory skin of the young girl beneath him and his lips closed over hers in a slow, sweet kiss.

She pulled away and cradled his face. "What of your mistress?" she whispered. "If she discovers us—"

"Put those thoughts to rest, my sweet. She will not bother us."

"Yes, but she has powers. She knows things others cannot see."

He kissed the tip of her nose and brushed his cheek against hers. "Her powers are strong, but her will is weak."

He replayed the night, a fortnight ago, when he and Silura had lain intertwined after making love under the starry night sky. He had heard her murmur words he felt certain he was not meant to hear.

"I love you," she had whispered.

After that claim of love, Maksim knew he would always have the upper hand.

Now, his latest lover softened under his touch.

"You are quite certain we have nothing to fear from her?" she asked.

A laugh rumbled in his throat. "Silura has taught me well. It is she who should be afraid now."

~ ~ ~

Chapter 20

*His thoughts tie him to her, tangled with emotions
that only delay the inevitable. Yet still he rises against
me. He is stronger than the others, it is true, but my
patience is thin. I summon what strength I have, and
reach out ...*
~ *Maksim*

Dani had become such a part of my routine, such
a part of me, that not being with her was painful.
Going from seeing her every day, touching her every
day, to this—staying away from her on purpose—was
like cutting off my air. Nothing felt right. Everything
seemed so out of place.

This entire week seemed like forever. Dani
avoided me and I let her keep her distance. I watched
her, though, every day. She seemed to have kicked
the habit of tucking her hair behind her ear, and now
she let the strands act as a shield over her face.

There was no cutting the bond between us,
though. Nothing could do that. What we felt for each
other wasn't ordinary. From the moment I saw her, I
knew she was the one I'd want to be with forever. I'd
do anything for her—even die for her.

Which led me to my decision today. I couldn't let
this chasm grow any larger. I needed to be stronger. I
wouldn't let Maksim take control of my life. If there
was a way for Dani and me to be together, I was
going to find it.

I glanced over at Justin, who was leaning against
my truck with his arms folded over his chest, looking

across the parking lot. Justin never mentioned what had happened when we took that drive last week, and never spoke of Dani. I wonder if he had spent any time with her. I knew he wouldn't betray our friendship, even though I'd asked him to. Yeah. The guy was loyal.

Then, over the tops of the cars, I saw her. Dani walked slowly across the lot, head down, from the far corner where she had recently begun parking.

I pushed myself from the truck and headed towards her, covering the distance between us in a heartbeat.

"Dani." I grabbed her elbow but quickly let go when she shot me a scathing look. "Listen, I'm sorry for what happened. *Please.* Can we talk?"

"There's nothing to talk about." Her eyes shifted quickly to Justin, who hung back, then turned to face me.

We stood for a long time looking at each other. I hadn't realized just how much I missed her. And what I saw nearly broke me. The sparkle had gone out of her eyes. She looked defeated. And sad.

"I love you so much, Seth," she said softly, breaking the silence. "But you… you've been so different. I really thought you loved me. That's the part that really sucks. I truly thought you loved me."

How could she think that I didn't love her? If only I could wrap myself around her to get her to *feel* how much I loved her, maybe she would listen.

"Dani, I do love you. I love you more than anything. I'm so sorry about what happened. Let me make it up to you. Please."

Let her know. Yes. She needs to know how much you… love her.

Dani stared at me, daring me to give her reason to trust again.

168

And I was desperate. I closed my eyes and let Maksim take over. The rush of heat through my veins was instantaneous, burning random paths through bone and muscles on its way out of my skin. My waves of hot energy swept up and over her shoulders, across her back, up the curve of her neck and back around, brushing against the underside of her chin. It was good to feel her again. I wanted so much to actually touch her with my hands and feel the softness of her hair and skin.

Her eyes softened a little, and in those few seconds there was no one but us. We were connected, just like we used to be—before I invited the demon into my life and into my body. The corners of Dani's lips came up just a little, letting me know she felt the connection, too.

But, *damn it!* Maksim couldn't let it be, could he? Cramping pain shot through my neck and shoulders and the thread that connected Dani to me thickened. It was no longer gentle and warm, but grew heavier and darker. And in that thread, a story was told, a memory so vivid, so horrifying, I couldn't look away—like watching two trains about to collide and not being able to do anything about it.

I didn't blink, couldn't blink, because I was afraid not to see, or maybe the demon inside forced me to see: a woman's red-stained mouth, opened barely enough to take in air, formed a plea that slowly died on her lips, as her fingers dug uselessly into hands wrapped around her throat.

My elbows and wrists swelled with shards of fire, and my hands grasped at the air, and still I could not look away. Then instead of empty air, my fingers warmed against skin—her skin—pressing down on the flesh of the woman's neck, my thumbs pressing against her windpipe until the pressure crushed it, choking a garbled cry from the her mouth. As the life drained from her face, her skin whitening, the woman's hair, short and blonde, morphed, growing long and dark. Her lips pinked and her skin softened into the perfect likeness of Dani.

What the *hell!* I pulled back, suddenly realizing the energy had reached past my fingertips. Clenching my hands in fists, the energy pooled into my hands and burned my palms, but I would not let it escape.

Dani's eyes narrowed and raked me up and down, confused and annoyed by my sudden change. She frowned and slowly shook her head. "You just don't get it, do you?" Dani backed up two steps then turned and ran toward the building.

Go after her!

No! My heart pounded against my chest. *Who was that? Who was dying?* How stupid was I to take a chance like that?

"What is wrong with you, Seth? You can't keep playing her like a freakin' yo-yo!" Justin pushed past me to catch up with Dani.

Damn it! My stomach rolled and I almost puked. *Who was that?* I demanded again. *Why did you kill her?* I screamed in my mind. *Answer me!*

Silence was all I got, but it was all that I needed. Maksim suddenly made it very clear what his intentions were. I had no idea why, but I knew without a doubt what I needed to do.

Chapter 21

*Now he knows what I am capable of. Now he
fears for her—as he should. Now that he no longer
has her light, I now have room to breathe.*
~ Maksim

"Look at me." Dani grabbed my arm and tried
pulling me towards her, but I resisted, unwilling to let
her get too close.

I hadn't expected to see her again so soon,
actually not at all, but she'd texted me, telling me she
was on her way over to my house. She was pissed off
and she was coming over to set me straight. I didn't
tell her not to. Partly because I knew it wouldn't do
me any good, and partly because I had to set her
straight about us, too. So I'd met her out on the
driveway. There was no way I was going to be inside
my house with her. If something was going to
happen, better it happen out in the open, where
someone could see and could get help if Dani needed
it.

Pulling my arm out of her grip, I glanced away,
not wanting her to look too deeply into my eyes,
afraid she would see the demon looking out, because I
knew he was there. He had to be.

She maneuvered herself around me and grabbed
my face in her hands. "Look at me!"

I fought against her pull. I didn't want her to see
me this way. The constant pressure and fight for
control over my body was breaking me down. Every
morning I had bloodshot eyes and lack of sleep

pooled into dark circles under my eyes. But I wasn't tired—I was never tired. My mind was constantly racing from past to present to future, back and forth. I felt like a ferret on crack.

I closed my eyes to shut Dani out, so she couldn't see how horribly my insides were twisting up. I was possessed by something that, for some reason, hated Dani. I was certain the demon was out for blood—*her* blood.

"Damn you, Seth." Her voice was quiet, but demanding. "Look in my eyes."

Even through all of this, even though I've done things to hurt her, she was still here, still trying to help. And I wanted her help. I *needed* her help, but I was afraid for her. I still had control over the demon, but it was shaky at best. I needed to convince her to stay away. So I opened my eyes.

Whatever she saw caused her breath to catch and her eyes to open wide.

"What's wrong? Are you sick?"

I took her wrists and yanked her hands away from my face. "I'm not sick. I'm fine."

"Don't lie to me, Seth," she hissed, wrenching her wrists free.

How could I possibly tell her the truth? I hardly thought she'd understand that I had bought a soul and now it was crawling around inside me, talking to me, giving me the ability to do things that no human should be able to do. Not to mention that he wanted to hurt her. She'd think I was nuts.

Dani's stood still, her fists balled up and her feet planted, ready for a fight. "What is so wrong that you can't tell me?"

I shoved my hands in my pockets. "Just let it go!" I said louder than I had wanted. I stepped back, feeling the fray of the bond between us. "Don't come near me."

Her shoulders quickly sagged and her hands released the anger. "How do you expect me to do that, Seth? I love you!"

A throb pulsed in my temples. *Damn!* I loved her so much. All I wanted to do was hold her against me and never let her go. I wanted to go back to the day I bid on this demon and delete, delete, delete. I wanted to be happy with what I had. I'd try harder and just believe what I had would be enough for the both of us.

But I couldn't do any of that. Not now. I managed to screw this one up royally. There was no way out and being with Dani was just too dangerous. If only I could tell her the truth…

"Why are you doing this?" Her voice cracked and a tear slowly rolled down her cheek.

My chest ached with both love for her and anger toward myself. "You'd be better off without me." I turned my back to her, my hands fisted tightly.

"That's what Justin said you told him! But I don't think it's up to you to decide what's best for me." Her voice challenged me.

She had absolutely no idea what we were up against. Dani was strong, I knew, but until I could figure this out, I had to protect her. I spun around and stared her down. "Don't you get it? It's *over* between us! Over!"

That shocked her into silence. This morning, I'd been begging her to take me back and now I was telling her we were done. Minutes that seemed like hours crawled by, minutes I'd wish would hurry up and get going because every minute I stood here with her was another chance for the demon to show his ugly head.

Then squaring her shoulders and lifting her chin, she pierced me with such a look of contempt, I flinched and stepped back.

She turned and walked away.

Triumphant. That was the only word to describe what I felt as I watched her yank open the car door and get in. And relief, knowing she was safe from me.

I watched her car speed down the street, taking my heart with her. She would stay away, I knew, at least for awhile. Now I could focus on this shotgun-riding freak, and maybe somehow figure out what the hell to do about it.

DANI

"Breath"

I see nothing in your eyes, and the more I see the less I like
Is it over yet, in my head?

I know nothing of your kind, and I won't reveal your
evil mind
Is it over yet? I can't win

So sacrifice yourself, and let me have what's left
I know that I can find the fire in your eyes
I'm going all the way, get away, please

You take the breath right out of me
You left a hole where my heart should be
You got to fight just to make it through,
'cause I will be the death of you

This will be all over soon
Pour salt into the open wound
Is it over yet? Let me in

So sacrifice yourself, and let me have what's left
I know that I can find the fire in your eyes
I'm going all the way, get away, please

You take the breath right out of me
You left a hole where my heart should be
You got to fight just to make it through,
'cause I will be the death of you

Chapter 22

I walk with him. I sleep with him. I breathe with him. I encourage some thoughts and banish others, but he has woven threads of his woman into his soul, keeping him alive.
~ Maksim

"Why? *Why*?" I furiously swiped at the tears that refused to stop. "What the *hell* is going on?" I drove my car as fast as I dared down Fourth Street, across to Lake Street, and then towards the Long Bridge. The car heater was going full blast, but I still couldn't stop shaking.

At the south end of the bridge, I pulled off and parked at the Café 95 restaurant. The ache in my heart hadn't let up, my tears hadn't stopped, and my hands hurt from squeezing the steering wheel. I was out of the car and running back towards the bridge before the car door had slammed shut.

I ran to escape the hurt and to push out the ache. I ran to forget the cruelty in Seth's eyes and anger in his voice. I ran to find my breath that he had taken from me. But it wasn't helping. Nothing was. It was no use. I ran halfway across the bridge before I could accept the fact that there was no running from any of this. I sank down on one of the benches that sat against railing of the bridge and wrapped my arms around my legs, hot tears soaking through my jeans. Resting my chin on my knees, I saw nothing but the emptiness in Seth's eyes. It was as if he wasn't there. At least he wasn't there for me.

Alyx seemed to have this one all figured out, but I was having a hard time buying into it. I'd never really spoken to Alyx because I didn't think we had anything in common. After all, Alyx was into all that Goth stuff; vampirism and voodoo, or whatever it was they were involved with in their world.

Her very first words to me this entire school year were at Seth's practice. I couldn't forget what she said. *"He's got it bad."* She'd been watching Seth practice and then dropped that one on me without sticking around to explain what she meant. I followed her to War Memorial Field to get some answers and I ended up with way more than I wanted to know.

She'd looked so confident sitting on the bleachers, cigarette smoke curling like a serpent around her fingerless black gloves. Every so often her thumb would flick the end of her cigarette before she'd bring it to her lips to take a deep lungful. But I was struck by the intensity of Alyx's blue eyes, the intelligence and confidence that rolled off her. She didn't seem to be afraid of what anyone thought and didn't need to convince anyone of anything. She knew something.

No. She knew a lot of things.

It was that confidence that had me telling her everything. I told her about the dogs at the shelter, about how Seth's eyes got all smoky or shadowy sometimes, about how he made me melt when he kissed me. I even told her how at the Winter Dance Dirk was trying to get me to dance with him and he made a grab for my elbow, but stopped when Seth put his hands up. Dirk had just... stopped. I'd never seen Dirk so confused. It was like he couldn't help himself, like he *had* to listen to Seth.

And she took note of all of it – everything I said went down in a notebook she carried with her in her messenger bag.

Then she mentioned Seth's size, how much bigger he had gotten lately. That made me think, well, maybe he was taking steroids. I thought I read somewhere that steroids caused mood swings, but she shot that one down. Her answer wasn't at all what I had expected: "*Pfff! Steroids? You think your boyfriend is on steroids? Believe me when I tell you that would be the least of your problems. No, his problem is deeper and much more complicated than that.*"

She was so evasive, dropping hints or speaking half thoughts so I never really grasped what she was leading to. She mentioned Reiki and energy transfer, but the real kicker was when she said that Seth was a "dark, angry, possessed jock." Before I could ask her what she meant by that, Seth had shown up and she had left, obviously not too thrilled about being in the same space with him.

Maybe Seth was right. Maybe I did need to stay away from her. She was into all of that dark magick stuff. Besides, Reiki wouldn't explain why other girls were so obviously flirting with him, even with me around. It wouldn't explain why he didn't discourage them. Maybe he was getting buffed out because of them. Maybe he *was* tired of me. Maybe he didn't want the same future that I did.

I wiped the tears from my cheeks. I sure hadn't seen this coming. I'd thought I knew him. I'd thought he loved me.

I guess I was wrong.

~ ~ ~

"What's wrong with him, Justin?" I pressed the heels of my hands into my burning eyes, hoping to at least delay the tears. "I don't get it. I thought we were solid." I locked my arms around my legs, pulling them tight against my chest.

After I'd cried out all the tears I could, I left the bridge and went to the one person who knew Seth better than I did.

It felt strange being in Justin's room, just the two of us. I'd been there many times over the last couple of years, but it was always with Seth. My *life* had always been with Seth.

I looked around the room, so neat and orderly. The shelves were lined with trophies and ribbons and pictures of family vacations, most of them with Seth in there somewhere. Seth's arm was usually slung over Justin's shoulder, a huge grin on his face, his eyes happy.

So different from what Seth looked like now. It was like there was no light to him anymore; like someone had shot out the sun inside him and created a black hole.

Justin sat on the edge of the bed, his elbows on his knees, looking down to where I sat on the floor. He shook his head. "I really don't know what his problem is."

"It's not like him to keep secrets from me," I said. "I don't know what I did wrong." The tears broke free again and I dropped my forehead to my knees, wrapping my arms tighter around my legs.

"Shit," Justin muttered. He slid down the side of the bed and sat next to me. "Dani…"

"This hurts… so… bad," I told him.

"I know," he said gently, draping an arm around me. He ran his hand through his hair and took a big breath. "I asked him if he was doing drugs. I mean, it would explain a lot if he was."

I looked up. "What did he say?"

"He said he wasn't, but I'm not so sure."

"What about steroids or something? I mean, doesn't that mess with your moods?"

"Now that he's hanging out with Dirk, who knows what he's into," Justin seemed to be just as clueless as I was.

"I don't see you two fighting, though. It *looks* like you're still friends."

"Yeah. I wouldn't be too sure about that right now."

"Justin, did I do something to push him away? Was this all my fault?"

He shifted around to face me, then cradled my face in his hands and looked at me with an intensity that sent a shiver up my spine.

"Don't think that. *Never* think that." He leaned in closer, his voice just above a whisper, "It could never be you."

His grip tightened and suddenly there was no space between our faces. He touched his lips to my cheek and then drifted to the tip of my nose. Our breath mingled when he lingered at the corner of my mouth, so close our lips almost touched. I held my breath, afraid to move.

With a barely suppressed groan, Justin pulled away and kissed my forehead, then shifted around and put his arm around my shoulder.

Relieved, I wrapped my arms around his waist and buried my face in his shoulder.

"I love you, Dani." He said it so quietly, I wondered if he wanted me to hear it.

"I love you, too. You're such a good friend," I whispered. I wanted him to hear that because I meant it. I felt totally safe with him. He'd never cross that line.

"Yeah, that's me. A really good friend."

Not understanding the sarcastic tone in his voice, I pushed myself back from his arms and studied his face. His jaw went rigid, his teeth biting down rhythmically, making his smile seem forced.

"No, really, you are. After all this stuff going on, you're still standing by his side. And mine, too." I took his hands and squeezed them tightly. "I'm having a hard time forgiving Seth for how he's treating me—treating us. If I didn't love him so much..."

His jaw tightened even more.

"You know," I said, remembering. "I looked into his eyes tonight. They were *so* dark. Just so freakin' cold. There was something really weird about his face, too. It was like he had a million thoughts going on. He was there, but not there, you know?"

I wrapped my arms around my knees again, bringing them up hard against my chest. Even though he told me it was over, I knew deep down that Seth still loved me. What I didn't know was why he pushed me away the way he did. Something was very wrong. If I had no clue, if his best friend didn't know, maybe I had to look for the answer with someone who didn't know him at all.

~ ~ ~

"So the gossip is true," Silura said.

The girl took a step away from her mistress, back into the shadows, wringing her hands. "Yes," she whispered, her voice shaking.

"Repeat the words you heard."

Silence fell, broken only by the shuffling of pebbles beneath the girl's feet.

Silura reached out and stroked her servant's hair, then lifted the girl's chin until their eyes met.

"You have nothing to fear from me. Your honesty will put you in my good favor."

The girl licked her dry lips before finally speaking. "He said... he said... that he loved her. That his soul soared to great... heights when she was near. That she was the missing piece in his life. That... that..."

Silura's throat tightened. She knew the next words her servant spoke, whatever they were, would undo her. "Go on." She squared her shoulders, feigning strength she did not have. "Do not be afraid."

"He said that he would gladly die for her."

A small gasp escaped Silura's lips. Those were words she had longed to hear Maksim say to her, but he had said them to another woman. *I am a fool,* Silura thought. *I gave my body freely to him. I gave him power and unconditional love. Now he loves another.*

A searing ache welled in Silura's chest, making it hard for her to breathe. *A thousand bites from a viper would have been less painful,* she thought, *for poison would kill her instantly. But this—this would fill her veins with sorrow and pain so intense, life would be unbearable.*

Her fingers crushed the girl's thin shoulders, but the servant said nothing, not wishing to anger her mistress any further.

"Where are they now?"

"In the gardens," the girl whispered.

~ ~ ~

Chapter 23

I want out. I want vengeance, but the river of
death is hindered by unexpected forces. The taste of
familiarity is bitter upon my tongue.
~ Maksim

"We need to talk," I told Alyx.

Six sets of eyes suddenly found something more important to look at on the walls of the Commons or down on the table in front of them.

Alyx took one look at her friends and rolled her eyes. Balling up her empty potato chips bag and licking her fingers, Alyx slid her chair back and motioned to the bench along the back wall. "Let's get away from these weenies."

"So, what's going on? Why did Seth tell me to stay away from you?" I asked, a little too loudly. Unfortunately, it was one of those moments when the noise in the Commons hit a lull.

Alyx stopped and turned around so fast, I ran into her. "I don't think everyone heard you."

I looked around and, sure enough, we were the object of considerable interest. Alyx and I were a mismatched pair; me in my jeans, tennis shoes, and hoodie, and Alyx, in her knit sweater, tights, calf-length skirt, and clunky Doc Marter's, head-to-toe in black.

"Maybe we should talk outside," I suggested.

"Yeah, probably a good idea."

The air outside was cool and the walkway wet. We both crossed our arms tightly across our bodies to protect ourselves from the drizzling rain and cold.

"He broke up with me." I swallowed against the tightness in my throat. I still couldn't believe it, and saying it out loud only made it more real. It hurt even worse now than it did yesterday.

Alyx's brows arched. "What? Barbie and Ken aren't dating anymore?"

"Look—" I started to say, but Alyx interrupted me.

"What reason did he give you?"

"He really didn't give a reason. He just said I'd be better off without him."

"Huh. I wonder who instigated that."

"*He* did. I didn't. *I* wasn't the one who wanted to break up."

"I'm not talking about you," Alyx said. Her dark eyes cut into me for longer than I felt necessary. "Are you sure you want to hear what I think? I'm assuming that's why you wanted to talk to me."

I met her stare head on. "If it has to do anything with why he doesn't want me talking to you, then yeah."

Alyx pressed her lips together for long seconds before she let out a sigh. "Okay. A soul—a dark soul—has attached itself to your boyfriend," she said matter-of-factly.

My jaw dropped. I stopped walking.

Alyx grabbed my sleeve. "Keep moving."

"Attached? You mean like a leech?" I asked.

She glanced at me again, her eyes narrowing just a little, as if to decide if I were worthy enough to hear what she had to say. I was afraid for a second that she would decide I wasn't, but then she went on.

"Everything has a vibration—us, the buildings, trees, rocks, animals—everything." Alyx swept her hand in front of her. "And we put out vibes that attract other vibes just like them. Simple Law of Attraction."

"Huh?" I frowned, not getting it at all.

"Okay. Let's say you're thinking about, like, I don't know, um… animal abuse."

Boy, she knew what button to push with me. Right away my body reacted like it always did when I think about abused animals. My fists balled up, ready to fight if I had to. Alyx was quick to notice it.

She nodded at my balled up hands. "So now, that thought that you have in your mind, whether you say it out loud or not, radiates outward at a certain vibratory frequency."

I followed her hand movements, as she gestured to the air around us. "If you hold that vibration long enough, other like-minded people will eventually hook up with you. That's when groups are started, movements, clubs, all that stuff." She fixed her eyes on me again. "Are you following me?"

I didn't know. I was worried about what I was thinking all of a sudden.

"The same thing goes for souls—the dead kind. But they're really not dead. They're an energy form, just like us, only without the body. Even though you can't see them, they're around all the time. You can't kill energy. Energy doesn't go away."

Goosebumps took over my entire body. I would have sworn there were a hundred pairs of eyes on me. Even with my arms hugging my body, I couldn't stop the chill. Alyx noticed that, too. Was there anything she *didn't* notice?

"These souls can attach themselves to us because of the energy we're putting forth. We attract them with our vibes, and unless we've protected ourselves, they'll make themselves right at home in our bodies. It happens all the time," she said knowingly.

I just stared. What could I have said to that?

"Most of the time a person won't even realize they have an attachment," Alyx continued "Picture this. If someone is a mean drunk or a woman is PMSing, they could attract a soul with a lower vibration. These entities are everywhere around us, but at a party or a bar, those things are a dime a dozen."

"But what do these souls have to gain by attaching themselves?" I lowered my voice, in case "they" could hear.

"When they attach, they get to feel our emotions. It's like an extension of them. If the soul died an addict, for example, then it would find a living addict, or someone who is on the edge of becoming an addict, who is weak and vulnerable, to feed from. If someone feels completely worthless and depressed—"

"Then a depressed soul attaches," I finished her sentence. "So," I said, doing my best to process this. "You're telling me that *Seth* has this soul attachment thing?"

"I'm pretty sure he does." Alyx frowned. "Most of the time, the attachments move on when the person gets enough sleep or sobers up or gets happy because there is nothing for them to leech off of anymore. It's usually not a big deal because there isn't enough time for the attachment to tie itself to the body.

"But I've heard stories of souls who refuse to leave. They like what they've found and aren't willing to give it up. Sometimes the host actually likes having the attachment because it validates what they're thinking. Just like having a private chat room.

I've even heard of the host dying with the attachment's hooks still in their soul and the attachment taking them *both* into another body." She shook her head hard. "Freakin' unbelievable."

Alyx took a few more steps and then stopped walking, her eyes vacant—not looking at me, not looking at anything, really. Or maybe she did. At this point I wouldn't put anything past her.

"If the attachment gets out of control, though," she said almost as if reciting the words, "there's battle that goes on inside the host. Sometimes it's too much and the host will just go nuts. These are the people doctors tend to lock up because everyone thinks they're over-the-top schizo, especially when they say they're hearing voices, but they actually have these souls that are talking to them—the 'voices in their heads.'"

I hated to admit how much sense it made in Seth's case, but I still wasn't ready to buy into it. "This sounds flat-out crazy, you know."

Alyx rolled her eyes, shaking her head. "I knew you weren't ready for the truth."

"I'm wasting my time," I snapped. "I should have *my* head examined."

Alyx turned and headed back to the building. "Yeah, you go ahead and do that."

I watched her walk off, thoughts whirling around in my head so fast it made me dizzy. Soul attachment. Yeah, right. A totally ludicrous idea.

On the other hand, something major *had* changed in Seth lately. I couldn't explain his mood swings. And his eyes. A shiver ran up my spine and exploded in my body. I'd seen something in his eyes that I'm pretty sure had nothing to do with drugs.

"Alyx! Wait!" I jogged to catch up with her. "I'm sorry. I really need to know more about this. Please. Help me."

She didn't slow her pace.

"You never answered my question," I said, taking hold of her arm. She stopped, and I pushed a little on Alyx's arm to make her face me. "Why doesn't Seth want me talking to you?"

The tiny hairs on the back of my neck stood up under Alyx's steady gaze. The blue of her irises seemed darker, grayer, as if reflecting the color of the sky above us. I couldn't look away even if I wanted to.

"We're dealing with something big here, and your boyfriend knows that I know about it. And so does the soul that's attached to him."

"The other day at the bleachers, before Seth showed up," I remembered. "You said something about possession. Is that the same thing?"

"Yes and no." Glancing at her watch, Alyx said, "My parents told me that it's possible for a person to invite a soul to jump in. Inviting a soul makes the bond much stronger. But it has to be a mutual agreement or else it won't stick. If it *is* mutual, and the host is weaker than the attachment, that's when it can turn into possession."

The speed of her words picked up. "People don't understand it's not a game. A soul is another entity. You invite one in, and it's an energy with a life force all its own."

"But why would *Seth* do that? He was happy!"

Alyx cut me a sidelong glance, raising the ring pierced through her brow. "Really."

"Yeah. Really." I snapped back.

Alyx shrugged. "Maybe he wasn't as happy as you think. Maybe he needed a quick fix."

190

"Oh, this is *stupid*." I spat out the last word. "He doesn't even know stuff like this exists."

"It makes sense, though, doesn't it?"

"No. No, it doesn't." Tears stung my eyes. "Maybe it's me—maybe he doesn't want to go out with me anymore."

Alyx pursed her lips, thinking. "Or it could be that this guest crawling around inside him doesn't like you."

"The *soul* doesn't like me?" I brushed away the tears. "I don't have any enemies, alive or dead."

I was so glad when the bell rang, keeping me from having to hear Alyx's explanation anymore.

She followed me to my locker and leaned her shoulder against the locker next to mine. At least she stopped talking about the whole attachment thing.

I yanked down on the lock and opened my locker, grabbing my biology book then slammed the door shut. Leaning against my locker, I watched the parade of students walking by.

Alyx nudged me with her elbow, jerking her chin toward a group a little way down the hall.

"Oh." The book slipped a little from my grip. "Really, Seth?" I whispered, hoping what was left of my heart wouldn't hear.

"Hey, *Danika*." Dirk winked at me as he sauntered by. "Looks like Seth found someone else already."

Seth had done more than found someone else. He had her backed against the wall, caging her in with his arms. The girl said something to him. My guess? *Hey, your old girlfriend is watching us,* or something like that, because he didn't bother uncaging her when he looked at me over his shoulder. Stone freakin' cold was the kind of look he gave me, and with the smug

191

little smirk that *she* added to my humiliation, it was just too much.

One step was all I was able to take before Alyx grabbed my arm and yanked me back.

"It won't do you any good, Dani. That's not Seth doing that."

"Then what am I supposed to do?"

"For starters, stop the dumped girlfriend act," Alyx said. "Get tough."

"But did you see the way he looked at me?" Turning my back on him was the only way I was going to keep it together. "I don't know which is worse, Alyx—Seth treating me this way, or some whacked-out soul jumping on his back."

"Oh, there's no question which would be worse," she said quietly. "None at all."

Grabbing a pen out of her pocket, then grabbing my wrist, she shoved my sleeve up to my elbow and scribbled a phone number onto my skin. "Call me when you're serious about helping him."

~ ~ ~

Strange that she had not noticed it before. The vines draping the garden wall hung limply, as if bereft, the leaves drooping down to the dirt below. The vibrant hues of the flowers she'd so carefully tended to only weeks ago had faded. The birds were singing a song so sad, she would swear they wanted to die. Even the breeze that brushed against her skin was cooler than it should have been in the midst of summer.

There was no point to life now, not if Maksim turned his back on her. Love's death had robbed her of all joy. Love had brought her senses alive, had inspired her to see beauty in her existence. Now only dreary grays and blacks remained for her.

The cold... it burrowed its icy fingers into her soul and wouldn't let go.

She would be left a bitter woman with nothing to live... or die for.

"I will have his love," she murmured, "or I will die trying."

~ ~ ~

Chapter 24

I look at her through his eyes. I taste her with his lips. He wants to tell her, but how can one explain something such as me? He hopes to save her. She hopes to save him. Fools.
She speaks of forever. She has no idea what forever truly is.
~ Maksim

The next week passed in a blur. I buried myself in my schoolwork, staying as far from Seth as I could. I had no idea how to handle this. I'd given up on the idea that he didn't want me anymore, because I'd seen him watch me in the halls, at lunch, and in class... and most of the time, he looked miserable.

But I was also having a hard time accepting Alyx's explanation about a "simple" soul attachment, let alone this possibly being something bigger. And what exactly did she mean by "bigger"? Did souls come in different sizes? And what had Seth been feeling that could have attracted it?

I just wasn't sure about anything anymore.

Today, when Seth walked into our lit class, I slouched down. I didn't want to talk to him. I didn't want to see what was in his eyes. But at the same time, I missed him so much. I clamped my hand to my chest, pressing down on the void beneath it. It hurt every day, and it was getting worse.

"Hey, I need to talk to you." Seth's voice was low and controlled as he slid into the seat next to mine.

I turned my head a little to look at him. His eyes were desperate and his body tense. I wanted to reach out and smooth away the tightness of his jaw and the veins that bulged in his neck, and hold his hand that so tightly gripped the edge of his desk. I wanted to, but I didn't.

"Will you meet me after school?" he whispered.

When I didn't answer right away, his knuckles turned white.

"Dani, please? I really need to talk to you. I love you."

What could he possibly say that would help us get past this? Did he even know what was going on, *if* that was what was happening? I peered into his bloodshot eyes and sniffed the air—just enough to see if there was any odor of pot or beer on his breath. Nothing. But his eyes were a dead giveaway and what I saw in them planted me firmly in Camp Alyx.

"You can't have him," I whispered. "He's mine."

Seth eyes clouded and his brows pulled together. "What?"

"You heard me. I'll meet you out front after school."

He leaned back and settled into his chair, sliding down a little in his seat, flashing me a small grin.

Despite his slouch and the easy sprawl of his legs, his tension was still there. Whatever part the soul was attached to, right now it didn't matter because part of him was still my Seth.

~ ~ ~

Seth made me wait a long time after school. So long that I thought he had bailed out on me.

Damn this weather. I shivered. *Will it ever be warm again?* I doubted I would ever shake the chill, not until Seth was better.

I turned around when I heard footsteps behind me. Seth steps were quick, his head down, and his shoulders hunched over.

I met him halfway. Every inch of me missed him, missed his touch. My body craved his arms around me, but I knew that wasn't going to happen, at least not now. But I wanted to at least touch him and somehow connect, to let him know I was here for him, but when I reached for his arm, he pulled back.

"Listen to me Dani. I need to explain. It's all so complicated. I don't even think I *can* explain." He looked up at the sky, his eyes searching for something. "I love you. More than you'll ever know. And I miss you so much. Every day that goes by, this separation," he gestured between us, "it feels worse and worse. But I can't be with you. Not now. I'm just not myself."

"Then when can we be together?"

"I don't know." He slowly shook his head. "It's bad, Dani. There's a side of me that wants to hurt you—"

My sharp intake of breath made him wince as if I had slapped him.

"And it's getting harder to control. Being around you is the best thing for me, but at the same time you're not safe. I'm trying my best to protect you, but I'm totally screwed."

Hurt me? Part of him wanted to *hurt me?* His look of utter hopelessness started to undo me, and his next words finished me off.

"I wasn't messing around when I told you that you have to forget about us. It's the only way. Please stay away from me. No matter how I might beg you to come back, you need to stay away from me. I am not who you think I am." Then he whispered, "Not anymore."

"Seth." Despite my fear, I started to reach for him, but pulled back. "I think I know what's going on. I don't understand it, and I didn't want to believe it, because it all sounds so crazy to me, but if it is true, we can fight it. Together."

Seth's face contorted as if shocked with pain. Then darkness spread like black ink across his eyes. His body tensed, and he straightened up to his full height, his face unreadable granite, chiseled lines cornering his mouth.

And just like that, Seth—my Seth—was gone. I searched his face for any sign of him, but saw nothing. His eyes went dark, as if the light in his eyes had been snuffed out.

"Seth? Seth!" I grabbed his arms. "Talk to me! What is it?"

But he was gone.

No! That soul had *no* right to take him! I launched my fists against his chest. "Say something, Seth!"

All of my pent-up frustration now released the tears I'd promised myself I wouldn't cry. My fists pummeled against his chest for a few seconds before his iron grip held them away.

Within his eyes, copper swirled against black. I winced, not at the force of his grip, but at the coldness of his stare and the hate that lined his eyes. The air thickened and wrapped around me, pulsating, leeching me of my strength. I fought against it, and for long, drawn-out seconds, we stared at each other, neither backing down.

Being this close felt like being next to a highly-charged transformer. Something stood between us. Something real… and evil. I focused on his face.

"I know you're in there, Seth," I whispered. "I love you so much! Let me help you."

His grip tightened.

"Mr. Thompson? Miss Parsons? Is there a problem here?"

Ms. Cambridge, our principal, stood a few feet away.

Seth quickly let go of my wrists and threw his hands up in surrender, backing up a few steps. But he didn't take his eyes off me.

Then I saw it—a momentary flash of fear and pleading. A flash that glowed through the blackness. Seth.

"Seth, I think you need to go home," the principal suggested.

He responded by turning his back to her and walking away.

"Dani, are you all right? Do you need to talk?" I turned towards her.

"Um, no. It's okay." I pulled my cell phone out of my back pocket and pulled up my sleeve. I glanced across the parking lot, watching as Seth climbed into his truck and drove away. I went in the opposite direction, dialing Alyx's number as I walked. I needed her help. Desperately.

Chapter 25

I marvel at this boy's determination. He refuses to step aside, purposefully blocking my path, but his fear is palpable. Time will tell if his fear will strengthen or weaken him. Time that he does not have.
~Maksim

How could Alyx even think I wasn't serious about helping Seth? Of course I was. The only problem was that I didn't really know what she was talking about. I'd never, ever heard of all this stuff about energies and dead people hanging onto living people and I was pretty sure none of my friends had either. I mean, how do the souls even get in? Do they just stand around? Where do they fit? And what did Alyx mean by protection? How do you protect yourself from something you can't even see?

I wanted to help Seth, but I also needed to learn for myself what this was all about. I wanted to make sure that Alyx knew what *she* was talking about. This was serious—if Seth did have an "attachment"—and I didn't want to make any mistakes. Alyx probably thought I was being a dork about this, so I'd gone to the library to do my own research, and what I found about soul attachments led me to the gem store in town.

I'd never been inside Zero Point. I'd driven past the store almost every day and I'd look through the front window out of pure curiosity, but I thought the pretty stones and crystals on display were nothing more than something to hang on my rear-view mirror.

But even then, I was never motivated to see them closer—until now.

The moment I stepped inside the shop, I realized that there was more to stone energy than I'd thought. It was a completely different world! For there to be a store this big, with so many different types and sizes of stones, it was obvious people put a lot of faith in them. The front of the shop held mostly jewelry, necklaces, earrings, and rings—not the fashion kind with gold and diamonds sparkling under lights created only for the bling effect. With these, each piece had a definite... purpose. That was the only word to describe what I felt when I dragged my fingers across the necklaces that hung against one of the walls. Even though the stones were crowded together, each one definitely held its own place, almost as if creating a space around itself. They were absolutely beautiful. Perfectly imperfect.

"Those are nice, aren't they?" The sales clerk smiled from behind the counter. "Are you looking for anything in particular?"

I smiled and shook my head. "I'm just looking."

"Go right ahead," she said. "Let me know if you need anything."

The shop was filled with stones from all over the world: Brazil, India, Africa, China. There was even obsidian from Oregon. Small cards sat on display for each one, explaining the name of the stone and its purpose. Raising vibrations, centering, grounding chakras, healing. In a corner, next to a table displaying a couple dozen compartments of stones, sat the biggest stone I've ever seen. An amethyst, the card said, a stone of healing.

"Can you explain something to me?" I turned and asked the clerk.

She glanced up from the box she had placed on the counter. "Of course. What would you like to know?"

"How can a stone do anything that these cards say they do?"

"Well," she said, rounding the counter to stand in front of the huge amethyst. Her fingertips gently grazed the outer surface, then down the smooth inside of the gigantic stone. "It is the belief of many native tribes, ancient civilizations, as well as modern thought, that the earth is a living, breathing entity. The rocks and mountains are her bones. The lakes, rivers, and oceans are her blood. Just as a mother carries a child in her womb and she passes on characteristics to the child, the earth passes on her characteristics to the stones and crystals that she holds in her womb. And since everything has energy, they receive theirs literally from 'mother earth.' Stones and crystals are like batteries that store this energy. Does that make sense?"

I nodded. "Yeah, it does."

She smiled and reached to the containers of stones on display behind me and picked out two different types. She held one in each hand, opening and closing her fingers over them as if feeling the texture and weight.

"Since different parts of the earth have different energy, these stones get their energy from their birth place, just like everyone has different energies from our own individual families. Some crystals are found in lakes and rivers, so their energies may be different than the ones from within the ground. The blue lace agate, for example," she held up a pale blue stone, about the size of the top of my thumb, "was formed in a more calming environment and was created slowly. It had time to gather various energies around it." She put it in my palm and closed my fingers around it. "This is a stone of communication and can help bring on stronger intuition.

"Now obsidian," she held her palm flat, showing me a large marble-size black stone, "comes from volcanoes and is glass. It needed strength to come from the center of the earth. It was formed when the lava came in contact with water, which forced it to cool quickly and provided the shiny glassy texture. Since it needed strength for it to form in the first place, it radiates strength and protection for others."

"Okay, I think I understand what you're saying, but how does anyone know what these are vibrating? I mean, you say this is for calming, and that one," I said pointing to the obsidian, "is for protection. How can anyone prove that?"

The ring of the phone—so quiet and so appropriate for the shop—stole her answer from me.

She smiled and held up her finger. "Hold that thought. I'll be right back." Placing the obsidian back in its box, she skirted around the table toward the front counter to answer the phone.

I turned to the other stones on the table and quickly glanced at the cards. Citrine dissipates and transmutes energy. Bloodstone centers and grounds energy of the heart. Black tourmaline can be used to repel and protect against negativity. A lot of those stones protected. Which would be the best one to protect me from the soul? Which one would protect Seth?

The woman finished her call and came back to where I stood.

"I apologize for the interruption. As for your question as to how we know which stones vibrate what..."

I nodded for her to go ahead.

204

"Before science, during the time of ancient civilizations, our minds were wide open to the spiritual aspects of the world around us. We used more of our brains," she tapped her forehead, "especially the frontal lobe, when we knew less about the world around us. In our ignorance, we were more open to the unknown. In ancient times, the spiritual leaders would learn this knowledge through instinct and being aware of their spiritual guidance from the celestial. Then that knowledge was taught to the people, and those having the same instinct and openness would preserve it and pass it on to the next generation." She sighed. "Unfortunately, we're losing that connection. Science and the turning away from instinct and toward empirical facts have made us rely *less* on our natural ability to sense things and *more* on technology."

"Wow," I sighed. "That's a lot to take in." I supposed this was like any other piece of knowledge passed down through the centuries—in this case it was like eons. But I had nothing else to go on, so I had no choice but to trust what she was saying.

I looked around at the choices of crystals and stones lining the walls and tables. "Okay then. I need a stone for protection against dark souls. Will this work?" I pointed to the box holding the tourmaline.

She nodded and waited until I picked one up and tried to give it to her.

"Does that one feel right to you?" she asked, putting the other stones away.

I shrugged and then nodded, still holding the stone. I had no clue.

"Okay," she said. "Now you can carry it with you loose," she said, "or you can make it into a necklace. We have small wire casings you can use to make your own."

Awesome. Then I'd have one like Alyx. "Do you know anything about... soul attachments by any chance?"

"Here, I'll take that for you." She took the wand-like stone from my hand and side stepped me on her way to the cash register. "Soul attachments, huh? I know a little bit about them. My ex had one."

"For real?" I followed her to the counter. "Did it hurt him? How'd you get rid of it?"

She smiled. "I didn't, and as far as I know, he still has it."

My hope deflated like a slashed tire. I thought for sure she'd have an answer to help Seth.

She reached under the counter and pulled up a small plastic bag with a silver wire casing and chain for my stone. "I just couldn't be around him any more and he wasn't willing to give it up. That's why I ended up leaving."

I handed over some money as she rang up the sale. That was so not what I wanted to hear. I didn't want to leave Seth. I *couldn't* leave him.

"But," she said, wrapping the stone and the casing in a small piece of tissue paper. "I lived with it for a long time."

"How did you know for sure he had one?"

She shrugged. "I just did. I felt it. Sometimes he wouldn't act like himself, sometimes he would just look different, you know?" She looked at me, but didn't wait for an answer. "What got us through so many years, I think, is that I loved him so much. Love is light. And light, given with the right intent, will always chase away the dark." She carefully folded the top of the small paper bag closed and handed it to me. "And in the meantime, this will help."

Chapter 26

She breathes into our mind. She will not go away.
In another time, another place, if I did not have to kill
her, I would have loved her, too.
~ Maksim

I'd been expecting Alyx's house to be a decrepit hovel with a cauldron and skulls in the yard, and maybe a mongrel chewing on a human bone.

I certainly hadn't expected *this*! Looking down at the address I had scribbled on a piece of paper, I double-checked the house number. It was the right one.

Taking a deep breath, I pressed on the tourmaline that hung from a chain around my neck, waiting for a sense of protection it was supposed to offer. Right now, I'd take anything. As I pushed open my car door, I knew full well that I'd be stepping into a world I'd more than likely be happier not knowing existed.

The beautifully carved front door of the house opened silently and Alyx stepped under the archway, leaning against the door frame, crossing her arms over her chest.

Her home was a sprawling, perfectly-tended, two-story brick mansion set back from the street, with a three-car garage jutting from one side of the house and a row of manicured shrubs alongside the other, secluding the property from the other mansions on the street.

"My mother is a trust-fund baby," Alyx said.

My face heated. "I didn't think… I mean, I wasn't thinking…"

"Don't worry about it." Her expression was blank. "I'm sure it's a surprise to you. It is to everyone."

"It's a beautiful house," I said, tipping my head back to look at the windows of the second level.

"Yeah, thanks." Alyx raised her hand in a half-hearted wave to a passing car before looking back at me. "So, are you coming in or what?"

I adjusted my backpack on my shoulder and nodded. She moved aside, waving me in. For a moment I stared at the most unusual furnishings I had ever seen. Instead of the rustic, casual décor I was used to, the house was decorated in varying shades of gray and black with shocks of color—red, yellow, orange—in the pillows, lamps, and rugs. The effect was ultra-modern and really… interesting. Not exactly relaxing, though.

"This way," Alyx said, closing the front door behind us.

My tennis shoes were quiet against the stone floor that ran through the lower level of the house.

"Are your parents here?"

"Not until tonight," she said over her shoulder. "They're up in Bonners Ferry teaching a class on Reiki." Alyx pushed open the door of her bedroom and scooped up a pair of black pants on the floor, tossing them into the closet.

A poster bed filled the room, dwarfing the small desk next to it. A small chair sat in the corner, half hidden under the mostly black clothes that were thrown over it. A sliding glass door on one wall led out to a spacious balcony overlooking the lake. Shelves lined another wall, holding a crystal ball, pendants, stones, and other objects I had never seen before.

I slipped my backpack off my shoulder and let it drop to the pale silver carpet as I crossed the room to her book shelves. Tipping my head to the side, I read the titles. There were mostly books on chakras,—and "magick," whatever that was—some zombie stories, and a few trashy romance novels. I ran my finger along the spine of the one titled *Magick Murders* and stopped. There was more to Alyx than I'd thought. Taking a deep breath, I turned to face her.

"Alyx, I need your help."

"Won't work."

"What won't work?" I asked.

Alyx pointed to my necklace. "That."

My hand flew up and grasped the stone. "Why not? Aren't these supposed to give protection?"

She let out a short laugh. "*Supposed* to. But not in this case. For what we're dealing with, that stone is just something pretty to look at. Believe me," she said, rolling her eyes, "I know."

What little confidence I'd had dissolved. "So what *are* we dealing with? How bad is it?"

"This isn't some poltergeist that needs to be exorcised, Dani. Like I told you, it's a living, breathing energy, trying to be the top dog."

"Yeah, I know. I can see it. And Seth told me that it wants to hurt me."

Her brows rose. "He told you that? When?"

"Today. After school. He said it was getting harder to control it." I pressed my fingers to my eyes. "Then all of a sudden his eyes turned black, and I couldn't *see* Seth anymore. It was like he vanished. I mean, his body was there, but Seth definitely wasn't."

"I have to give your boyfriend credit," Alyx said thoughtfully. "He's putting up a good fight. It can't be easy." She wandered across the room. "When did you first notice a change in him?" Alyx pulled a book from her shelf and flipped through the pages.

"I don't know, two or three weeks ago, maybe." I sank down onto the floor and leaned up against the bed, pressing my hands over my face. "I don't know how long Seth has known about this, and I don't think he'd told anyone until now." I groaned. "It makes me sick to think he's been dealing with this all by himself." I uncovered my face and looked at Alyx. "What if Seth somehow could keep control," I said slowly. "If the other soul refuses to leave, can the two co-exist?"

"Sure, it's possible," Alyx said, returning the book to its place. She turned and leaned against the bookshelf. "But it would be crowded—like too many rats in a cage. It would be survival of the fittest, one being the dominant one. Or it could be like—did you ever see the movie *Sybil*?"

I shook my head. I had heard about it, but… no. Not my style.

"That's an extreme example, and that particular case has been completely discredited. But, it's a good example of what can happen to someone who really does have a soul attachment. Or attachments. It could look like schizophrenia. Multiple personalities. His lowered vibration will start attracting other lower-vibrating entities. His best hope is to be on psych meds to mellow out the attachments."

Oh, my God. Seth was strong, I knew, but I wasn't sure his inner strength was enough to fend off one, let alone a few!

Alyx picked up her messenger bag and took out her notebook. Opening it, she scribbled something down. "What exactly did you say to Seth before the soul took over?"

"Nothing that bad, I don't think," I said, shuddering, remembering how his face had become so different, so angry. "I just told him we could fight this together."

Alyx finished writing and then checked her watch. "I need to ask my parents about this. I've heard of an invited soul being aggressive to the host, but never this bad."

"Ugh," I grimaced. "You make it sound like it's a parasite or something."

"It is. These bad ones, once they are called to a host, tend to hang on, and some take over. The constant battle for control will eventually overwhelm the host."

"But if Seth had invited this soul, and now he doesn't want it anymore, why won't it just go away? I thought it had to be mutual," I said.

"There is a certain protocol these souls follow, but there are renegades, bad-ass types who don't think the rules apply to them. Your boyfriend was obviously an easy target. The other soul is gaining strength somehow. What I don't get is why it wants to hurt *you*. They are usually so self-serving." She chewed on her bottom lip and shook her head.

I waited for her to go on.

"It's almost like the soul has some ulterior motive. This is definitely not a textbook soul attachment."

There are textbooks on this? I thought.

We dropped back into silence.

"He got a tattoo," I said, suddenly remembering.

Alyx looked up. "Really? What is it?"

"An Egyptian symbol of power."

"A Sekhem?" Alyx sat straighter, her eyes widening, not much, but enough to tell me she knew what I was talking about.

"I don't know. He didn't say."

I doubted she heard me, because it looked like her mind was off processing something somewhere else.

"I have to help him, Alyx. Tell me what I can do."

"Um…" She shook her head as if to scatter her thoughts away and regain her focus. "Help him, yeah, he needs help." She picked up a book from her desk and thumbed through the pages, stopping almost at the end. "It says here," Alyx started, reading from the book in her hand, "that 'any object blessed through the church or belonging to or associated with goodness and light, can be used to repel evil spirits.'" She nodded. "What Seth needs is an object of yours. Something that's infused with goodness—your goodness," Alyx grinned faintly. "For that matter, just being around him might help."

"But he told me to stay away," I said. "Remember that thing wants to hurt me."

"Of course he said that, or at least the soul said that. Don't you get it? This love thing the two of you have going on gives your boyfriend strength—the one thing the soul doesn't want him to have. You," Alyx gestured to the space around me, "your energy, coupled with his, will overcome darkness any day of the week. You're a threat. The soul probably is using his own threats to keep that extra light out of his eyes so he can do what he intends to do."

"Well, then me being around him is a good thing, right?"

"It can be, but on the flip side, you could very well be a reason for your boyfriend's death," she said, shrugging her shoulders.

"What?" I nearly choked on that.

"It's a double-edged sword. Sure, he has strength because you love each other, but because of that, your boyfriend will keep fighting. He'll never let the soul hurt you. That could push your boyfriend over the edge mentally and physically, unless we can find a way to get rid of it."

"Okay, so let's do it. How *do* we get rid of a soul?" I asked.

She either didn't hear me or wouldn't answer.

"Alyx?"

Alyx's voice sounded deflated, with no inflection of tone, no emotion, just like her eyes. "If the soul is determined to stay, if it's as bad as I'm guessing this one is… there's only one way. The host has to die."

~ ~ ~

"I do not understand." Tears welled in Silura's eyes, but she refused to let them fall, to show him how much she hurt. "You so willingly took... everything."

"You so willingly gave... everything," Maksim countered.

"I turned a blind eye to your infidelities." Her fingernails bit into the flesh of her palm, drawing blood.

He shrugged. "You were not enough for me."

Outrage replaced her tears, and she cried out. "I gave you everything! I adored you!"

"You grew old." He stared at her, his eyes cold.

"I should kill you for that," she hissed.

He raised a brow.

"In exchange for your powers, your body and soul belonged to me," she said quietly. "Was that not the bargain? Or perhaps you have forgotten?"

His fists clenched and his jaw tightened, but he said not a word.

"You will answer me!"

"Yes," he said through gritted teeth, "that was the bargain."

"Then you must never have contact with her again."

"You would force yourself upon me, knowing I love another?" he asked.

"Was it not you who told me that you feared love?" she spat. "Yet now you claim you love her."

"I do not fear it anymore," he declared.

Her spine stiffened at his declaration. "And if she should die? What then?" Silura asked.

"She will not die." The usual edge to his voice was gone.

Silura could not recall a time when his expression had been so unguarded. This woman he claimed to love had made him weak and had turned Maksim away from her. Fury rose, choking her.

"Really," Silura managed to say. "And what is to save your lover from me?"

He closed the distance between them and glared down at her. "I will save her."

Lifting her chin, she said softly, "And who will save her from you?"

A crease formed between his brows. The meaning of her words escaped him. "I would never harm her."

"Really." Turning her back on him, she walked away, a slow smile spreading across her face. He was certain about that, was he? Well, it might have been too late to reclaim their relationship, she thought, but it was not too late to inflict on him the same pain he had made her feel.

~ ~ ~

Chapter 27

The boy reinforces his will. It is a pitiful attempt, but sufficient to protect the last part of him. I poke, I prod, I burn into him, but he is determined to withstand the pain to stand next to her, still hoping for salvation. But hope, like anything else, can be snuffed out.
~ Maksim

I woke up more determined than ever. If being Seth's "light" helped, then I sure as hell was going to blast as much sunshine into that dark soul as I could muster. Alyx and I figured there was a fifty-fifty chance that I was going to make a difference, but if I didn't try—like that was even an option—the odds would be a hell of a lot worse. Could I get hurt? Yeah I could, but there was no way I could stand back and watch Seth take the hit for this.

I slammed my car door shut and, slinging my backpack strap over my shoulder, I jogged across the parking lot to where a group of the wrestlers—Seth among them—stood talking, their breath sending out puffs of white into the cold air. As I got closer, I slowed down and imagined the rays from the sun soaking into me. I soaked it up like the stones at Zero Point so I could turn it on when I needed to.

"Hey, guys," I said, finding a place between Justin and Seth.

I got a few nods and a couple of *wassups*, but the boys mostly just stared at Seth and me. Apparently they had heard something had been going on between us.

I wrapped my free arm around Justin's shoulder and gave him a quick hug. "Hey, you."

"Hey," he said, his eyes sweeping my face.

He was watching me too closely these days, as if I were a fragile piece of glass, ready to shatter with the next gust of wind. Little did he know I was there to kick some dark-soul ass.

Tilting my chin up to look at Seth, I put my entire heart into my smile and slid my hand into the crook of his arm.

"Good morning, Seth."

My heart leapt when I saw his eyes brighten and the corners of his mouth curve up in a small smile.

"Morning," he said before dipping his head down and pressing his lips against mine.

The spark that was Seth was back in his eyes when he pulled back to look at me, and for a few minutes the conversation between us all was like it used to be.

Justin was unusually quiet as he watched me, but even he looked relieved.

Seth frowned and rubbed his eyes. He blinked a few times, and ran his hand over his face.

"Dude, you okay?" asked one of the guys.

"Just a headache," Seth muttered. The spark in his eyes had muted to a dull glow.

"I'll catch you two later," Justin said, when the bell rang, reaching over to slap Seth on the shoulder. He took a step backwards and mouthed to me, *Are you okay?*

Flicking my gaze back to Seth, I wasn't sure I could answer that. Seth seemed to be losing his focus and was fighting for control. Still, I nodded at Justin and smiled faintly. Precious seconds were being wasted. I needed to get through to Seth.

218

"Walk me to class?" I asked Seth in a cheery voice. My smile didn't waver, though my stomach knotted up in a tight wad as I watched the struggle in his eyes. His irises, still a golden brown, turned a shade darker and then back to golden with every beat of his heart.

"I thought I told you to stay away from me," he said through gritted teeth.

"Oh, you won't be getting rid of me that easily," I told him

He closed his eyes and pressed my hand against his cheek, relief washing over his face.

"Come on, then," he said. "Let's hurry."

~ ~ ~

I sat next to Seth in the Commons, my arm hooked into his. So far, my plan was working. Shadows had crossed his face more than once during our morning class, but he wasn't pushing me away.

I scanned the room, looking for Alyx. I spotted her a few tables down, dressed in her usual black. The only color that jumped out was a bright red ribbon, wrapped around her head and tied into a bow on the top, the color perfectly matching her lipstick. Staring directly at me, her raised eyebrows asked: *"Okay?"*

I gave her a quick thumbs up before putting my hand back on my lap. Yeah, it was all good.

Then without warning, Seth's body tensed up, flipping my senses to full alert.

"Damn it," I muttered.

Seth's profile had changed. His jaw clenched and the muscles tightened up to create serious angles on his face. He laced his fingers together and placed them on top of the table as he looked toward the door.

I saw what changed him. When Dirk had sauntered in, Seth's gaze was intense and focused.

Dirk was clueless, as usual, as he headed towards the gym.

Keep going, keep going! I screamed silently, as if I had the power to push him through the gym doors. *Almost there. Grab the handle and pull it,* I pleaded.

Just as he put his hand on the handle he hesitated, as if listening to something, then he whipped around and locked stares with Seth.

Looking from one to the other, my heart sank when they smiled at each other and tipped their chins in that barely perceptible way guys did. Dirk gave up on whatever it was that he was going to do and wound his way through the tables to us.

"Hey, bro," Dirk said as they fist bumped. "Hey, Danika," he leered, giving me a once over.

"Go away, Dirk," I shot back. I turned to Seth... and my heart dropped. This *wasn't* Seth. It couldn't be. His features were too hard, too unforgiving, and too cruel.

"Seth?"

His harsh gaze crushed me, but I refused to show him how much that hurt. Twisting to face him, I slid my hand behind his neck to pull him into a kiss. It was like pulling down on a massive tree branch and he wasn't about to bend.

"No," he hissed, with enough malice to scare the hell out of me. "Not this time."

A hand pulled on my arm, gently insisting I let go of Seth.

"Come on, Dani," Justin interrupted. "I need to copy your notes for next period."

I resisted. "You won't win," I sneered into Seth's face. I really hoped that the soul was listening.

Justin tugged harder on my arm, getting me to stand up. "Come on." His breath warmed my cheek. "Don't look back," he murmured.

But, of course, I did.

"Bye-bye," Dirk waved to me, and then burst out laughing.

My face went hot and I sagged into Justin as he wrapped his arm around my shoulder and led me away.

~ ~ ~

"Don't do this to yourself, Dani." Justin stopped and faced me, holding both of my hands in his.

"You don't get it, Justin. I *have* to stay with Seth. He needs me."

His teeth clenched and his nostrils flared. "You're right. I *don't* get it." He slammed his hand into the locker behind me, making me flinch.

My teeth bit deep into my bottom lip. I had no idea Justin would react like this. How could I possibly explain this when Alyx and I didn't have any answers ourselves? I wrapped my hand around his hand and squeezed. I couldn't afford to have him jumping to conclusions, but I couldn't let him in yet on what little we did know.

Holding his hand seemed to smooth things over just a little, because he cupped the side of my face and turned me to face him. "I don't know what his problem is," he said quietly. "You deserve so much better."

I pressed into the warmth of his touch. Justin would do anything for me, I knew. But there wasn't anything he could do to help Seth. I wished I could confide in him, but he'd think I was crazy. He'd probably look at me with pity, and I didn't think I could stand that.

"Thanks, Justin. Thanks for being here."

He held me a second longer before pulling back and shoving his hands in his pockets. He nodded, pressing his lips together as if shutting off what he wanted to say.

"Justin, it's just that…" I let out a big breath. "It's just complicated."

He was quiet for a few seconds. Again, he shook his head and sighed. "Be careful, Dani. I don't want to see you hurt."

"I know." I stood on the tips of my toes to kiss him on the cheek.

"Pssst!" Down the hall Alyx stood at the entrance to the Commons, waving me over.

"I've got to go." I gave his hand a squeeze and turned to leave, but he hung on, pulling me back again.

"Hey," he said. "I'm here for you. Anytime. Day or night, okay?"

"Thanks, Justin." He let go and I hurried towards Alyx.

"Does Justin know?" She asked when I reached her.

"No." I shook my head.

She lowered her voice. "Good. Did you catch what happened in the Commons?"

I frowned. "Which part? When Seth shut me down or when Dirk laughed at me?"

Alyx shook her head hard. "I watched the whole thing! It looked like your boyfriend got Dumb Jock's attention without even saying anything—from across the freakin' room! I mean, that was crazy!" Alyx dug into her pocket and pulled out her cell phone. "I've got to call my mom. I'll catch up with you later."

222

She left me standing in the hall alone. So now what? I had to go back in and face Seth, because I wasn't about to back down. I may not have any answers or know all the stuff that Alyx did, but I had a few strengths of my own, the most important one being that I loved Seth. And, according to the lady at the stone shop, love is a pretty powerful weapon.

I peered around the corner into the Commons. Seth and Dirk sat with their backs to me, talking with a group at the next table. Seth's shoulders were slumped, his elbows planted on the table, his forehead pressed against his fists and his new sidekick, Dirk, was busy talking to the others.

That was my chance. I made my way to Seth and slid my arms around his waist, kissing him lightly on the ear. "I need a study buddy tonight. Will you help me?"

He nodded his head ever so slightly, as if giving a secret signal.

"Good," I whispered, giving him a squeeze. "Seven o'clock tonight at your house."

Another nod.

I knew what I had to do and I was going after that freakin' soul with my barrels fully loaded.

Chapter 28

*I raged. I shook the bars of the cell he tried to
contain me in. I burned the blood that ran through his
veins. He forced his body to function by sheer will,
knowing that she would come tonight and offer him
an elixir of light.*
~ Maksim

Seven o'clock. The porch light over the front door
glowed like a beacon. Seth had heard. Seth had
remembered. I'd been wondering what was going on
in Seth's mind, if Seth had any control over what the
soul heard, or if the soul allowed Seth to hear
anything at all.

What I had planned for tonight could be the
stupidest thing I'd ever done... or the smartest. The
odds, I thought, were in my favor, but it all depended
on who would open the door.

I singled out Seth's house key from the others on
my keying and headed towards the front door. There
was no way I was going to let this soul destroy what
Seth and I had.

The door was yanked open before I could get the
key in the lock and a hand shot out from behind it,
grabbing my wrist, and pulling me inside the door.
My foot caught on the threshold, but strong arms
steadied me before the door closed behind me. A rush
of air escaped my mouth when Seth pulled me to his
chest and covered my lips with his. I would give up
my breath for him if that is what he needed.

Letting the keys fall onto the floor, I tangled my fingers in his hair to get closer. I wanted to be inside him, fighting for him. I wanted to be his strength.

Maybe Seth knew what I wanted to do, maybe he wanted the same thing, because his grip tightened across my back and the taste of Seth's desperation was unmistakable.

The moments slipped by until his hold on me finally relaxed, breaking the contact between our bodies. A shiver rippled through my body. It felt good to have Seth so close again.

"I missed you, Dani," he said.

Blinking, I focused on the face peering down at mine. To my huge relief, it was Seth, not the creep inside.

"I guess I should have said 'hi' first," he said, laughing a little, "but I need you... so much." The last two words were full of pain.

My skin was still warm where he'd gripped my waist, and the heat of his stare warmed me again, releasing the tension from my muscles, but I wasn't about to let my guard down. This wasn't over. This was just Round One.

"Come on," he said.

He still held tightly to my elbow, almost too tightly.

Letting his hand glide down my arm before entwining our fingers, he scooped up my keys and led me to the kitchen.

"Thirsty?" he asked over his shoulder. Without waiting for an answer, he opened the refrigerator and grabbed two sodas.

Peering around his shoulder into the lit fridge, I gasped. "When was the last time you bought food?"

It was empty except for cans of soda and two half-eaten sandwiches. That made no sense. Seth liked cooking *and* he liked eating what he cooked. Spinning to look around the kitchen, I realized it was spotless. Not a dish, a wrapper, or anything that would suggest this part of the house was ever used.

He avoided both my gaze and my question and pulled me down the hall to his room.

"I'm glad you came over." Tossing my keys on the desk, and putting the soda cans next to them, his grip on my hand tightened. He pulled me to the side of the bed and we sat down. Shifting his body, he faced me and focused on tracing small hearts on my palm with his thumb in a methodical way.

I listened to his breath, the tone of his voice, anything that would give me warning of a change for the worse. Seth's shoulders drooped as if completely defeated. He wouldn't even look at me. It seemed like he was ashamed of what was happening. Would he confide in me or would the soul keep him from telling me? Even more important, how much longer did we have before *it* came forward again?

I pulled my legs up on the bed and sat cross-legged to face him. "I know what's wrong."

He took a ragged breath and shook his head, still not looking up. "No, you don't. You have *no* idea what's wrong."

His thumb stopped mid-stroke and pressed deeply into the center of my palm. No way was I going to tell him it hurt like hell. But it was probably nothing compared to what he was going through. The way his shoulders cinched up all of a sudden and the muscles in his arms corded up and shook a little, like he was bracing for something to hit him, nearly made me cry.

"You probably wouldn't believe me." His voice was strained.

"Try me, Seth," I said quickly.

One more shudder and his muscles relaxed again. "At first I thought I was losing my mind. I kept hearing a voice. I thought I was schizo," he laughed softly, as if it were an inside joke—and it may well have been. "I really wanted that to be the reason, because what was really happening was starting to scare the shit out of me." The hearts he traced had mutated and were buried under Xs, each one progressively bigger, until it filled my hand, before they shrank back into a small point in the center of my palm.

"Then things started happening," he said. "Really weird things. Things I couldn't explain. Like the dogs freaking out on me at the shelter, my truck, my keys."

"What about the dogs? Did you do something to them?"

He shook his head. "At first I didn't understand, but then I realized. They felt him. They knew he was there. They *knew* he was bad. But I had no freakin' idea. Not a clue."

"Who, Seth? Who was there?"

"*Him,*" he whispered. He lifted his head just enough to look at me from under his brows. "I thought he was an angel. He *told* me he was an angel. Ha! Imagine that. An angel." He went silent for a few seconds. The Xs on my hand were warming up. Then without warning, he let loose and he slammed his fist onto the bed.

"He *LIED* to me!" His fingers shot through his hair, stopping when they got tangled up in the strands, then his fingers squeezed tight as if that would help him hang onto his sanity. And when he finally looked at me straight on, his eyes were wild and desperate. "It was all so cool in the beginning. I was thinking I had it all together. I had his help and I could do anything, be anything. I'd make you and Dad so

228

happy and proud. Then I started to realize I was losing control. He started hurting me if I didn't give in." He grabbed at his shirt as if to loosen invisible ties that bound him in. "He wanted me to hurt you. I don't know why, but he wanted to hurt you.

"I've tried to keep it from you, Dani. I've tried to keep it from everybody."

I held his face between my hands, forcing him to look at me. His brows were scrunched together so tightly, the space between them almost disappeared. He had to be feeling overwhelmed with this soul that was proving to be so horribly strong. I pressed my hands closer against his cheeks. He leaned into them as if he were transferring his heavy burden onto me. It seemed to help because the lines on his face smoothed out a little.

"You have no idea, Dani. If only you understood, you'd be running." His voice dropped to a whisper. "I wish *I* could run away from it, but I can't."

"Help me understand," I said. "Start at the beginning."

His fingers wrapped around my wrists and pulled my hands from his face. He straightened up, taking back his burden again. "He's not just in my mind, Dani. He's in my body. He's trying to take over."

A shiver raked my body with brutal force. It took everything I had not to let it show. Seth didn't need to know how scared I was for him—for us. "Seth," I said as gently as I could. "Who is he?"

He looked right through me at first, his eyes wide before he finally focused on my face. "A soul. Another soul is inside me." He shoved his fingers through his hair again, then dropped his hands to his lap. Blowing out a big breath, he stared up at the ceiling. His shoulders slumped once again. "It tries to make me to do things that I don't want to. Like treat you badly, treat Justin badly. He wants me to be friends with Dirk." Glancing back at me, he made sure I was listening. "I really hate that." He let out a shaky laugh. "If you could only see what goes on inside of me. God, I feel like I'm bleeding."

His brows pulled together. "And then there are the things I *do* want to do. He gives me these... powers. At first, it was cool. Then I realized that the more I used the powers, the more power I gave *him*." He shook his head. "I'm trying not to use it, but sometimes I have no choice."

"What powers?"

"You never noticed, did you?" He slowly shook his head. "I thought you might ask, but you never did." His finger lightly traced the line of my jaw towards my chin and his finger brushed over my lips. His touch was just warm enough and sensual enough to melt my spine. It was my turn to lean into his touch. My lids dipped a little, and a subtle white noise echoed in my ears, almost washing out his next words.

"Didn't you ever wonder how you turned to putty in my hands lately?"

I snapped up, my eyes wide—really wide—and I pushed Seth's hand away. Oh, my God. It wasn't Seth. It had been that soul. That *demon* soul that touched me. How *dare* he violate me! How *dare* he violate Seth! He was going to pay dearly for that.

"You can't stop fighting it, babe," I said, determined to fight. "We *have* to find a way to get rid of it."

Seth shook his head. "There's no way, Dani." He took a deep, shuddering breath. "I've screwed up. I've tried to push him out, but he won't let me." He added, his voice low, "I won't give in, but it's not

230

getting any easier." He put his hand over mine and I winced at the pressure of his squeeze.

"Is he listening right now?" I asked quietly. As if whispering would help.

Seth hissed out his breath. "He's always listening. And waiting. Waiting until I get too tired to fight him off. I don't want you to go away because I need you. But you're not safe around me," he said, lacing his fingers with mine. "Even now we're taking a big risk. I just had to see you one more time."

"What do you mean, one more time? What's going to happen?"

He wouldn't meet my eyes. "I don't know."

"Where did you get him, Seth? How did he find you?"

"I…" He stopped, a small choke cutting him off. "… bought… it." He let go and shoved both hands over his hair, his fingertips digging into his scalp. Air pushed past his lips in short bursts.

I leaned into him, sliding my hands up his arms, gripping them to pull him closer. "I'm here, Seth. It's okay. Don't talk. Just stay with me."

"I don't know how long I can do this, Dani." This time when he looked up his eyes glistened from tears that threatened to erupt and his voice became raspy. "I feel like I'm getting weaker."

"No, Seth. You are the strongest guy I know."

Again, he shook his head. "I bought it because I wanted so much for you. I wanted to give you reason to stay with me. I wanted to get Dad off the road and home with me." He swiped at his eyes and took a deep breath. "Now it looks like everything I've ever wanted, everything I had, is about to be taken from me."

"We can fight it. Alyx and I can help."

He clutched his stomach. "I bought something bad. Really bad. And now it is a part of me. A part of me I can't let go."

I couldn't take it anymore. To see him suffer like this, to blame himself for this, this, demon. I ran my lips across his brow, his eyes, and over his lips. I put everything I had into those kisses.

At first Seth wouldn't respond, his lips too rigid, but I was relentless, not knowing how much time we had. I gently coaxed him to kiss me back, and was rewarded when he pulled me close and pressed his lips hard against mine. Our breath mingled before fusing into a soul-searing kiss, and I mean *searing*. I launched into an all-out assault on Seth's senses, using everything I had. My fingers threaded through his hair and held on. There was no way I was letting go now. Our tongues tangled in a frenzy. I hoped like hell that Seth wouldn't stop me, because I needed him to feel my love and give him whatever strength he could take away from it.

Seth pushed me up the bed before covering my body with his. I had every intention of taking this all the way. Any reason I'd had to hold back until marriage washed away with my tears because this was where I needed to be, exactly what I needed to do.

I pulled up the edge of his t-shirt, desperate to have skin-to-skin contact and to have nothing between us. I wanted Seth in me, on me, around me. I wanted him to take pieces of my soul back inside him.

Breaking our kiss, he sat up and peeled off his shirt. His eyes, though heavy-lidded, were still golden, still burning bright.

Still Seth.

His wide chest rose and fell with his breath, but caught and held when I ran my fingertips down his stomach.

I knew there was no turning back now. My intensity matched his as I pulled him back down over me. My clothes felt like a barrier between us, keeping my energy from reaching its destination—inside Seth to where the monster lay waiting.

Our bodies moved in rhythm with each other. Soon I would be Seth's and he would be mine. Soon I would have victory over the dark soul. I closed my eyes and arched my back, pressing my body into him, my neck exposed to his kisses. I ached for more of the heat that consumed us both, burning away the dark soul.

Then…

Seth stopped.

A chill spread across my skin and I opened my eyes to see Seth towering over me.

"Get out of here, Dani." He turned his face away.

"No, Seth!" I reached for him. This couldn't be happening! "Seth…" Frustration stuck in my throat. "Don't stop! Please!"

He pushed my hand aside. "I know what you're doing. *He* knows what you're doing."

I scrambled to sit up. "Then hurry up and take me, Seth!" My fist landed a solid punch on his thigh. "Damn it! Take me!"

The muscles of his chest flexed hard, and his breathing pushed out fast and shallow. "He's trying to get back in control. Shit. He's really pissed." He groaned. "This is going to hurt."

My one chance and it hadn't worked!

Seth's thick lashes covered his eyes for a moment. My gut rolled at the empty dullness in his eyes when he finally looked at me. Sadness turned to regret, and then…

I could see the shadows smoking in his eyes and the hardening of the lines around his mouth. I was losing him.

Rising to my knees, I grabbed his face between my hands. "Fight it!" I pushed through my gritted teeth. "Seth! Look at me and fight it!"

He shoved me backwards. "Go, Dani! It's too late!"

"No, damn it!" I wasn't scared. I knew Seth wouldn't hurt me.

Which explains my complete shock when Seth backhanded me. Hard.

The right side of my face was throbbing even before I hit the floor, a shrill whine ringing in my ears. My skin was already hot against my palm as I stared through my fingers at Seth. His face was contorted with rage… and pain.

I scrambled backwards along the floor, crab-like, to press against the wall. He took a step off the bed towards me.

Okay, *now* I was scared.

But Seth's legs buckled underneath him at the same time he clutched his stomach.

"Dani." He swallowed hard. "I'm *so* sorry!" Pulling himself up to one knee, he tried to stand up. He collapsed onto all fours, panting like a hurt animal. Determined to get to me—to protect me or to hurt me, I didn't know—he tried to crawl, but his arms gave out and he flattened onto the floor.

I pushed myself off the wall, "Seth!"

He didn't move. I pushed his hair from his face, afraid of what I might see. But his features were disturbingly peaceful. Except for the imprint of creases between his brows and around his eyes, that was the Seth I knew and adored.

Finding a pulse in his neck, I relaxed a little. The pain must have caused Seth to pass out. For now, I thought, he was safe. But for how long?

I put my hands under his arms and yanked his body until I had his head resting on my lap. I let my fingers trace Seth's face, his brows, nose, and lips. Cradling his head, I kissed him, wishing desperately he would kiss me back.

"Fight, Seth," I said against his lips. "Fight for me. Fight for us. I *won't* lose you."

But emptiness poured into me and hope was slipping away.

Drawing a ragged breath, I took my cell phone out of my back pocket and dialed my mom.

"Hi. It's me." I hoped I sounded calmer than I felt. "I'm staying here tonight. Seth is sick and I need to take care of him." My jaw set hard. "No, Mom. It's nothing like that." I winced as I gingerly touched my cheek. "Trust me, okay? No. No doctor. He just needs me right now. He'll be fine. Okay. I love you, too." I let the cover slap closed.

"He'll be fine," I said out loud to the eerily quiet room. "He has to be. He *has* to be."

I leaned my head against the bed, holding Seth, getting ready for the long night ahead.

~ ~ ~

Thoughtfully, she tapped a finger to her lips, staring at him from across the blanket she had spread out over the grass. Here, under the trees and surrounded by the elements, Silura would have the power she needed, should it come to that.

"So you love this girl?" she asked him.

Maksim remained silent, staring cautiously at Silura.

What he didn't know, what he couldn't know, because she had never taught him how, was exactly what she was thinking. After much contemplation, she had devised a curse that she knew would cause him the most pain. The kind of pain he had caused her.

She softened her voice. "Would it sadden you greatly, Maksim, to lose this girl? Would it break your heart to see her die? Die by your own hand? I would imagine your lover's death by your hand would be devastating."

"What is this you speak of?" he spat out. "I would never cause her harm."

"So you do love her." She smiled sadly. "Well then. I have decided on the price you must pay for the all the knowledge I have given you... and all the pain you have caused me," Her voice suddenly hardened. "You will be forced to have the blood of your love on your hands. As well as the blood of every lover you will ever have—throughout eternity," she said coldly.

His eyes narrowed at the implication. "But... that would include you, Silura."

A moment passed as she contemplated his words. "Yes. Yes, I suppose so," she agreed.

He hesitated. "You wouldn't."

"Yes. I would." She shrugged. Life was no longer attractive to her. She did not mind sealing her fate along with his.

His eyes raged, but his voice betrayed little. "You seem to forget that you have taught me well. I am a powerful sorcerer in my own right." He leaned forward to cup her face with his hands, stroking her cheeks with his thumbs before sliding his fingers down her neck. "I will not be commanded, or threatened, by a mere woman."

"You think to break a bargain with a high-ranking sorceress?" she challenged. "A dangerous attempt."

"Ah, but I am in no danger." He laughed. "You cannot force my hand in this."

"Oh, but I can." A knowing smile flashed across her face.

"Whatever you do, I can counter," he said.

She tried to pull out of his reach, but his hands held her still.

"Not everything." Silura chose her next words carefully. "I never intended to teach you everything I know." She watched his face change from confidence to confusion and then to rage. It seemed that Maksim now understood that she had kept secrets from him. He'd blindly trusted that the devotion she felt for him would also render her without sense.

Fool. He had been so very wrong.

~ ~ ~

Chapter 29

The virgin sacrifice. The ultimate act of love. Had
she surrendered her body to him, her light would
have become his. Now he lives in purgatory within his
body. I would have killed her then had he not shut
himself down, rendering his body useless to me.
~ Maksim

My chin fell to my chest, waking me up with a
jolt. I saw pale gray light brightening the
neighborhood beyond the window, but it still felt like
the middle of the night in this room. The air was
heavy, dark, and stagnant, smelling of decay. It took
me a few seconds to get my bearings.

Underneath my hand, Seth's chest rose and fell
with steady breaths. He looked peaceful, the crease
between his brows now gone. Whatever was in his
mind made his eyes move slowly behind his lids. I
hoped he dreamed of me.

Seven o'clock in the morning.

I rested my head against the bed, sorting out my
options. I didn't want to leave Seth like this, but I
didn't see a choice. I couldn't see how I could help
him now, especially after last night. Seth wanted me
out of his house. No, not Seth, but that *thing* inside
him wanted me gone.

My cheek ached. I was obviously no match for
either of them. Staying all night had been risky and
staying any longer was just plain stupid. I wasn't any
good to Seth if I was injured… or worse. I needed to
get help. I had to talk to Alyx before school started.

Trying my best not to wake him, I grabbed a pillow off the bed and put it under Seth's head as I slid my legs out from underneath him. I stifled a groan. I was surprised I could even move after being in one position for the last eleven hours.

First I made a bee-line for the bathroom. I came out, and seeing he was still passed out on the floor, I sneaked past him and out the bedroom door. I would come back later to check on him, maybe with Alyx and Justin. Maybe the three of us could handle him.

I made it to the front door before I realized I didn't have my keys. *Damn!* Seth had tossed them on his desk! I turned to go back and when I got just inside the bedroom door, I froze.

Seth was gone.

The room was completely empty and the pillow that Seth had laid on still had the imprint of his head.

A shiver rolled across my skin, making the hair on the back of my neck stand at alert. "Seth?" His name came out as more of a croak than a whisper.

I was afraid to see him just as much as I was *not* to see him. Something told me, though, that it wouldn't be Seth I would find.

The keys were still where Seth had left them, but too far away. Grabbing them too fast would mean noise, sudden movement, and attracting attention. Inching towards them slowly would mean I'd spend too long being an easy target.

Where the hell *was* Seth? Where could he have gone so quickly, and without a sound?

Cold sweat broke on the surface of my arms and neck, like tiny pricks of ice. I was beginning to feel like I was in a really bad horror movie. Screw it. I didn't have time to think about this anymore. I went for it and grabbed my keys. Even though I'd dozed off with the demon soul practically in my lap, I'd felt

240

relatively brave because Seth was asleep, but now that he was *moving around*, I wasn't so anxious to see either of them. Not now. Not until I had some help.

Inching backwards until the door jam stopped me, I took one last look around me before turning and jogging past the pictures of the baby boy with his beaming parents that lined the walls leading to the front door.

Once outside, once in the growing light of the morning, the reality of Seth's situation hit me. I was stupid to believe that I could take this on myself. I wasn't some superhero or someone with magical powers. All I had was love and determination. How can that possibly stack up against something as evil as this attachment was? I could have gotten myself killed in there. Then what good would I be to Seth? The only hope I had now was Alyx. Yanking open my car door, I got in and started up the engine. I didn't want to be here any longer than I had to.

I gunned it down the road, checking my rear-view mirror at least a dozen times in the few seconds it took me to drive the block to the grocery store parking lot.

My hands were shaking as I opened my cell phone and dialed Alyx's number. She answered on the second ring.

"What's up?" She asked.

"Are you at school?"

"Almost there now. What's up?" she asked again.

"Can you meet me at the south portables in ten minutes?"

"Yep."

Just like that. No questions. I got the feeling she wasn't surprised to hear from me.

As soon as I hung up, my cell phone rang. "Hey, Mom," I said, trying to sound cheery. "I was just going to call you. I'm on my way to school right now." I rested my head against the headrest. What could I tell her? "Yeah. Seth will get better. I'll probably check on him later." I checked my watch. "Okay, Mom. I love you, too."

I pulled into a space at the south end of the building and got out of my car, catching my reflection in my window. Ugh! Nice look, you got there, I thought. I draped my hair over the side of my face where the bruise was beginning to turn a dull shade of purple. I'd figure out later how I was going to explain that one.

I ran across the lot and then over the soggy grass to the portable classrooms. I was relieved to see Alyx waiting for me, but not so happy when I saw Justin following her. Why was *he* here? I hadn't planned on explaining things to him as well.

Alyx sauntered over and raised her brow. "What happened to your face?"

"It got bad, Alyx," I said, trying to stop my voice from quivering. "Last night... I... I was trying to give myself to Seth. You know... I was hoping that would help Seth somehow." My eyes welled up. "But it didn't work. Seth just got mad and... the soul..."

Alyx looked over her shoulder at Justin and then back at me. She lowered her voice, "This morning my mom mentioned something that might be important and I need to look it up."

"So let's do it," I urged.

Justin walked up behind Alyx, staring at my face. "What happened?" His features hardened as he ground out the words. "Where's Seth?"

"I don't know where he is," I snapped back. "When I left his house this morning—"

"You spent the night with him?" Justin stepped back, like I had slapped him.

242

"Oh get off it, lover boy," Alyx snapped at him. "She didn't *sleep* with him."

"No! I didn't! Seth got really sick and he passed out. I *had* to stay."

"Why didn't you call me? Why didn't you call 911? What happened?" Justin demanded. "And what happened to your face? Did Seth hit you?"

I glared at him. I so didn't need this right now.

"We need to tell him," Alyx said to me. "We're going to need his help."

"Tell me what?" Justin glanced at Alyx, then past her to the parking lot. "Oh, look who's here." He was glaring at a truck that pulled up at the curb. "Speak of the devil, huh?"

"You don't know how close you are," Alyx muttered.

"Seth," I whispered.

"Yeah, dude!" Dirk yelled from the front of the school.

The three of us turned to see him lope across the lot and jump into Seth's truck. Even with the window rolled up and the car driving away, we could hear Dirk laughing.

"Come on, let's go." Alyx said.

"Wait a minute!" Justin grabbed my arm, yanking me back. "*What's* going on?"

"Later, Justin," Alyx said. "Right now we're going to follow Seth and see what he's up to."

"Come on, Justin," I said, pulling my arm free. "We'll explain it in the car."

He took one more look at my bruise, and then nodded.

We followed Alyx to her car, and the closer we got, Justin slowed down, his jaw dropping.

"You think you're going to catch them in *this*?"

I had to admit I was a bit skeptical myself. The car was pretty beat up.

Alyx wasn't offended. Instead she grinned and patted the hood.

"Of course we will. It's a Subaru. North Idaho's finest!" She unlocked the doors and we piled in. "Did I tell you my brother is a Porsche mechanic down in L.A.?" She smiled at Justin before slamming the door closed.

~ ~ ~

We followed Seth's truck to City Beach and down toward The Witch's Hat, the huge picnic pavilion at the far end of the beach. Alyx stopped her car just before getting to the boat ramp and parked far enough away that—we hoped—Seth and Dirk wouldn't notice her car. As long as they didn't look back, we were good.

Alyx pulled a pair of tiny binoculars from the glove box and adjusted them.

"They're headed over to the statue." She shook her head. "Whoever thought of putting a mini-Statue of Liberty here at the beach? Freakin' bizarre."

She handed me the binoculars. "Why do you suppose they're here?" I asked her.

Justin leaned forward from the back seat. "Hey, when are you two going to explain what's going on with Seth?"

Alyx glanced at me. "Now, I guess. But we have to keep an eye on Seth and Dirk. This could be important."

I kept the binoculars up to my eyes while Alyx gave Justin a crash course about dark souls.

"If you haven't noticed, your buddy hasn't been acting like himself lately."

"Well, yeah. Look who he's been hanging out with." Justin leaned forward and pointed toward Seth and Dirk.

"That's not it. Something's making him behave differently," Alex said.

"What, like a disease?"

"Sort of," Alyx said.

I glanced at her out of the corner of my eye.

She caught my look and took a big breath, letting it out through puffed cheeks.

"Seth has a soul attached to him. It's very common," she waved her finger, indicating the three of us, "for anyone. Most of the time they're just drifters and they don't do any harm. But the one he's picked up won't leave." She twisted in her seat to face him. "This one is dark, like Darth Vader dark. Full of bad juju. We're still trying to figure out why it's here and how to get rid of it."

Justin sat back and laughed. "You expect me to believe all this crap? Come on!"

"It's true, Justin," I said, watching Seth and Dirk standing next to the mini-statue. "I thought Alyx was crazy, too—sorry, Alyx!" she shot me a look. "But she's totally right about this."

"Yeah, right." Justin sat back, mumbling to himself. "You guys *are* crazy."

"I'm afraid not," Alyx said quietly.

Justin went silent. Fifteen minutes crawled by while Alyx and I handed the binoculars back and forth to each other, taking turns watching Seth and Dirk. At first there was just a lot of talking between them, or so it looked, but then Seth kept pointing to things, the concrete underneath them, the rocks, the water, and the statue, all with hand movements that reminded me of a street magician. At one point Dirk stumbled backward, almost falling off the concrete

pier, but Seth grabbed his shoulder to steady him
After a couple of seconds, he lightly slapped Dirk's
cheek, like they did in those Mafia movies, getting
Dirk to snap out of whatever stupor he had fallen into.

Then they stood toe-to-toe. Seth cupped his hands
together in front of him and Dirk leaned in to look,
passing his hand over Seth's.

"What's he doing, Alyx?" I handed the binoculars
to her. "It looks like he's holding something."

I heard Justin shift in his seat.

"I can't tell." Then Alyx gasped. "Oh, man! He
did it. He actually did it!"

"Did what?" Justin and I said at the same time.

"Let me see!" Justin reached his hand between us,
trying to get the binoculars, but Alyx wouldn't let him
have them.

Seth had squatted down and put something on the
ground at the base of the statue and then stood up.

"Do you see it?" Alyx said, shoving the
binoculars in my hands. "He actually did it! He
manifested a fireball!"

Justin leaned closer. "What the hell are you
talking about?"

Alyx was right. Seth *had* created a small fireball
and had placed it on the ground. As he stepped back,
we could see an orange-red ring starting to snake
around the base of the statue and circle around,
winding its way up like a snake slithering up a tree.

Seth raised his arms up, as if encouraging the light
to rise.

"Oh, my God!" Alyx whispered. "He's going to
light the torch!"

The trail of fire twisted its way up the torch
handle until it touched off a small blast of fire at the
tip. Seth then brought his arms up again, drawing

246

water up from the lake, splashing the torch, and putting the blaze out.

We were treated to the obnoxious hoots and whistles of Dirk, jumping around and fist pumping the air as Seth stood calmly, looking out over the lake.

Then my blood froze. Seth had looked over his shoulder in our direction and our eyes locked through the binoculars for a fraction of a second before he turned back to Dirk.

I gave the binoculars back to Alyx. That. Was. Not. Seth.

"What was that all about?" Justin asked, leaning forward and touching my shoulder.

"We'd better go," I said, ignoring Justin's question.

"He saw us, didn't he?" Alyx said.

I nodded. "Yeah."

"Not good."

Alyx started up the car and made a u-turn to get us out of there.

Chapter 30

The girl. The vortex of my curse. So innocent in her devotion. So blind in her pursuit. She will soon learn that love is not light. Love is dark. Yes. I can already taste the sweetness of overwhelming grief of a lover lost. My moment of release.
~ Maksim

Seth didn't come to school that day.

I was torn between wanting to see him and wanting to stay as far away from him as possible. I wished I'd known if he was okay, though.

Dirk was at school, unfortunately, and every time I saw him, he had a stupid smirk on his face. I wanted to hit him over his head with my history book. He looked so smug, like he had a dirty little secret. Somehow he had gotten himself involved with Seth and the dark soul and I had the feeling he was making the situation worse.

Justin was even more protective of me than usual. At lunch, in the halls, and in the one class that we had together, he shadowed me, looking over both his shoulder and mine. It was endearing, sort of, but I didn't need protection. I needed information. While Alyx was doing her research, I needed to do mine.

"Hey! Where are you going?" After school, Alyx caught up with to me as I headed towards the parking lot.

"I'm going over to the library," I told her. "I thought of something that I want to check out."

She nodded. "Then I'll meet you there. I need to look up something, too."

At the library we found two empty computers next to each other. We dropped our packs on the floor and settled in.

When Alyx had told me that maybe the soul didn't like me, I thought she was joking. I mean, I don't have any flesh-and-blood enemies at all, let alone any *dead* enemies. I'd wondered if we were missing something obvious. That book that was on Alyx's bookshelf, *Magick Murders*, got me thinking. If this was as common as Alyx said it was, then maybe there were archived records of evil attachments where people got hurt—and how they may have been stopped.

"Looks like you and I have been thinking the same thing," Alyx whispered, leaning over to look at my screen.

"It's a start, anyway," I whispered back. I scrolled down, found nothing of value, then added "unsolved" before the word "murder." A few possibilities, but not good enough. I added "lover" to the search. High-profile murders were listed halfway down the page. Okay, worth a try. One link had a list of cases dating back to the 1800s, unsolved, with the suspect never charged due to lack of evidence, but all of them involved the man killing his lover. Some of the men committed suicide afterwards, some disappeared, and others were institutionalized.

I started with the first on the list: Rose Harding, a servant girl found strangled to death in 1900 by an unknown assailant. She was six months pregnant at the time, supposedly by a local Baptist minister. He was tried, but found not guilty.

"Go to that one." Alyx pointed to my screen.

That article was about a Dr. Samuel Miller, convicted in 1953 of murdering his pregnant wife, though he claimed that "someone else" did it. The trial ended with no conviction, but the doctor ended up in a psych ward because he "heard a voice telling him to do awful things."

A woman named Cristi Harmon, in 1964, was found dead in a hotel bathroom. She'd been strangled to death. Her rock star boyfriend had been arrested and charged with her murder. He confessed, saying, "I didn't mean to kill her. I loved her." He'd tried to commit suicide but recovered, only to die of an overdose a week later. A note found in his pocket read, *I kept my side of the bargain, but I can't live with it.*

"They were all strangled," I said. "Weird."

"Yeah, I noticed." Alyx did her own search. "I can't believe this. There are so many others!" She opened a link and began reading. "In 1836, a prostitute and one of her customers fell in love. Apparently, he was obsessed with her and ended up killing her." She went silent as she read more of the story. "They said he went into a jealous rage and— oh, get this—he strangled her. The guy just vanished afterward."

And there were others, many of them involving movie stars and their girlfriends or wives.

"Here's another one!" Alyx didn't keep her voice down this time. "Holy crap!"

"Copycat murders, maybe?" I whispered.

"Or maybe a serial killer," Alyx suggested.

I looked at her. "'Serial killer' implies one person. These murders," I pointed to the screen, "are spread out over two hundred years!"

"Exactly." Alyx kept clicking on different pages, talking to herself. Finally she closed everything out and stood up. "I've gotta go."

I started to ask what she was thinking, but she spoke before I had a chance.

"I'll call you later," she said, looking distracted. She slung the strap of her messenger bag over her shoulder and walked away.

I stared back at my screen. What *was* she thinking? Murders by strangulation over a period of 200 years. Most of the suspects claimed to have heard voices or that "someone else did it." Suspects who ended up committing suicide, disappearing, or institutionalized. Serial killer, Alyx had said. But how could one person commit all of these murders? Nobody lives that long.

Then I remembered what Alyx told me. A soul lives forever. Like a ghost. A spirit that hangs around and doesn't cross over to "the other side." I straightened up. I'd bet that's what Alyx was thinking. Was it possible a soul had taken over these men and had them kill their lovers? Who the hell was this thing? And why was he doing it? And how long had he been doing it? It could go back centuries, and have gone unrecorded.

I closed down the screen and logged off. Gathering up my backpack, I made my way to the section of the library where I had gone the other day with Seth. I walked quickly down the aisle where the books on ancient civilizations were shelved. Maybe something would trigger an idea. There wasn't much, but I opened a few books and thumbed through the pages, just in case I'd missed something. I went through six books on ancient cultures, two on old civilizations, and three on prominent historical city leaders and rulers. I didn't find anything related to murders. Pulling each book off the shelf again, I went through the pages, slower this time. When I reached the thinnest book of the group, I remembered. This was the book Seth had taken from me that day. Since

when did Seth have an interest in ancient civilization?
He isn't even taking history this year.

I opened the book and flipped through the pages,
one by one. A dog-ear at the top of page 51 stopped
me.

*Hotep, the Egyptian symbol of
peace, depicting both a snake and the
sun. Very similar to the Asian yin
yang, the Hotep unites contrary forces:
The snake, representing the
underworld, and the sun, representing
the light of the gods, come together
and balance one another. There is
written a story of a chamber deep
within the labyrinths of Egypt that
encases a sacred altar. A stone slab,
measuring two meters on all sides, has
embedded within it a circle,
surrounding which are what appear to
be wave-like divots. By day, the slab
rests empty and cold, devoid of life,
dark and foreboding. By night,
movement stirs the stagnant air and
brings with it vitality to please the
gods. A serpent soundlessly glides
along a well-worn path and ascends
the wall of the slab to the outer edge of
the circle and winds to and fro, the
sides of its body folding upon itself in
a precise, methodical motion,
mastered over centuries. The final
motion of this ritual brings the
serpent's jeweled head to rest in the
center before it stills its body for the
night. Many ancient drawings capture*

the magnificence of this creature and the complex, yet simple interconnectedness it has with the world. Its movements are purposeful, yet seemingly random, but when the serpent completes its winding path to slumber and it aligns its scaly pattern with the wave-like divots on the stone slab, the markings along its back casts the appearance of the sun. See illustration page 52.

As I turned the page, my breath caught. There it was, staring back at me. A little smaller, with faded outlines. The caption beneath it referenced the page before it. There was no explanation as to what the origins were, only that it was thought to be from some past Egyptian civilization, but there was no mistaking it.

It was Seth's tattoo.

~ ~ ~

"Check this out," Alyx jabbed her finger at a page in the book she'd shoved into my hands. "Read this. It all makes sense now."

Alyx had called me twenty minutes after I had gotten home and insisted on coming over, saying what she had to show me couldn't wait, which was great timing, because what I had to show her couldn't wait either.

One page of the book she held out to me was a story titled *Legend of the Order,* and the opposite page held a solitary symbol.

"That's Seth's tattoo!" The excitement of finally getting somewhere was almost too much for me.

254

Alyx grabbed the book back from me before I could read the story. "Your boyfriend hit the jackpot. This particular soul is saddled with a curse. A really nasty one."

"A curse?" My jaw dropped, along with my excitement.

Alyx nodded. "The soul who hijacked your boyfriend has been called a lot of names through the centuries, but his original name was Maksim."

"Maksim." Just saying the name gave me the creeps.

"He was a regular guy who attracted the attention of Silura, an important sorceress in Egypt, back in the third century. Apparently, he was a player but she wanted him anyway. So, in exchange for his loyalty to her, she promised to teach him magick and to give him the power of a sorcerer."

"But those are just stories, aren't they?"

Alex frowned. "Every story or myth is based in fact, Dani." She went on. "Anyway, he behaved in the beginning, especially when she was teaching him how to manipulate the elements and teaching him the way of The Order, but after awhile he must have gotten bored, because he didn't keep his part of the bargain. He cheated on her—a lot. Silura knew it, but didn't do anything about it. *Until,*" she held up a finger, "until he fell in love." Alyx snapped the book closed.

"And that was a bad thing?" I wasn't quite following.

"Well, yeah. He fell in love with a village girl, *not* Silura. All Silura ever wanted was for Maksim to love *her*, not some other woman."

"And Silura didn't take it very well," I guessed.

"Hell, no! She gave him an ultimatum: leave the girl or the girl would die. Now here's where the curse comes in. Lover boy thought he could stop Silura because he had become so powerful, so he killed her.

"And get this," Alyx leaned closer and looked me in the eye, "before he *strangled* her to death, Silura apparently managed to recite an incantation, one she'd never taught him. The curse bound him to fall in love and then kill his lovers, just so he could feel the same pain she did. She cursed him to destroy anyone he ever loved—*throughout eternity.*"

"Wait a minute," I protested. "How did anyone find out about the curse if she died right after that?"

"The book says Silura was a part of the Rahotep of sorcerers, a tight society and well-respected group. Apparently she went to Rashidi, who was her mentor and old sorcerer, and told him about her suspicions as a back-up or protection, so in case something happened to her, he would know who to search for. After Maksim killed her, lots of sorcerers from Rahotep searched for him, but gave up after awhile because Maksim apparently hid himself so well. But once they realized that a string of murders pointed to Maksim, they tried to track him down again and have him destroyed. Maksim moved around a lot, always managing to keep one step ahead of them. Then the murders just... stopped. There was no record of these types of killings until about a hundred years later. Then the pattern started up again."

"So you're saying all the articles we found at the library are part of the pattern?" I asked.

"Exactly." Alyx said. "We only have legend to go on for all these murders—until about 200 years ago, when newspapers and records became more common. Those are all the stories we found at the library. But all these murders through the centuries, they've all been done by the same soul—*the soul inside of Seth.*"

I tried to swallow the lump that started to form in my throat, but I couldn't. The words were too thick on my tongue and I instinctively reached for my throat. "So that means Seth is supposed to kill me next."

Alyx's pressed her lips together.

"So why hasn't he done it yet? He's had plenty of chances." Just like the time in his room. Just the two of us, alone. He could have done it then. Had I known, would I have still gone? Yeah. I would have.

"I think it's because Seth's love for you is so powerful, he's managed to fight off Maksim's curse… so far."

"Maksim loved his women, too, and he still killed them," I said.

"True, but there were also a lot of other factors that came into play, like drugs, alcohol, jealousy. All of those things can give the attachment some kind of loop hole."

Jealousy? Oh boy.

"But the woman at the stone shop said that love is light and it would chase away the dark. If we have that, and Seth is fighting, why won't Maksim just go away?"

"It's all about the curse," Alyx explained. "Silura was making damn sure Maksim wasn't going to get off easy after what he did to her. I wonder if what we need is to give it a reason to leave, maybe a distraction. Kind of like a clown at a rodeo, you know? A decoy to take the attention off the cowboy. But right now Maksim is so close to fulfilling his curse, I doubt even that would work. As soon as he does, though, he'll be released. But then it'll start all over again."

I shook my head. "Just like you said—a serial killer."

"Exactly! He can't be destroyed, at least according to what I've read. Seth and Maksim are locked in a stalemate." She flopped back on my bed, staring at the ceiling. "I can't believe Seth has held out this long. It sounds like it's usually a slam dunk. I'm really impressed."

I sat on the floor and leaned weakly against my dresser. "I can't believe this. This is so freakin' unreal." I searched the ceiling hoping to find some answer in the smooth surface. "This is all because we love each other. Who'd ever think that would be such a crime?" I swallowed hard to get past the tightness in my throat.

A long minute passed before Alyx broke the silence. "That's probably why Seth broke up with you. He was trying to protect you." She sat up. "Seth is probably thinking that if you're not around him, then Maksim can't hurt you. I don't think not being around you is going to make any difference, though. As far as Maksim is concerned, you're Seth's lover."

"But Seth would die before he let Maksim hurt me!" I said, a sob breaking through my words.

"We have to figure out how to undo the curse or get rid of the soul. We'll follow Seth the next time he goes out, just to see what he's doing. Maybe we can find something to help us." She sighed and said, "Right now, it's all we've got."

~ ~ ~

Maksim's fingers tightened around the slender column of Silura's throat and she tore and scratched at his hands. The pale skin of her neck was already bruising under his touch, but he did not waver. This woman had dared to try to control him, tried to temper his appetite for power and women. She had dared to test her strength against his! For that, she would die.

He squeezed his hands tighter, if not to end it quickly, then at least to stop her lips from moving in their silent prayer. No god would answer her now. None would dare defy him and pull her from the edge of the abyss from which she was about to plunge.

He pushed her onto her back and straddled her. Tiny blue veins beneath the delicate skin of Silura's eyelids were pulsing as she struggled. Where was that powerful sorceress he had once adored? His beautiful, compelling queen who once stood so tall and forbidding, now crumpled beneath him, praying!

"Open your eyes and look at me while you die, you bitch! Tell me now who your master is."

Her pale, pink lips continued to silently recite words as her lids opened enough for him to glimpse the malice in her eyes. Then, as a pale purple hue replaced the fine white of her skin, she moved no more.

Silence whispered across the grass. His shaking hands loosened as he stared at her.

He'd killed her. Her lids spared him from seeing her lifeless orbs. Even so, he thought with a bit of hatred, he could still feel her malice.

The fine hairs on the back of his neck crept upward, sending a chill up and over his scalp. He

259

broke his gaze away from Silura, quickly looking around. Had someone seen him? Oh, but her friends would have vengeance should they discover him. They had never liked him. They had always been jealous of his ability to learn and master their art, and he being a mere commoner. And his affair with Silura... well, that was more than they could tolerate.

Silura was the one person who stood between him and his enemies, for they respected her and held her above all else. Now that she was gone, with her demise by his hand... But, her death was not his fault! This was her doing, he told himself. Had she not loved him so much, had she not been so controlling, she would still be alive.

His head whipped around to scan the trees. A rustling in the leaves at the base of the mighty oaks from a rabbit both frightened and incensed him. I am Maksim, he said to himself. I will not cower from this or anyone who tries to take retribution on her behalf. He closed his eyes and sent his energy through the trees, ensuring there was no one in hiding. Narrow was his mind's eye at the moment, as he searched for his enemies far from where he was, straddling the body of his mistress and teacher. Too narrow, for he missed the subtle shift of the blanket beneath his knees.

His eyes snapped open and he cried out in pain when red-painted nails slashed at his face, raking the skin from his cheeks.

Silura's voice reverberated through the air as she spoke in a language he had never heard her use before. He knew by the way sweat beaded on his brow and how his ribs constricted around his lungs that he faced something more powerful than anything he'd ever known. In his desperation, he squeezed her throat harder to stop the words.

Ice ran through his bones, failing to quell the fever that raged within. He now understood, down to his soul, that he would never escape her... even after her death.

~ ~ ~

Chapter 31

I gather him in my arms and cradle him against me, whispering encouragement. He is mine now, too tired to fight any longer.
~ Maksim

The chance to follow Seth came three nights later. The three of us had spent the last two nights parked down the street from Seth's house watching to see if he would leave. Dirk came and went, but there was no sign of Seth. Until tonight.

Now Alyx, Justin, and I were headed north in Alyx's car, just past Selle Valley, on a two-way road. There was so little traffic here that Seth and Dirk had to have known we were following them. It was a game of cat and mouse and I had a feeling we were the mice, driving right into a trap.

But Alyx had absolutely no fear. She was fascinated by what was happening. I was afraid, though, afraid of what we might see. Afraid I was going to lose Seth. As for Justin, he wanted to help Seth, but I think he was more scared for me.

"Hey, grab the backpack, will you?" Alyx told Justin, holding the wheel with one hand as she gestured to the space behind his seat. "Open it. There's one inside for each of us."

"One of what?" Justin asked, dragging a backpack over the seat. He unzipped it and pulled out the first thing he found. "Um, if this is what you're talking about, I don't think it's the right size for me." He gingerly dangled a black lacey bra from his fingertips.

"Of course, it is. Just…" Alyx glanced at him in the rear-view mirror. "Ugh!" she cried. "Put it back! Not *that* backpack! The camo one!"

He shoved the bra back in the pack and reached back again. "How was I supposed to know? Black is your color, isn't it?

I stared at her in amazement. "You do camo?"

"Are you kidding? Not on *this* body." She took the pack from Justin and put it in her lap. "I found this pack at a garage sale."

Steering with her knees, Alyx's attention shifted between the road and whatever she was digging for in her backpack. "Here they are." She threw one pair of night goggles back to Justin and another pair to me. She adjusted hers with an ease that said she'd done it before.

"Night goggles?" I asked. I was skeptical, but when Alyx explained how to adjust them, I was amazed at how much I could see along the highway and into the dense woods on either side.

"Look," she said, pointing ahead of us. "Seth's turning." She turned off the car's headlights and crept along the road.

"What the hell are you doing?" Justin demanded.

"Duh, trying *not* to be seen," Alyx said to Justin.

The moonlight barely broke through the cloud cover. Wow. It was off-the-grid dark, and the trees and shrubs around us were creepy. I breathed easier as she guided the car into a stand of trees and turned off the engine. We weren't too far from where we'd seen Seth's truck pull over.

"We have to do it this way," I told him.

"Fine," he said. He opened the door and slid out, then closed the door as softly as possible. "Dani, stay close to me, okay?"

"Yeah, okay." I walked around to meet him and squeezed his arm. "We'll be all right." I turned to Alyx. Through the goggles, she glowed a pale green.

"With these," Alyx pointed to her goggles, "we're leveling the playing field."

"You hope," Justin muttered.

"Stop it, Justin." I punched his arm.

Alyx stood still, turning her head from one side to the other.

"Let's go this way." She gestured toward the east and we began to make our way in the direction of Seth's truck. She added in a low voice, "I wouldn't be surprised, though, if Seth's little sorcerer sees perfectly in the dark."

"Sorcerer?" Justin asked. "Seriously?" He glared at me. "What else are you leaving out?"

"Later!" Alyx hissed. "Quiet!"

We could hear Dirk's voice now, but we couldn't make out his words. Off a little way in front of us, Dirk was shifting his weight from foot to foot and moving his hands around animatedly, like he was jacked up on something, like he just couldn't contain himself. Seth, on the other hand, hardly moved, but when he did, his body was fluid, measured, and deliberate.

Dirk shifted to stand on the other side of Seth, and in the truck's headlights, we could see a limp rabbit draped over Seth's hand.

I shuddered and turned away. I've never seen Seth mistreat anything. He may not be as passionate about animals as I am, but he would never hurt one. I refused to believe Seth was in control—it had to be Maksim.

"Oh, shit. That's just sick!" Justin coughed and turned away. "He's lighting the rabbit on fire."

I whipped back around to see, and my stomach rolled at the sight. A flame sat in Seth's palm, its tendrils stretching up and greedily flicking at the rabbit's face. Dirk egged Seth on, but Seth didn't seem to need any encouragement. The smile on his face told me he was thoroughly enjoying the performance.

The flames crawled up the rabbit's fur before Seth tossed it away into a burning heap on the ground.

"Yeah! Yeah!" Dirk's voice broke apart the quiet air. "Dude! That was freakin' awesome! Yeah!"

They did a high five, but when their palms hit, Seth grabbed Dirk's hand and held it. Dirk's knees buckled just a little bit.

"Dude! That—"

Seth's lips moved and Dirk went silent, then they both turned around to stare at us.

"We have to get out of here!" Alyx whispered, now clearly agitated. The tone of her voice made the hair on the back of my neck stand up.

We turned and ran back towards the car. Nervous sweat made my goggles slip down my nose and I had to hold them onto my face with both hands.

"Holy crap!" Justin said. "That was crazy!"

I let out a scream when wood splintered directly behind us. Beside me a tree toppled, its branches thudding on the ground. Alyx grabbed my arm and we ducked behind the widest tree we could find, trying to catch our breath.

"Bastard," Alyx muttered.

"You mean *Seth* did that?" Justin panted.

My heart pounded against my ribs so frantically, my entire body was shaking. "That wasn't Seth," I said. "Seth isn't in control now."

Alyx peered around the trunk. "It was Maksim giving us a warning."

Through the trees we could still see Seth and Dirk silhouetted against the headlights. Another spark blazed, lighting up their faces.

"Get to the car! Now!" Alyx's command had us moving.

Justin grabbed my hand and we started to run. We thought Alyx was right behind us, but I realized I couldn't hear her footsteps.

"Wait!" I stopped and whirled around.

Alyx was walking towards Seth.

"Alyx!" I hissed. "Get over here!"

"What the hell is she doing?" Justin asked from behind me, still pulling on my hand. "Come *on*, Dani! We need to go!"

"I can't leave her!" I was terrified. Alyx was the one who told us we needed to run—and now she was walking right into danger! Had Maksim somehow compelled Alyx to go to him? Could he *do* that?

The tiny, solitary flame Seth held in his hand had swelled into a fireball. His arm was cocked back, and he was aiming the fireball at us.

None of us moved. I refused to believe that Seth would throw it, not if there was some part of him that still cared.

But he launched it. It was an easy toss, but the fireball headed toward Alyx like a rocket.

"Alyx! Run!" I forced my feet to move forward, stumbling in her direction.

Alyx yelled, like a warrior diving headlong into a battle and shoved her hands at the air in front of her.

"No!" My scream burned my throat. "Move, Alyx!"

But she knew exactly what she was doing. The fireball came within an inch of her, then ricocheted off to the side. It exploded, orange and red lighting up the trees.

My mouth dropped open. She had created a barrier, just like the one Seth did at the dance to keep Dirk back.

"How did Alyx do that?" There was awe in Justin's voice.

"I have no idea," I whispered.

Alyx turned and ran, grabbing my arm in passing. "Why aren't you guys in the car?" she growled.

Our survival instinct took over and we sprinted.

"Shit," Justin spat out as he turned in mid-stride to check on Seth. "He's making another one!"

Behind us a tree exploded. Seth had missed his mark—us.

As soon as we got to the car, Justin shoved me into the back seat ahead of him and slammed the door as Alyx floored it.

Justin pushed me down, covering my body with his. "Good thing Seth never had very good aim," he muttered.

Yeah, a very good thing, too. Out here no one would find us for a long time, I thought, pushing Justin off so I could sit up.

"He *meant* to miss us with that one," Alyx said calmly.

"Why would he try to miss?" Justin asked.

"Because of Dani," she answered. Alyx looked at me in the rear-view mirror. "Your boyfriend is doing something to keep some control. He obviously isn't going to let Maksim hurt you." She added, her voice suddenly angry, "But the first one was definitely for me. I don't think either dude likes me much."

I looked back again, half expecting to see Seth and Dirk materialize behind our car, but I saw nothing except the glow of the Subaru's tail lights.

"I don't think we need these any more," Justin said, ripping his night goggles off. "Alyx, what exactly did you do back there?"

She shrugged.

He turned to me. "What if she's the same as Seth?" he demanded. "I mean, look at her, Dani. She's part of that Goth group. Don't you think—"

"She's been *helping* me, Justin!" I said. "And she isn't like Seth. She doesn't have an attachment! She just knows a lot about this stuff."

"*Why* does she know so much?" he demanded. "You know, I think maybe we should just walk from here."

"Knock it off, Justin," I snapped.

"Alyx, let us out!" He fumbled with the door handle.

Alyx jammed on the brakes, and the car skidded to a stop. Her finger tapped against the steering wheel. "Go ahead. Get out."

"Come on, Dani." He opened the door, tugging on my arm.

"No." I pulled away.

"What the hell do you know about her? Maybe she's as dangerous as Seth!"

"She's my friend, Justin! That's all I need to know."

The car lurched forward, rocks spitting up behind us.

"Discussion over," Alyx murmured. "He's following us."

The car bumped off the dirt and back onto the highway. The glow of headlights lit up the darkness behind us.

"We need to get out of his sight," Alyx said.

Justin said nothing, and wouldn't look at me, but he did reach over to squeeze my hand.

And I squeezed back, but I wasn't sure who was comforting whom.

We were all silent as Alyx drove toward Ponderay, a nondescript town consisting mainly of strip malls. I seriously doubted that we could escape Seth and Maksim, especially there—not if Maxsim truly wanted to find us.

The car slowed as Alyx turned left onto a road leading to the back entrance of the JC Penny. "Maybe we can lose them if we hide here for a little while," she said.

As we sat behind the store in the dark car for fifteen excruciatingly long minutes, we realized Seth wasn't coming.

"So now what?" Justin had a good point.

"We need to find him," Alyx answered.

I shook my head. "No, *I* need to find him. Take me to my house and I'll get my car. You both have done enough."

Both Alyx and Justin shot down the idea before I even finished.

"Nah-uh. No way," Alyx said first.

"I don't think so, Dani," Justin said. "I'll go. Seth will listen to me. *I'm* not the one he's after," he shot a pointed look at Alyx.

Alyx turned in her seat. "Yeah? And what are you going to tell him? To stop playing with fire? Stop trying to hurt Dani? Why the hell would he listen to *you*?"

"Well, at least he doesn't try throwing fireballs at me."

"Listen, I think I'm a little better equipped to handle this than you are, Justin."

"Would you guys knock it off?" I glanced between the two of them and decided I couldn't let either of them be a part of this anymore. It was getting too dangerous. None of us knew what Seth was capable of and to what extent he'd go. And there was no way to know how much control Maksim had right now.

This was my fight. Between me and Maksim. I wasn't being all heroic or anything. I was definitely scared, and even though I was willing to die for Seth if I had to, I was not willing to put my friends' lives in danger for me.

I turned back to Justin. "You're right, you're *not* the one he's after." I looked at Alyx. "And neither are you. It's me he wants. I'll go to him." I held up my hand as they both started to talk. "I'm not saying I'm going to stand in front of him and sacrifice myself to him, but maybe if I can connect to Seth, I think we can fight it together."

"Absolutely not," Justin said, leaning back hard and crossing his arms over his chest as if that was the final word on the subject.

"Yeah, well, that's all romantic and smells likes pretty pink roses and stuff, but the reality is that he's unpredictable. Both of them are. We need to do this together or not at all. The three of us might stand a chance, but alone," Alyx shook her head. "Too risky."

"I agree, but I still think Dani should stay out of this," Justin said.

It was my turn to protest, but Alyx jumped in for me.

"She'll keep Seth focused. As long as he can anchor to you, Dani, he'll have a chance."

Justin made a funny little noise, a cross between a grunt and a snarl, but he didn't say anything more.

"So what's the plan?" I asked Alyx.

"No plan," she said, looking at herself in the rear-view mirror again, then back at Justin, then out the windshield. "Just winging it. I mean, how do you plan for something as unpredictable as this?"

"We've got to find him first. He could be anywhere," Justin finally said.

"Sandpoint isn't that big. I'm sure—" Alyx froze. "Wait." Alyx held up her hand. "Did you hear that?"

"Hear what?" I shook my head and glanced back at Justin who was watching Alyx through the rear-view mirror, his eyes narrowing just a little. They had this stare-down thing going on between them for a few seconds before Alyx looked away, to her own reflection. She gasped quietly but quickly coughed and started rubbing her eyes.

"Alyx," Justin started to say, but she cut him off with a hard shake of her head.

"You okay?" I asked, reaching for her arm, but she shook me off and nodded.

"Hang on a second." Alyx looked upward, turned her head slightly to her left, then to her right, tilting her head slightly as if straining to hear something. Her eyes widened in surprise. "He's back at the school."

"Who?" asked Justin. "Seth?"

My seat belt caught me tight across my chest as Alyx quickly put the Subaru in reverse before sending me back into my seat when she pulled out of the parking lot.

"Yep. Now's our chance to end this."

Chapter 32

He is a worthy adversary, not like the others. Weak, they were, pretending to be horrified at the atrocities committed. They shielded their eyes against the blood that spilled, condemning others for their crimes, while secretly peeking through their windows as the events unfolded. But not this one. He still believes in love. He still believes that he has a choice. I mean to teach him otherwise.
~ Maksim

Seth and Dirk couldn't have been here that long—fifteen minutes tops, because the doors on the south end of the school had been fried and the metal was still too hot to touch. As we stood staring at it, I shuddered. Maksim appeared to be back in control now.

"Let's go inside," Alyx said.

We edged past the still-glowing doors, hanging on their hinges, and moved down the halls towards the Commons. I swore under my breath at the sound of echoing laughter—Seth's and Dirk's voices.

"Dude," Dirk said. "You know the cops are going to be all over the place with the doors all blown apart like that."

"There wasn't a choice. There was no other way in. I had to get them away from the woods. It was too secluded there," Seth answered.

"What are you talking about? We were fine out there."

"I need to keep her safe."

"Whatever," Dirk said. "I'm going to take a piss."

In the dim light, we could see Dirk move away from Seth, who stood motionless in the middle of the room, his hands shoved into his jacket pockets, his head tipped forward.

"Freakin' asshole." Alyx fixed a hard stare at Dirk's back.

It's now or never, I thought, steeling my nerves. I took a step into the Commons, but Alyx grabbed my arm.

"What do you think you're doing?" she hissed.

"Seth doesn't have Dirk to help him now. I *have* to talk to him."

"And what if you can't?" Justin shook his head. "It's too risky, Dani."

"We don't have time to talk about this." I said firmly, pulling away from Alyx.

I walked quickly toward Seth, Alyx and Justin right behind me. As I got closer, I could sense the intense darkness engulfing Seth. His achingly handsome, high-cheek-boned face was like granite. Cold, gray, unmoving.

"Seth?" I whispered, staring into his black eyes. I put my hands against his chest, feeling his muscles tighten under them.

"Careful, Dani…" Alyx warned.   She moved to Seth's side while Justin came around to flank me.

But I knew my touch had re-connected the two of us and I staggered at the jolt of emotion.

"Please, Seth, talk to me," I begged.

The dim lights above us flashed to bright, full power and I jumped.

Dirk leaned against the wall, grinning. "He doesn't want you anymore, bitch. Time to move on."

Alyx whirled around to face Dirk, planted one foot in front of the other, and pressed her palms against the air. "Back off, numbnuts."

"*Pfff!* Are you kidding me? What do you think you are, a Power Ranger?"

Alyx's arms dropped to her side and her shoulders slumped, like he had just taken the wind out of her sails.

Dirk pushed himself off the wall and began closing the space between them, strutting like there was nothing that could stop him.

My whole body tensed up. I wanted to scream at her. It seemed to take forever for Alyx to react. At first she fumbled with her amulet and mumbled something as Dirk's steps got faster and the distance between them shorter. Justin and I, and I think even Seth, stood perfectly still, watching the inevitable clash between them. It was too close, too fast. My warning got stuck in my throat and I couldn't look away.

I don't know what it was that Alyx did, but Dirk's face was suddenly vulnerable and confused.

"I… don't… What… the… ?"

Seth moaned, "No!"

I forgot all about Alyx and Dirk. I grabbed at Seth's waist and glanced over at Justin. "Help me," I pleaded.

But Seth lifted an arm in Dirk's direction, and like a frightened dog coming to his master, Dirk slunk toward him.

Justin and I grabbed Seth's arm, but Alyx was already a step ahead of us. Pockets of air pulsed around us, then, just like in the woods, she shoved what was like an invisible wall at Dirk so fast and hard, his hulking body stopped short.

"Huh?" Dirk's jaw dropped when he realized he couldn't get past the wall. Looking first at Seth and then to Alyx, he understood. It was Alyx who held him back.

"Don't even think about fighting me, you dumb jock." Alyx stared at Dirk, daring him to test her.

Seth's—or rather Maksim's—fury was obvious as he turned his attention to Alyx.

"Seth! No!" I tried desperately to hold him back, but his body had turned rock-solid and he shook me off as if I was nothing more than a pesky fly. Whatever objects that stood between him and Alyx didn't stand a chance. Shoving and kicking chairs and tables, dragging us along with him, he got within a few feet of her in a matter of seconds.

Alyx's eyes narrowed into determined blue slashes and with one palm keeping Dirk grounded, she used the other hand to scoop the air around her. Then she threw enough force at Seth to slow him, but not enough to stop him. I'm not sure anything could have stopped him at that point.

My hands slid from Seth's waist as he pulled away, out of my grip. "Stop it, Seth!" I cried.

"I can't hold him, Dani," Justin's voice cracked. "I... can't..."

Alyx's body shook with the strain of stopping both Seth and Dirk. I could see the indecision in her eyes as she looked at Dirk then at Seth. But it was too late. Seth broke through her barrier and she gave up.

Alyx took two backward steps to Seth's one forward step before she ran out of room—backing right into Dirk.

Dirk caught her and laughed, fisting Alyx's hair and throwing her on the floor.

She scrambled back up. "It'll take more than that to stop me, you asshole!" Alyx spat.

Dirk grinned. "Wanna bet?" He pushed her down, straddled her, and wrapped his hands around her throat.

Justin pushed past me. "Get off of her!" he yelled, grabbing Dirk's arm and pulling him off Alyx as Alyx jumped up again.

I whirled around and faced Seth. "Seth! Make him stop!"

But there was no reaction from him, not a blink, nothing.

There was no way I was taking silence for an answer. I had to *get through.* "Hey, Maksim! This is between you and me, *not them*!" I pulled back and slapped Seth's cheek hard, so hard I felt the pain from the contact shoot up my arm and straight to my jaw.

But that got his attention, because his eyes, like stone, bore down into mine, and his lips pulled back in a snarl.

"Yeah, you bastard! I'm talking to you! There is no way you can win! Love is light and light will always—" The rest of my really great speech died on my lips because Seth's body suddenly jerked, then seemed to fold up into himself, before he stood up to his full height.

"Seth?" My voice faltered. His eyes were blacker than black now.

Before I could take a step towards him, his arms flew outward, his head whipped back, and I could almost *see* a blast of energy shoot out from Seth. The blast threw me off my feet, sending me backward into the trophy case. My back and arms stung as shards of glass pierced my skin. Sports trophies fell from the shelves and around me.

Seth turned and faced Dirk, his hands fisted at his sides.

"Seth!" I yelled, pushing myself up and away from the case. I ran towards him. "Fight it! Fight it!"

With an agonized cry, Seth raised his hands and threw energy at Dirk's back. The force of it lifted the tables, flipping them on their sides, sending tables and chairs skidding toward Justin, Alyx, and Dirk, knocking them down like pins at a bowling alley.

Seth's lips pulled back and his eyes rolled back until all I could see was white. Then his balance started to waver.

"Get. Off. Me!" I could hear Alyx yell from the other side of the room.

Seth clutched his stomach and before I could reach him, and he went down hard, his head hitting the floor with a sickening thud.

I ran to his side and rolled him onto his back, crouching down next to him. He was so still, his forehead smooth and the hard lines around his mouth gone. Running my fingers down his neck, I was able to find his pulse—a weak one—but it was there.

"Oh, Seth. Where are you?" I smoothed his hair back from his face, not knowing what to do next. He was in there, somewhere. But then again, so was Maksim. How much time did we have before he came back? A scent of… something metallic caught me off guard. I pulled my hand back and saw the smear of blood across my fingers.

"We have to get Seth to the hospital!" I shouted to Justin and Alyx, who stood over Dirk.

Alyx shoved against Justin's shoulder and lifted her chin in my direction.

"Come *on*!" I screamed.

Justin ran back to me and squatted on the other side of Seth. "Get under his arm," he said, doing the same. "On the count of three. One… two…"

On three we lifted, wrapping our arms around Seth's waist.

I strained under Seth's weight, ignoring the stinging wounds on my back and arms.

"A little help here, Alyx?" I called out.

But she was bent over Dirk, passing her hands over his still body.

"Is Dirk alive?" Justin grunted loudly as he shifted Seth's weight, slinging Seth's arm over his shoulder.

Alyx's hands came down. "Yeah, unfortunately," she said. Her foot came back and she gave Dirk a hard kick in the ribs before turning on her heel and walking towards us.

She helped Justin and me drag Seth down the hall, back the way we'd come in. By the time we got to her Subaru, my shoulders were screaming from the strain and my knees were shaking.

"Geez, he's heavy," Justin grunted.

Alyx climbed in the back seat of the car. "Lift him up," she ordered us, "and I'll pull him in."

After getting him all the way in, Justin got into the front passenger seat and I got into the back seat with Seth. As gently as I could, I lifted Seth's head onto my lap.

"What exactly did you do back there?" Justin asked Alyx.

Alyx rested her head against the steering wheel, worn with exhaustion. "It was something I'd read about. Never had a chance to try it out until now, though."

Justin stared at her. "It looked like a… a spell or something."

She shrugged. "Yeah, kind of." She started up the engine and threw the car into gear.

"Right." Justin slapped the side of his head with his hand. "I *had* to ask." He added, "Okay, so what was it supposed to do?"

"Well," she said, "if it works, his penis will fall off."

Justin's jaw dropped. "You're joking, right?" he asked, shifting uncomfortably in his seat.

"And if it doesn't work," Alyx said, grinning, "at least he has some broken ribs."

I put my hand on Seth's forehead. "He's burning up, Alyx," I said anxiously. "Justin, can you call Seth's dad and have him meet us at the hospital? I'm going to call my mom."

Alyx looked at me in the rear-view mirror. "Are you sure taking him to the hospital is a good plan?"

"What other choice do we have?" I demanded.

"Well, what are we going to tell everyone? Seth has an ancient sorcerer inside him and he's, like, really dangerous?"

"Alyx, I don't care *what* we tell anyone. I won't lose Seth!" Tears welled up in my eyes.

Justin twisted around towards me. "What if that thing decides to make an appearance when Seth wakes up?"

"*If* he wakes up," Alyx said grimly. "That soul is pissed off because Seth isn't doing what he's supposed to be doing. He'll rip him up from the inside out."

"Oh, God, no," I moaned. I gripped Seth tighter.

Justin looked at me and then at Alyx. "Do you have to say shit like that?" he hissed at Alyx.

She shrugged. "It's the truth."

With shaking hands, I pulled my cell phone out of my pocket and dialed my mom's number. She answered on the first ring.

"Mom? Mom, Seth is really sick. We're driving him to the hospital right now. Yes, *I'm* okay." I choked up. "But I'm really worried about Seth. He's unconscious. We're taking him to the ER. Yeah, Justin is calling his dad now. Okay. Thanks."

I closed my cell phone and stared out the window. We didn't think this out too well. What *would* happen when—not if—Seth woke up? All hell could break loose, that's what. We could be putting other people in danger. Maybe if the doctor would sedate Seth…

I looked down at Seth, lying still, except for his arms twitching a little.

"Stay asleep for just a little longer, Seth," I whispered. "Keep that thing away long enough so we can help you."

Justin snapped his phone shut and turned in his seat. "His dad is taking the next flight home tonight. He'll meet us at the hospital."

I nodded and tucked my hand around Seth's waist, hanging on to him as if my life depended on it.

Because maybe it did.

~ ~ ~

Maksim stared sightlessly at the ocean far below him.

It had happened again.

Silura's curse had consumed him, as it always did, at the moment he was most vulnerable, when his heart was most exposed. When he was in love.

Leila. His strong, beautiful Leila. She had seen the shadows that moved within him, had felt the tremors that moved under his skin, yet she caressed his body with a touch that soothed the shadows away. He thought she would be the one to free him at long last, but her devotion was rewarded with death by his hands around her lovely neck.

Her light—his light—had drained from her eyes along with her breath. Her eyes had been fixated on his face, but saw him no more.

His fists clenched. The people of the town suspected him, though he'd covered his tracks well. He almost wished they would discover his secret and do what they had to do to make him stop. It would be far easier to suffer their torture than to suffer his own.

But now he grew weary. This vicious pattern would never stop. After he took a lover and his heart led him into hopeless love, he'd always killed her.

He wanted to be free of the madness. He wanted never again to feel life slipping away under his hands.

So he had traveled far and now stood at the edge of the world. The ocean breeze swept up and over the cliffs on which Maksim stood, cooling a path up his body, carrying with it a promise of eternal peace.

He looked down, over the tips of his sandals that perched over the rocky cliff's edge. He would jump *and end the curse. For once his body lay draped across the rocks far below, he could never again fall in love; and never again kill.*

Never, ever again.

~ ~ ~

Chapter 33

I wasn't alone. The boy lay in a pool of agony.
Beaten down by his own resistance, battling a force
far more experienced and far more adept at rendering
control, more powerful than he had imagined. He
simply wore out as he searched for the end.
But the end never comes because forever stretches
beyond the edges of the stars.
I have learned.
There will never be an end.

Beep. Beep. The lines on the heart monitor pulsed rhythmically, though faster than normal. Not even massive amounts of sedatives were slowing down Seth's heart. Tubes snaked out from beneath the surgical tape, which stretched across his wrists and hands and reached up to the plastic IV bags full of fluid.

I heard the nurses say something about how erratic his heart was, almost as if there were two heartbeats. That made me sick. I wanted to beat on Seth's chest, to pound on it until that soul was forced out.

The doctor kept asking me if he had taken any drugs, anything "cardiotoxic." I could tell she didn't believe me when I said Seth was clean. She went down a list of anything and everything that could have put him in a comatose state—steroids, amphetamines, barbiturates, meth, cocaine, heroin, over-the-counter medications—and I had emphatically said no to each one. When the tests all came back negative, the doctor's disbelief turned to head-scratching bewilderment. In the doctors'—now there were four physicians on the case—determination to solve Seth's "mysterious illness," more tests were ordered: MRIs, EKGs, CT scans, blood cultures. Nothing shed a sliver of light or gave the slightest glimmer of hope for treatment. All they could do, they said, was wait and see and keep him comfortable. For that, at least, I was grateful.

Seth's hair felt coarse under my hand as I smoothed it off his face. I shifted uncomfortably under my own bandages. Before we went into the emergency room, Alyx had thrown a heavy coat over me to cover the blood all over my shirt from my cuts and scrapes. Once we'd had a free moment, she'd whisked me away to her house and patched me up. She'd told me, in her normal half-irritated tone, that I'd been damn lucky the smashed glass from the trophy case hadn't severed an artery.

Looking down at Seth now, I didn't feel very lucky. He laid deathly still, his face pale, his dark lashes flat against his cheeks, but he looked at peace, finally. After trying to fight the soul on his own, he had no choice now but to let someone else try to help him.

The soft squeak of rubber against the polished floor registered somewhere in the back of my mind. I watched numbly as the nurse checked the IVs and pulled out a thermometer to recheck Seth's temperature.

"Is it still up?" Justin's voice broke the oppressive silence in the room. He'd been keeping vigil from a chair in the corner of the hospital room.

The nurse nodded. "A bit, but it's stable."

It was an effort to focus on the nurse's words. "Thank you," I managed to say. "For everything."

The nurse left the room, and Justin followed, closing the door behind them. leaving me alone with Seth.

"I love you so much, Seth," I whispered. "You *can't* die."

Who knew? Who knew that simply loving each other would come to this? I removed my earrings, my beautiful, sparkling birthday earrings, placed them carefully in his limp hand, and closed his fingers around them. There was nothing more I could do.

~ ~ ~

Alyx and Justin were waiting for me in the hospital lobby.

"Any news on Dirk?" I asked.

The police had no idea who had trashed the high school because the security camera tapes were mysteriously blank during the time we had been there.

"No one has seen him," Justin said tonelessly.

I knew it was wrong of me, but I simply didn't have the energy to worry about Dirk. The last few days, it had taken everything I'd had to hold onto Seth, to try to keep him here. with me.

I slumped down into a white plastic chair beside them. "I can't believe this is happening," I told them. "If only Seth had told me what was *really* happening. Maybe I could have stopped all of this."

Alyx was leaning against the wall next to Justin, her arms folded across her chest. "He probably didn't know—" she started.

"But *I* should have known," I said. "I mean, I *knew* something was up. Right before my birthday, weird things were happening even before *you* noticed." I stared at Alyx.

"Right before your birthday?" Justin ran his hands through his hair and his eyes flitted around as if he was trying to remember something. "eSouled! He bought it off of eSouled. *Shit!*" He slammed his hand into the wall. "And I was there!"

"What do you mean you were *there*?" Alyx glared at him.

He glanced at Alyx. "He was stressing big time on what to get Dani for her birthday, so he was looking online. I don't know how he ran across it, but he found an ad that said 'Soul for Sale.' It said something like it would 'give you power and control.' He was thinking that might be pretty cool to have, even though he knew it was a joke." Justin looked at me. "He laughed and said that maybe it would help him give you anything you wanted."

"Did you actually *see* him buy it?" Alyx asked, her voice tense.

Justin shook his head. "No, I left. I didn't even think about it. I mean, come on. It was a dollar and there were no bids. We *both* thought it was a joke."

"So," I said, slowly, "if he did buy this thing online…"

"Then we can get rid of it by *selling* it online!" Alyx finished my sentence.

Hope surged through me. "Alyx, would you stay here and keep my mom and Mr. Thompson from asking too many questions? I'm going over to Seth's to get on his computer."

Could this *possibly* work? I felt a twinge of guilt at the thought of someone else buying the damned soul. But this was Seth's life and honestly, at this moment, I didn't care about anyone else.

"Sure, no problem," Alyx said.

"I'll come with you." Justin grabbed his jacket.

~ ~ ~

I pulled my coat closer against the drizzle. "Do you think this will work?" I asked Justin.

"I sure hope so. I just wish I'd figured this out sooner." He shook his head.

"How could you know? You thought it was a joke. Anyone would've." I glanced at Justin. "What do we say on our ad? 'Do you want unlimited power? Buyer beware? This soul will kill you and anyone you love'?"

"I don't know," he said, "but we'll think of something. Let's hurry."

I looked behind me at the hospital, up at the patient room windows, scared that we were running out of time.

We started to break into a run across the parking lot, but stopped when Dirk suddenly lurched out from behind a car, clutching his ribs.

"Wait! What's wrong with Seth? Why is he here?"

Dirk blocked my way, but I side-stepped him. "Get out of our way, Dirk."

Justin was right behind me. "Move it, Dirk," Justin said.

Dirk grabbed my arm and pulled me back. "Tell me." His voice was hard and threatening.

I turned and rammed my fist into his ribs. A perfect shot. "There. I told you."

Dirk winced. He let me go and wrapped his arms around his ribs. "You're going to pay for that, bitch!"

Justin stood between us and shoved Dirk away.

"Come *on*, Justin! We don't have time for this!" I urged.

Dirk made the mistake of going around Justin to grab me again. He didn't get very far because Justin had him on the ground in an instant.

"Go, Dani! Just go! I'll handle him." Justin grinned wickedly. "I've wanted to do this for a long time," he said, leaning over Dirk.

We were running out of time. I turned and ran.

~ ~ ~

I threw open the front door of Seth's house, pocketed my keys, and ran down the hall to Seth's room. Sliding into his chair, I jiggled the mouse to wake up the computer. I went straight to eSouled and Seth's account popped up.

"Okay," I said to the screen. "Let's get this over with." I started typing. *Power, strength.* I added a few key words of my own. *Control over others. Learn the secret of ancient sorcerers.* There had to be a few fanatics out there who would bite. God, this felt so cold, but what was I supposed to do? Watch Seth be beaten down by this thing? One way or another, it was going to be set free to do this all over again. So why not fight it? Why not beat him at his own game? Annihilate him before he annihilates us. I just wanted this to be over. I wanted things to be back to how they were.

The front door opened and closed. Panic pricked at my skin. *Crap!* I hadn't locked the door behind me. If it was Dirk...

I looked around frantically for some type of weapon. Great. All I had was a pencil. But even a pencil, if aimed correctly, could maim. I stood and faced the door, my pathetic weapon behind my back, my heart thudding to the urgent pace of the footsteps down the hall.

290

My breath rushed out at the sight of Justin. His cheek was swelling and starting to bruise, and his lip was oozing blood.

"Oh, Justin," I cried, dropping the pencil. "Are you okay?"

He waved me off. "Did you do it yet?"

I sat back down. "Almost finished. I'm going to give it two days and a 'Buy it Now.'" I finished putting in all the info I could think of, skipped the image, and sat back. I pulled my sleeves over my hands and pressed them to my eyes. I didn't want to cry. I needed to stay strong. I took in a deep breath.

"How are we going to get anyone to look at this stupid ad?" I asked Justin. "Someone *has* to buy it right now!"

It was quiet in the room except for the steady hum of the computer.

Justin knelt down in front of me and tugged at my wrists, exposing my face.

"It's okay. Seth means a lot to me, too. You both do. I'd do anything for you guys."

"I know. Oh, Justin, what if we're too late? What if this thing doesn't let him go?" I let Justin hug me against his chest.

"It *has* to. One way or another, it has to," he said.

The seconds ticked by. I was comforted a little by the steady beat of Justin's heart against my ear, but at the same time, it reminded me of Seth, and that hurt.

I pushed myself away and looked at the screen, then refreshed the page.

Nothing.

"I can't stay here," I said. "I need to be with Seth. Justin, will you please stay and watch this and call me right away if anything happens?"

"You don't even need to ask. Go. Let me know if there is any change in Seth, okay?"

I hugged him tight. "Justin, you're the best friend anyone could have." I pulled back and touched his cheek. "Thank you."

He gave me a crooked smile, but it didn't hide the shade of sadness in his eyes. "No problem, Dani. Go. Go take care of Seth."

~ ~ ~

"Mom!"

My mom stood outside Seth's room, talking with Alyx.

"How is he?" I asked.

She shook her head. "No change, Sweetie." Her touch was comforting as she pushed my damp hair back off my face. "Seth's dad is in there with him now."

Alyx raised her eyebrows at me and I gave her a small nod.

"I'm going in," I said.

I opened the door to see Marty sitting next to Seth with his forehead resting on the edge of the bed, his shoulders shaking with sobs. He loved Seth with all his heart and soul. Ever since his wife died, Marty had done whatever he could to make up for the loss. I knew he hated not being at home more. And now this. Coming back home only to find he might lose the only person he lived for.

I gently placed my hand on his shoulder. "Hey."

Marty looked up, his eyes red-rimmed, his cheeks stained with tears. He wiped his face with the back of his hand, then stood and encircled me within his arms. We held each other tight for a long time.

"When Seth wakes up, I think I'm going to have to ground him for scaring me like this." Marty's voice was a little shaky. He pulled back, his eyes full of concern. "How are *you* doing?"

"I'm okay," I told him, doing my best to put on a smile, "but I think I'll have a talk with him, too."

He smoothed my hair back and kissed my forehead. "The doctors don't understand why he's so sick." He turned and faced Seth, adjusting the tubes and straightening the sheets. "You'd think with all their fancy tests, they'd know," he muttered.

They're never going to figure this one out, I thought. Even if I *could* explain to him what happened, it wouldn't make any difference. There wasn't anything this hospital had to offer Seth. They were doing the best they could, keeping Seth nourished with IVs, but that's all they could do. Somewhere in there, I hoped, Seth was fighting... and fighting hard. We needed more time to get rid of Maksim.

The door swung open and my mom poked her head inside. Alyx peered over her shoulder.

"Come on, you two. Let's go get some coffee," Mom said. "The nurses will let us know if there's any change."

Marty hesitated, then seemed to accept the fact there was nothing he could do. He squeezed my arm before brushing past me toward the door.

"Dani?"

"I'll be right there, Mom."

When the door closed, I turned back to the bed and held Seth's hand. I took in all the tubes going in and out of his arms and listened to the beeps and whirs of the machines. My eyes rested on his hand, still holding my earrings.

Leaning down, I placed my ear against his heart, counting the beats as they pulsed against his chest, finding some solace in the rhythm. I lifted my head and whispered against his lips, "Fight for me, Seth. Fight for us." Then I moved his hair back off his forehead and softly kissed him. I walked out of the room to join the others.

~ ~ ~

My phone rang, jolting me back from wherever my mind had been. I had turned the volume way up so I wouldn't miss Justin's call. And there it was. I think my heart stopped. I know my breathing did. I looked at Alyx and then over at my mom. She and Marty had finished eating and were talking quietly together.

"Justin?" I whispered into my phone.

"It sold," he said.

I pressed one hand against my chest to slow my heart. Something was wrong. I could hear it in his voice.

"Justin?" I said again. "What happened? Why don't you sound happy?"

"Are you with Seth right now?" he asked.

"No, I'm down in the hospital cafeteria."

He was sounding urgent now. "Go see if it worked!"

Why was I hesitating? Because I was so afraid it *hadn't* worked. So afraid of what I would find.

Alyx's eyes widened and I nodded at her.

Mom glanced up and started to say something, but I waved her away. "Later, Mom."

I bolted from the cafeteria, Alyx on my heels. We ran through the halls and up the stairs in a full sprint. Skidding around the corner, we saw the door to Seth's room swing shut. We shoved it open.

Two nurses stood beside the bed, blocking my view of Seth. One was checking his chart, the other was holding a stethoscope to his chest.

I felt sick all of a sudden. This didn't look so good.

"Go get Dr. Spencer," said one of the nurses to the other, shaking her head.

The other nurse turned around. I braced myself.

Her mouth broke into a huge smile when she saw us. "He took a turn!"

From the tone of her voice and her big smile, I knew it was a turn for the better.

She brushed past me, in a hurry to get the doctor.

I hurried to the bedside. Seth's color *had* returned, his cheeks and lips touched with a hint of pink.

"Would you mind stepping back please?"

The doctor's brusque voice startled me and I moved back. He flashed a light in Seth's eyes, checked his pulse, and listened to his chest with the stethoscope.

"It's the damnedest thing," he muttered under his breath. "Vitals are strong. Let's do some repeat labs on him, culture the blood."

Mom and Marty ran in, out of breath.

"Dani, when you ran out like that, you had us worried. Is Seth okay?" Mom took one look at Seth and the frown disappeared.

"He bounced back," the doctor said, shaking his head. "I still don't understand it, but his body seems to have purged whatever made him so sick. We're going to run a few more tests and do another CT. Then we'll see how he is in the morning."

Relief like I had never known before made my knees weak. I sank down into the chair against the wall. I was ready to laugh *and* cry. I couldn't wait for Seth to wake up. I wanted to talk to him, to hear his voice, and most of all, to look into his eyes and see *him*. I mean, really see his soul, *Seth's* soul.

Marty held Seth's hand against his heart, closed his eyes, and moved his lips silently before pressing Seth's palm against his cheek. A brilliant smile broke across Marty's face. He turned quickly as the doctor walked away.

"Hey, doc, I have some questions," Seth's dad trailed behind the doctor out the door.

Alyx slid inside the room before the door closed.

"I called Justin," she said. "He's on his way."

I nodded, too tired and overwhelmed to say anything. I gave her my seat so I could be at the bedside, holding Seth's hand.

Then we waited.

And waited.

And then it happened. A slight pressure around my fingers. I stared down at my hand, so small compared to his. My breath stuck in my throat.

I was afraid to look up. Still afraid this wasn't real. But when I finally did...

I cried.

Tears of relief. Tears of happiness. Tears of love. Seth was back.

ALYX

Do not wait for it, for the end never comes...
~ Maksim

It's funny how the universe throws unlikely people into unlikely situations with unlikely results. I never would have thought I'd be here right now, hanging out with Mr. and Ms. Popular. Dark, totally misunderstood, totally underestimated, misfit Alyx. But here I am.

This whole dark sorcerer thing spiraled down from the cosmos, winding itself through time to land in our laps, tying us all together. I hate to admit it, but I actually think Seth and Dani are pretty cool.

And then there was Justin. Another underestimated person. He tends to lay low, keeping pretty much to himself, but he's a bundle of emotion, that guy. His eyes say everything his mouth won't. He's an easy person to read—that is, if you take the time to do it. He'd rather stand in the shadows, letting the other guy have the glory. That's too bad, because I think he's pretty cool. He's someone you can depend on. Loyal to the end. Any girl would be lucky to have him as a boyfriend.

Not that *I've* considered it. Well, not really. But I'm not blind. I can look past his good looks and his great body to see what makes him tick. He has already proven how deep his emotions go. He has a lot of layers to him. Now, if only he would end this infatuation he has with Dani. It's the only obstacle between him and…

Whatever. It's not that I care or anything.

So here we were, the four of us just hanging out at City Beach. It was like even the sun was afraid to come out while Maksim was around. But now it was sunny, and it felt good to be sitting out here.

I had the place of honor—the hood of my car. Seth and Dani were sitting as close as two people could on a blanket Dani had spread out, and Justin was perched on a picnic table that he'd pulled over.

"I still can't believe you did that," Dani was saying for the umpteenth time. "Buying that damn soul."

"I just wanted to give you more reasons to stay with me. I thought if I had more power..." Seth's voice trailed away.

Dani punched him in the arm. "You went and did something so insanely stupid to make sure I would want to stay with you? You put yourself and everyone in danger!"

Personally, I was bored with the subject. And this devotion thing those two had going on was pushing Justin's limits. He seemed to find the lake a lot more interesting than the conversation. I would have thought he would be ecstatic that he had his best friend back, but something was hurting him in a big way. Probably his feelings for Dani. It made me want to rush over there and ask him what was wrong. Honestly. I kind of wanted to hug him and make it all go away.

But I don't care that much about him, right?

"You didn't believe in me. You didn't believe in us!" Dani said.

I wondered when the girl was going to move the conversation on to something else.

"I don't know if I should kiss you or hit you," she muttered.

Ugh! I'd like to see her hit him.

Seth laughed. "Do I get a say in that?"

Dani glared at him for a second, then smiled. "You don't need to worry, Seth. My love is for real."

It was kind of sweet to see Seth tuck her hair behind her ears and admire her earrings, ironically the gift that started this whole damn thing, before he wrapped his arms around her and pulled her close, resting his forehead against hers. It looked like *that* whole conversation was done. Finally.

The next few minutes of quiet were nice. Even Justin relaxed a little bit, though the pained look in his eyes didn't go away. For a moment it looked like he wanted to ask me something. And he might have if Dani hadn't let out a yelp before she jumped up and backed away from Seth.

My body went on full alert.

"It can't be! It's supposed to be gone! It was sold!" Her eyes were huge and scared. She pointed a finger at Seth. "You did that thing to me again! You made me feel all melted inside!"

Seth laughed. "Relax. Maksim *is* gone, but some of the stuff he taught me stayed. It's like it became a part of me." He shrugged. "Only the good stuff. I promise."

It did seem to make sense, I thought. An attached soul like Maksim's was bound to have left some psychic residue.

Dani sat back down and let him hug her again.

"It doesn't have control over me," he said. "I just remember how to do some stuff."

Dani shuddered. "I wonder who ended up with the soul. At first I didn't care, but now I feel horrible for whoever it is."

Justin looked like he was trying to swallow a golf ball, but he said nothing.

"I just wish that instead of dumping it," Dani said, "we could have found a way to break the curse.

Alyx?" She turned to look at me. "Did you and your parents ever come up with anything?"

I heard her voice, but the words didn't register because I realized there was something really off about Justin. He was too tense, too serious. He didn't seem… himself.

The hair on the back of my neck slowly stood up. I reached for my amulet.

"I gotta go," Justin got up and fist bumped Seth.

"Where are you going?" Seth asked.

Justin shrugged. "Just have to do some stuff."

"Okay. See ya, man."

I watched him go. Just as he passed me, our eyes locked.

"Alyx?" Dani was trying to get my attention.

"Huh?" I asked, not looking away.

"*Did* you find anything on how to break the curse?"

I stared after Justin as he got into his car.

"No…" I said, lost in my thoughts. "No. But I think I'll start working on it. Just. In. Case."

~~~~

AUTHOR'S NOTE

Thank you so much for spending your time with Seth, Dani, Justin, Alyx, and Dirk. I truly hope you enjoyed reading *Souled*.

I invite you to sign up for my newsletter to receive news about sales, new releases, and other fun news. Don't worry, though. I won't flood your email box with unnecessary stuff.

As a writer, I encourage any comments you might have. I would very much appreciate it if you would take a few minutes to leave a review on whichever site you purchased this novel and let me know your thoughts. If you do, please email me at dianamurdockauthor@gmail.com with a link to your review so I can thank you personally.

Thank you again for spending your valuable time with the teens from Sandpoint, Idaho. My next project in the Souled Series… Justin's and Alyx's story.

I'd love to hear from you! Please feel free to connect with me at any of the following sites:

Website: http://www.dianamurdock.com/
Twitter: @Diana_Murdock
Facebook: www.facebook.com/diana.murdock
Pinterest: pinterest.com/dianadmurdock/
Email: dianamurdockauthor@gmail.com
Just for fun: http://esouled.com/

ACKNOWLEDGEMENTS

I'd like to thank those who have helped me to bring this story to life. Some were with me in the beginning, others in the middle, and still others toward the end, but each one had so much to contribute at each stage. I must mention, though, the final push to write "The End" came from my fabulous sistas of HDSA, a group of talented writers I've been fortunate to be a part of. Thank you with all my heart.

My thanks reach out to my early readers: Jesse, Caleb, Maria, Natascha, Mala, Muzna, Ginger, and Teresa.

I also had great input from Sabrina and Alicia, awesome girls who know their stuff.

Special thanks to Coach Mike Randles of Sandpoint High School for his expertise on the wrestling scenes, and to Cassia, Judi, and Martha for their valuable insight of earth energy.

And to Toria, Kathleen, and Theresa, I am eternally grateful for the many hours you spent scrutinizing each page and making the words shine.

Cover Photographer: Victoria McCune
Cover Design: Steve McCune
Models: Scott and Elaina
Make-up: Kimberlee Langford
Tattoo Design: Crystalyn Abercrombie